Dear Readers,

With Valentin[e] ... letter month for love, and Bouquet ... romances to put you in the mood!

Legendary Zebra author Colleen Faulkner starts us off this month with **Maggie's Baby,** the story of one woman's painful loss—and her emotional reunion with the only man who can change her past mistakes into a future that holds the promise of love. **Cookies and Kisses,** from Gina Jackson, tackles the lighter side of love with this sweet story of a man who decides his wholesome neighbor would make a great weapon in his custody battle—until he develops "forever" kind of feelings for his temporary wife.

Sometimes love is found in the most unlikely places. In longtime Harlequin author Vanessa Grant's **The Colors of Love**, a sensible physician believes that the free-spirited artist he meets by chance is the wrong woman for him—until she convinces him that their attraction is not only red-hot, but true blue. Finally, Jove and Zebra author Ann Josephson offers **Coming Home**, the story of a successful businessman returning to his rural hometown, searching for a simpler life—but finding that the beautiful owner of a local quilt shop is an attractive complication.

A dozen red roses, a box of candy . . . and four fantastic, brand-new Bouquet romances—what better way to celebrate the only day devoted to love?

Kate Duffy
Editorial Director

WEDDING NIGHT

"What's wrong?" Neil crossed the floor in an instant and took Taylor into his arms. "You're not sorry you married me, are you?"

Taylor took a deep breath and hoped her voice wouldn't shake. Just being in Neil's arms again made her long for him desperately. "No. I'm glad we got married, but . . ."

"But what?"

"This isn't exactly the way I hoped my wedding night would be."

"I know. It's not exactly what I had in mind either. Just looking at you in my bed . . ."

"Should we amend our agreement?" Taylor held her breath, hoping that Neil would reconsider.

"We can't."

Neil's voice was thick with passion and Taylor heard it. He was having doubts, too. She let the sheet slip down slightly and was instantly rewarded as his arms tightened around her. "Could we make an exception, just for tonight?"

"Do you think we should?"

Taylor turned her head so her lips met his in a kiss of longing. And then she whispered, "Yes, Neil. I definitely think we should . . ."

COOKIES
AND
KISSES

GINA JACKSON

Zebra Books
Kensington Publishing Corp.
http://www.zebrabooks.com

ZEBRA BOOKS are published by

Kensington Publishing Corp.
850 Third Avenue
New York, NY 10022

First Printing: February, 2000
10 9 8 7 6 5 4 3 2 1

Printed in the United States of America

For Lois and Neal, my wonderful Minnesota friends.
And a big hug to Aunt Myrtle for some of my best recipes.

ONE

Taylor MacIntyre was at the end of her rope when she took the turnoff for Two Rivers, Minnesota. Barring death, she couldn't think of a single thing that hadn't gone wrong on her cross-country trip. She'd suffered through a series of minor vehicle mishaps: two flat tires, a broken fan belt that had caused her engine to overheat, and locking her keys in her car outside a truck stop in Atlanta. And even though she'd dressed in old jeans and faded sweatshirts from her college days, pinned her long, curly black hair into a severe bun, and worn sunglasses to hide her violet-blue eyes, she'd still been hit on by several truckers when she'd stopped for food and gas.

The pristine white sign Taylor spotted as she reached the outskirts of town made her smile. It read: TWO RIVERS, MN—POP. 1,344. Here she was, safe in Two Rivers, and all she had to do was drive to her grandmother's house and settle into her new, uncomplicated life.

Taylor drove through the outskirts of town, smiling as she passed rows of modest houses, painted in a rainbow of pastel colors. The front porches looked inviting, the yards were neat and filled with a variety of trees, and they sported narrow flower beds along the walkways. Some were still blooming with fall chrysanthemums and there wasn't a weed in sight.

The more houses she passed, the more convinced Taylor became that she'd made the right choice when she'd decided to move to Two Rivers. According to the letters that Grandma Mac had sent, there was no crime, the neighbors were friendly, and everyone took pride in their town. Though Two Rivers was small, Grandma Mac had boasted that they had all the modern conveniences. There was cable television, a movie theatre, and three restaurants. Taylor knew she wouldn't be able to dash down to the corner for cappuccino, takeout Chinese, or a hot bagel, but as far as she was concerned, Two Rivers had one crucial advantage over Manhattan. It was as far away from Blake Williams as she could get.

It was painful to admit that she'd been wrong about Blake. Taylor had thought her dream had come true when she'd married the new senior partner at Simmons, Gilby, Conners, and Williams. Of course she'd heard all the horror stories about secretaries who'd quit their jobs to marry their bosses and ended up getting dumped for their new, younger replacements, but Taylor had been convinced that her marriage to Blake would be the exception. It had taken her almost two years to find out that it wasn't.

On the afternoon that Taylor's marriage had come to a crashing end, she'd come home unexpectedly, her lunch plans with a friend canceled at the last minute. She'd gone straight to the master bedroom to change into something more comfortable, and she'd found Blake in bed with his young assistant, Stacey Randall. Taylor had stormed out of the apartment in a rage, and when she'd come back, several hours later, she'd found a note propped up on the kitchen counter. Blake had moved out. Their marriage wasn't working. He wanted a divorce.

Blake had filed the papers himself, and three months later their marriage was history. Since she'd signed a prenuptial agreement, Taylor had received a lump sum, equal to the salary she'd forfeited to leave the firm and become Blake's wife, and a small monthly alimony check. There was no way Taylor could afford to stay on in their expensive Manhattan high rise, and she'd been in the process of job hunting and looking for a cheaper apartment when the letter had come from Grandma Mac's lawyer. In two neatly typed paragraphs, he'd informed her that Grandma Mac had died quite peacefully in her sleep and Taylor had inherited her house in Two Rivers.

As Taylor had stared down at the letter, her eyes wet with tears, she'd realized that she had just been given a priceless gift. Grandma Mac had given her a way out of Manhattan and a ticket to a new life.

And now she was here. Taylor drove down the tree-lined streets, smiling broadly. When she'd been in grade school, her mother had sent her here every summer for a week's visit. Taylor remembered the warmhearted lady who'd taught her how to bake cookies in her kitchen as if it were only yesterday. She still had the first recipe that Grandma Mac had written out for her: "Cowboy Cookies," with chocolate chips and oatmeal. Every birthday and every Christmas, Grandma Mac had sent her a big box of home-baked cookies and a recipe, along with a gift. Taylor had kept every handwritten recipe. The cookies were delicious, and it always gave her a sense of family when she baked them.

Taylor's mother, Candice, hadn't been the type to bake cookies. To tell the truth, she hadn't really been the motherly type at all. Taylor's father, Rob MacIntyre, had died before her first birthday, but Taylor had learned a lot about him from the old photos and letters that Grandma Mac had kept. Taylor was certain that she would have loved her father very much. He'd made only two mistakes in his life, as far as Taylor could see. One was marrying Candice, and the other was dying before Taylor had gotten the chance to know him.

Taylor turned left at the corner of Main Street and Elm. She drove another block and then pulled up in the driveway of a two-story white house in the middle of the block. Her grandmother's house looked exactly as she remembered, and Taylor almost expected to see Grandma Mac at the front door, wearing a pretty bib apron and waving a greeting. But Grandma Mac was gone and Taylor sighed deeply as she got out of her car and walked up to the front door.

Three hours later, Taylor was almost settled in. She'd pulled her car into her grandmother's garage, carried in her suitcases, and unpacked them. She'd emptied the closet and the drawers in her grandmother's rosewood dresser, packed the contents in boxes to store in the attic, and put away all her things. She'd made up the bed with fresh sheets and blankets from the linen closet, hung fresh towels in the upstairs bathroom, and filled the medicine cabinet with her toiletries. And when these tasks had been accomplished, she'd walked through every room in the house and made a list of the few items she wanted to buy. She had just flopped down on the couch in her grandmother's living room to take a break when she remembered that she'd promised to call her grandmother's lawyer when she arrived.

There was a phone on the table by the couch and Taylor lifted the receiver. There was no dial tone. She should have thought to call ahead to have Grandma Mac's phone service restored in her name. Then another, even more dire possibility occurred to her, and Taylor reached out to flick the light switch. She was instantly rewarded by a glow from the old-fashioned lamp, and she gave a big sigh of relief. At least the power hadn't been cut off.

Taylor checked her watch. It was only two-thirty in the afternoon and the phone company office would still be open. She really didn't feel like getting back in her car and driving down there. It would be much easier to knock on one of her neighbors' doors and ask to use their phone.

A cold wind was blowing as Taylor stepped out the door, and she went back inside for her jacket. She remembered

Grandma Mac's description of the long, icy winters in Minnesota, and she took time to add two more items to her growing list. She needed to buy a warmer coat and a pair of warm boots. If Grandma Mac hadn't been exaggerating, she'd need them when winter arrived.

Taylor left the house, locking the door carefully behind her, and walked down the sidewalk to the light blue house next door. She fixed a friendly smile on her face and knocked, but no one answered. She knocked again, a little louder, but the door remained closed. Her neighbors must be gone for the day.

She retraced her steps and set out in the other direction, walking up to the solid-looking brick house on the other side. A couple used to live here, and they'd had a son.

Taylor patted down the curls that had escaped from the twist she'd fashioned at the back of her neck, but she knew it wouldn't do much good. Her hair had always been totally unmanageable when there was the slightest hint of moisture in the air. Realizing that she was frowning, she quickly put a smile on her face and then rang the doorbell. She could hear a dog barking inside and the sound of childish laughter. Someone was home, but they were making so much noise, they hadn't heard the doorbell. Taylor rang it again, and then she knocked on the heavy front door. She was about to knock again when she heard someone approaching the door.

The door opened and Taylor gasped at the sight that greeted her. A tall man with sandy hair and blue eyes stood there in his bathrobe. There was a towel draped around his neck, his hair was wet, and it was clear he'd just stepped out of the shower. Taylor knew she should apologize for disturbing him, but she couldn't seem to find her voice. He was gorgeous—the sexiest man she'd ever seen—and all she could do was stand there blinking.

Several long moments passed without a word. Taylor stared at the man, he stared at her, and at last she managed to find her voice. "Excuse me for bothering you, but I just moved in next door."

"Come on in." The man motioned her inside and closed the door behind her. And then he gave her a friendly smile. "You look so different, I almost didn't recognize you. You're Taylor, right?"

Taylor nodded. The man's smile was very familiar. It hadn't changed since Grandma Mac had introduced them, almost twenty years earlier. She felt a blush rise to her cheeks as she remembered that his disarming grin had been the object of every one of her schoolgirl fantasies. "That's right. And you're Neil DiMarco?"

"In the flesh. And you'll have to excuse me for that. I was in the shower and Angela can't open the front door by herself. It's too heavy for her to handle."

"Angela?"

"My daughter." Neil reached out with one strong arm and pulled her to a spot close to the wall. "You'd better stand over here, next to me."

He had his arm around her shoulders, and it had been months since she'd been this close to a nearly naked man. And Neil wasn't just any man. He was the boy next door—the one she'd wished was her boyfriend when she was eleven.

"Watch out. Here they come now."

Taylor was about to ask what he meant when a little girl with a blond ponytail came hurtling around the corner. On her heels was a massive dog that had to outweigh her by a hundred pounds.

"Slow down, gang." Neil held up his hand, and Angela and the dog skidded to a stop, almost crashing into him. "Where's the fire?"

The little girl giggled. "There's no fire, Daddy. We were just racing."

"I see that." Neil grinned at her, and then he held up his hand again, lowering it in a command. "Sit, boy."

The big dog sat obediently, his tail thumping against the floor. His mouth opened and he seemed to be smiling.

"This is my daughter, Angela." Neil introduced her to Taylor. "And this is Ollie. You'd never know it, but he was the runt of the litter."

"Really?"

Neil reached down to ruffle Ollie's fur. "He was just a little guy when we got him, but now he weighs in at one-twenty."

"I believe you." Taylor nodded. Ollie was so big, he looked capable of knocking over anything in his path. "Is he friendly?"

"He's *too* friendly. He likes to jump up and lick faces and he could bowl you right over if you weren't prepared. He's really very gentle, especially with Angela. It'd be different if one of us was threatened, but normally, Ollie wouldn't hurt a fly."

Angela giggled, looking up at her father. "Ollie *eats* flies, Daddy. He does it all the time. When he sees one, he just snaps it up."

"You're right, Pumpkin. I forgot about that." Neil smiled at her and then he turned to Taylor. "I stand corrected. Ollie doesn't hurt anything *except* flies."

"Are you my new baby-sitter?" Angela turned to stare up at Taylor curiously.

"No. I'm Taylor and I'm your new neighbor. I just moved into my grandmother's house, next door."

"Grandma Mac's house?" Angela's blue eyes clouded when Taylor nodded. "She died."

"That's right. It's very sad and I miss her a lot."

"Me too." Angela looked very serious. "Grandma Mac loved Ollie. She had treats in her kitchen for him. And she loved me, too."

"I'm sure she did." Taylor smiled at her.

Neil reached down and laid a comforting hand on the

top of his daughter's head. It was a completely natural gesture of affection and it made Taylor feel warm inside.

"I just came over to use your phone," Taylor explained. "The one in Grandma Mac's house isn't working. The phone company must have cut off the service."

Neil frowned slightly. "That's strange. Things don't usually move that fast in Two Rivers. If you wait until I'm dressed, I'll come over and take a look. There's no sense calling the phone company and confusing them if there's something else wrong."

"But they could tell by checking their computer, couldn't they?"

"What computer?" Neil laughed. "Our phone company's local and we don't have a computerized system yet. Until about ten years ago, they were still running off PBX boards with a live operator, and that gave us a real advantage over the automated systems."

"Really?" Taylor could see that Neil was teasing her. His blue eyes were twinkling with humor.

"Bertie Kusak ran the switchboard and she knew everybody in town. When we left the house, all we had to do was pick up the phone and tell her where we were going. If the call was important, Bertie made sure we got it."

"Call Forwarding without a monthly charge?" Taylor grinned up at him.

"That's right. We even had Caller ID and an answering service. Bertie told us about every call that came in while we were gone."

Taylor nodded. "I can see that living in Two Rivers is going to be a lot different than living in Manhattan."

"You'll get the hang of it." Neil gave her an encouraging grin. "All you have to do is remember that there's not much privacy in Two Rivers, especially on our block."

"What do you mean?"

"Our unofficial town crier lives right across the street in the yellow house. Her name is Mrs. Wyler, and she's probably on the phone right now, telling all her friends that you came over here. There'll probably be some gossip about us, but don't let it throw you."

"Gossip?" Taylor began to frown. "But why?"

"Because I'm divorced. And you're not married, are you?"

Taylor shook her head. "No. I'm divorced too."

"That's what I figured. I noticed that you weren't wearing a wedding ring. Mrs. Wyler is always trying to match me up with somebody. She feels it's her duty."

The thought of being matched up with Neil wasn't unpleasant, and Taylor was glad that he couldn't read her mind. "What should I do about it?"

"Nothing. The gossip will die down when there's no fuel for the flames."

Taylor was relieved. She wanted her new neighbors to like her, and the last thing she needed was to be the subject of local gossip. "Does Mrs. Wyler sit by the window and watch for something to happen? Or does she hire a whole network of spies?"

"It's a network. Mrs. Wyler is a widow and so are most of her friends. They have a lot of time on their hands and if something interesting happens in Two Rivers, they call each other to pass it along."

Taylor was a bit disappointed. "I thought Two Rivers was idyllic, but there seems to be a downside."

"There's an upside, too. If you ever get into big trouble, like a fire or some other kind of disaster, the whole town will turn out to help you. And there's really no crime. Mrs. Wyler and her friends are like a neighborhood watch. You've got to realize that nothing much out of the ordinary happens here. When a stranger moves to town, it's big news."

"So I can look forward to being treated like an outsider?"

Neil shook his head. "Not at all. Everyone loved your

grandmother and she talked about you all the time. Mrs. Wyler and her friends feel as if they already know you, and I think they'll accept you right away."

"I just hope Grandma Mac said good things about me!" Taylor gave a little laugh.

"She did." Neil nodded quickly. "She even asked me to look out for you. She said she wanted you to love Two Rivers just as much as she did."

When Taylor left to go back home, she was thoughtful. Neil was handsome, intelligent, and he'd let her know that he was available. But he'd also told her that the gossip about them would die down when there was no fuel for the flames. As Taylor straightened up the kitchen and waited for Neil's knock on the door, she wondered exactly what Mrs. Wyler would say about them, and whether she wanted to add some fuel to those gossip flames. It was tempting, very tempting, but she was newly divorced and she wasn't ready for another commitment. Taylor gave a deep sigh and banished any passionate thoughts about Neil from her mind. It wasn't the right time in her life for a new romance, but perhaps they could become really good friends.

TWO

By the time the doorbell rang, Taylor had found an unopened can of coffee in Grandma Mac's sunny kitchen and put on a fresh pot. She hurried to the door, pulled it open, and smiled at Neil and Angela. "I made coffee if you want some. And I found a box of pineapple juice for you, Angela."

"Pineapple?" Angela's face lit up in a smile. "Did you buy it just for me?"

Taylor smiled back and led the way to the kitchen. "It was in Grandma Mac's refrigerator. How do you take your coffee, Neil? I found some sugar, but the cream's gone bad."

"That's okay. I drink it black." Neil sat down on a chair at the kitchen table and accepted a cup of coffee. He opened Angela's juice, stuck in the straw, and handed it to her. "Stay right here, honey. Taylor and I are going to take a look at that phone. And don't drink my coffee while we're gone."

Angela giggled. "I won't. Go fix Taylor's phone, Daddy."

"She's still thinks that Daddy's a miracle worker," Neil explained as they went into the living room. "I'm just waiting for the day that she brings me a balloon and asks me to fix it. That's what happened with Michael."

"Michael?" Taylor turned to him in surprise.

"My son. He's twelve, going on fifty. You'll like him.

He's more adult than I am. I thought we were going to have some problems, a couple of years back, but everything's okay now."

Taylor opened her mouth to ask the obvious question, but she snapped it closed before Neil noticed. She didn't know him well enough to ask if Michael's problems were related to his divorce.

"This is the culprit?" Neil gestured toward the phone on the table by the couch.

"Yes. I clicked it a couple of times to make sure it wasn't sticking, but I still couldn't get a dial tone."

"Okay. Let me take a look." Neil examined the phone and then knelt down to look behind it at the wall. When he straightened up again, he was grinning. "Try it now."

Taylor lifted the receiver and a smile spread across her face. "Angela's right. You *are* a miracle worker! What did you do?"

"I fixed it."

Taylor noticed Neil's teasing grin and laughed. "I know, but *how* did you fix it?"

"With superior knowledge, a grasp of the mechanical, and an eye for the obvious."

Taylor groaned. "Okay. I'll concede that you're a genius. But I need to know how to fix it."

"Why?"

"So I don't have to bother you again. You don't want me to knock on your door every time it stops working, do you?" Neil didn't say anything. He just grinned, and Taylor felt her cheeks turn warm. "Come on, Neil. Tell me what you did."

"Okay, but if you tell anyone else, I'll have to kill you. It's a trade secret."

Taylor nodded. Neil was funny and she liked him a lot. "I promise. Now tell me."

"It was unplugged."

Taylor's mouth dropped open in surprise. "It was *what*?"

"Unplugged. I just plugged it in again."

"That was it?" Taylor was embarrassed when he nodded. "I'm sorry, Neil. You must think I'm a real idiot for not checking that first."

Neil just grinned. "Hey, it could happen to anybody. Besides, it was a great way to meet you again."

"You don't think that I used that as an excuse to . . . ?" Taylor stopped, too humiliated to go on.

"No. From what your grandmother said about you, you're definitely not the devious type. Will you be working here in town, Taylor?"

"I hope so." Taylor nodded quickly. "I was a legal secretary in Manhattan."

"There's only one lawyer in Two Rivers and his wife is his secretary. You'll probably have to commute to Minneapolis."

Taylor sighed. If she remembered correctly, Minneapolis was over fifty miles away, and she wasn't looking forward to the commute. "Are the roads good in the winter?"

"Minnesota roads are the best. Our snowplows get out there the minute the first flakes start to fall. Other states let it pile up and then try to plow it."

"That's good to hear." Taylor was relieved. "Then you never get snowed in?"

Neil looked at her for a moment, and then he started to laugh. "Of course we get snowed in. Last January, we got eighteen inches in one night. The drifts were over eight feet high in some places."

"What happens when you get that much snow?"

"We declare a snow day. The buses can't get through, so all the schools close, and nobody can get to work. It's kind of fun. There's a real sense of pioneer spirit, and we all get out there to help our neighbors shovel."

"But that doesn't happen very often, does it?"

Neil shook his head. "No. You should be fine, commuting to Minneapolis, as long as you have a reliable car."

"I think I do. It got me here."

"That's good, but it might not be winterized. I'll check it out for you and help you run a cord so that you can plug it in."

"Plug it in?" Taylor was puzzled. "But it's a regular car, not an electric."

Neil chuckled. "You still have to plug it in. You'll have to install a head-bolt heater before cold weather hits. It can get down to forty below, and your car won't start without it."

"Forty below?" Taylor's eyes widened. "Grandma Mac said the winters were cold, but I didn't realize they were *that* cold!"

"Don't worry about it. You've got a month or so before real winter sets in, and I'll make sure you're ready. It just takes a little getting used to, that's all. And now we'd better get back to the kitchen. Angela's going through that curious stage. It's courting disaster to leave her alone for too long."

When they stepped through the kitchen doorway, they found Angela standing in the middle of the floor looking sad. Neil walked over to scoop her up in his arms. "What's wrong, Pumpkin?"

"I was just thinking."

"What about?" Neil smoothed back her hair.

"There's no more cowboys."

"Cowboys?" Neil glanced over at Taylor, a puzzled expression on his face.

Taylor began to smile. She knew exactly what Angela meant. "You're talking about Grandma Mac's cowboys, aren't you, Angela?"

Angela nodded, but Neil still looked thoroughly mystified. "Will one of you girls let me in on the secret?"

"Grandma Mac baked cookies for Angela," Taylor explained. "And they were called 'Cowboy Cookies.' They're made with oatmeal and chocolate chips."

Angela nodded. "They were good."

"Yes, they were." Taylor smiled at her. "I have Grandma Mac's recipe. Would you like me to bake some for you?"

"Can you?" Angela looked hopeful.

"Of course I can. Grandma Mac sent me lots of her recipes, and if you help me look, I'll bet we can even find her cookbook."

"I can help." Angela nodded eagerly. "I know where she kept it. It's red and white and it's in the drawer under the spoons."

"Good. Will you find it for me?"

Neil had been watching their exchange with interest and he smiled as he set Angela down. "Thanks, Taylor. Angela's been talking about cowboys for weeks, and I couldn't figure out what she meant."

"Here it is, Taylor." Angela wore a huge smile as she brought the cookbook to Taylor. "I hope there's cowboys in there."

Taylor paged through her grandmother's cookbook. The sections were neatly divided and she quickly found the recipe. "It's right here, Angela. Now all we have to do is see if we have all the right ingredients."

Angela helped as Taylor explored her grandmother's cupboards. They found white sugar and a canister of flour, but there were no chocolate chips or oatmeal.

"I'll have to go to the store before I bake." Taylor jotted down chocolate chips and oatmeal on her shopping list, along with brown sugar, fresh baking soda, and fresh baking powder.

Neil smiled as he watched her lengthening list. "Why don't you come along with us? Angela and I were planning to go grocery shopping this afternoon."

"Thanks." Taylor turned to smile at him. "I'd really appreciate it. I don't remember where the store is."

"There are three, all within two blocks of each other. This week we're shopping at Baxter's. Next week it's Gibson's, and the week after that, it's the Co-op. We alternate."

"Why?"

"Because the stores are locally owned. I want all three of them to get an equal share of our business."

"Then I guess I'd better do the same." Taylor nodded, realizing that she had a lot to learn about Two Rivers. "What time are you leaving?"

"Just as soon as I can pick up my shopping list and check my answering machine for messages. But we'll wait for you to get ready."

"Okay." Taylor nodded. "Just let me grab my purse and a jacket, and I'll walk over with you."

Neil seemed surprised. "But don't you have to put on makeup or do something fancy with your hair?"

"I don't wear makeup unless it's a special occasion and my hair won't behave when there's this much moisture in the air. I'll just go as I am, if you don't mind."

Neil looked utterly amazed. "Mind? Of course I don't mind. I just thought . . . well . . . most of the other women I know would take a long time to get ready."

"Not me." Taylor picked up her purse and her jacket. "I'm ready whenever you are."

The trip to the store was fun. Angela gave up her spot in the front seat of Neil's Jeep Grand Cherokee so that Taylor could ride there. On their way, Neil pointed out the telephone office, the bank, and the elementary school. They pulled into the parking lot at Baxter's, and within minutes Taylor was pushing a shopping cart up and down the aisles.

"What's next, Taylor?" Angela kept pace with Taylor's cart.

"Brown sugar. Grandma Mac's brown sugar has too many lumps. I need some fresh."

"Aisle four." Neil pointed them in the right direction and veered off toward the frozen food aisle. "Come on, Angela. We'll meet Taylor at the checkout line."

Angela looked very unhappy. "Can't I go with Taylor, Daddy? She needs me to tell her where things are."

"I could use some help." Taylor smiled down at Angela and then turned to Neil. "Is that okay, Neil?"

"Sure, if you don't mind. I'll meet you girls up front."

Taylor was impressed at how well Angela knew the store. She'd obviously been here many times with Neil. She told Taylor, in a whisper, that Baxter's was her favorite because it was bigger and had more things than Gibson's or the Co-op.

As they were standing in the checkout line, Taylor noticed that several other shoppers were staring at her curiously. She remembered what Neil had said about Mrs. Wyler and her telephone habits, and she decided that it never hurt to be friendly.

"Hi. I'm Taylor MacIntyre." Taylor turned to smile at the heavyset woman standing behind her. "I just moved into my grandmother's house, and Mr. DiMarco and his daughter were kind enough to bring me to the store."

The woman smiled back, suddenly friendly. "I'm Edith Parker. I live just behind you, in the pink house with white shutters. We're all sorry about your grandmother. She was a wonderful woman."

"Yes, she was. I'm really glad to meet you, Mrs. Parker. I'd like to get to know all of my grandmother's friends."

Edith's smile grew wider. "Call me Edith. And you run right over if there's anything you need. I'm just across the alley and I'm almost always home during the day."

"Thanks. I'll do that. I've never lived in a small town before and it's wonderful to have friendly neighbors. Will you come over for coffee some morning?"

"Of course I will, and I'll introduce you to all the other neighbors. As a matter of fact . . ." Edith moved forward and tapped Neil on the shoulder. "Are you going to the potluck at the community center, Neil?"

Neil nodded. "I wouldn't miss it, especially if you're going to bring your chicken hotdish. It's got to be the best in town."

"I'm glad you like it, Neil." Edith looked modest, but Taylor could see that she was pleased. "Why don't you bring Taylor along with you? She wants to meet her other neighbors."

"That's a good idea. It's tomorrow night, Taylor. Would you like to go?"

"Yes, I would." Taylor nodded quickly and then she turned to Edith again. "You said it was a potluck?"

"That's right. Everybody brings a favorite dish. Of course, we won't expect you to do that, not the first time around. We all understand that you're just getting settled in."

"But I'd like to bring something." Taylor glanced down at her grocery cart. "How about cookies? I was planning to bake tonight."

Edith nodded. "Cookies would be fine. You can never have enough cookies at a potluck. Are you making one of your grandmother's recipes?"

"Yes, Cowboy Cookies. How many should I bring?"

"That's up to you, dear. There's always a big turnout, but everybody brings something and there's always way too much food. We pack up the leftovers and send them to the seniors' center."

It didn't take long to get through the checkout line. The clerk, who Neil introduced as Amy Meyers, packed their things in bags and loaded them into one grocery cart. Neil pushed it out to his Grand Cherokee and Taylor helped him load their groceries inside.

"I owe you an apology," Taylor sighed as Neil opened the car door and she climbed inside. "I didn't mean to rope you into taking me to the potluck dinner."

"That's no problem. I should have thought of it myself. It's a great way for you to meet people."

"What are you bringing?"

"Butter." Neil closed the door behind her and walked around to slide in behind the wheel.

"Butter?" Taylor was surprised. "I thought everybody had to cook something."

"Not the single men. They let us bring butter, coffee, cream, or sugar. Nobody expects us to cook."

"But you *do* cook, don't you?" Taylor remembered the items in Neil's grocery bags. There were lots of snacks and frozen microwave dinners, but that was about it. Perhaps he didn't cook.

Neil was smiling as he put the car in gear and drove out of the parking lot. "I only cook when I have to. I'm not very good at it. Just ask Angela what she thinks of my cooking."

"I like your chicken, Daddy." Angela spoke up from the backseat. "Michael says the trays are like the ones they use at school."

Neil chuckled as he glanced at Taylor. "Angela actually likes frozen microwave dinners. We have those on Tuesdays and Thursdays. On Mondays and Fridays, we eat at Mary and Bill's. And on Wednesdays, we go to Sammy's."

"Are they relatives of yours?" Taylor was curious. Neil hadn't mentioned any family in town.

"No." Neil chuckled again. "Mary and Bill own the café on Main Street, and Sammy's Pizza is out on the highway. On the weekends, we usually get invitations from a couple of local ladies who like to cook for the kids."

Taylor was amused. Neil was a handsome man and she suspected that more than one single woman in Two Rivers might think that the way to Neil's heart was through his children's stomachs.

"That's where we go to the movies." Angela pointed to

a small movie theatre on the corner. "That's the candy store, right next to it."

Neil smiled. "The Bijou is only open on the weekends. They have matinees for the kids and I let Angela go with Michael. The candy store is actually Foster's Drugs, but Ralph still carries penny candy in glass jars."

"Is it still a penny?" Taylor asked the obvious question.

"You bet it is. Ralph told me that he doesn't make a profit, but it's his way of turning back the clock."

"Are you baking the cowboys tonight, Taylor?"

Angela spoke up from the backseat and Taylor turned around to smile at her. "Yes. I think I need a test run, just to make sure I remember how. I haven't baked Cowboy Cookies for a while."

"I could help you, Taylor. Grandma Mac said that I was a good stirrer."

"We've been with Taylor all afternoon, honey." Neil glanced over at Taylor. "She probably needs some time by herself."

Taylor was about to seize the excuse. She was tired and she really wanted to just flop on Grandma's couch for awhile. But Angela looked so eager, she couldn't bear to disappoint her. "Your dad's right. I think I need some time to rest. But I could call you when I'm ready to bake. If your dad says it's okay, you could come over then."

"Can I, Daddy?" Angela's face lit up in a delighted grin.

"Sure, if Taylor's not just being polite." Neil glanced at Taylor again. "Are you?"

Taylor shook her head. "Polite has nothing to do with it. Angela seems to know where everything is in Grandma Mac's kitchen and I think she'd be a big help."

"I will be, I promise." Angela reached out to touch Taylor's hair. "You're nice. And you're my very best friend, except for Michael and Daddy."

Taylor was still smiling as she got out of Neil's car and carried her groceries into the house. Angela was really a sweet little girl and Neil was an excellent father. But a father couldn't make up for the loss of a mother, and it was clear that Angela needed a mother in her life. Perhaps she could help with the mother-daughter things that Neil couldn't do. Baking cookies was a good start and Grandma Mac had paved the way for her by taking Angela under her wing. Later, when Angela grew older, there would be lots of advice to give about clothes, and hair, and boys.

And then there was Michael. He'd need her help to get through his teenage years. Boys needed a mother every bit as much as girls, and Neil couldn't be both a mother and a father to his son.

Neil needed her help most of all. The kids shouldn't have to go out to a café for dinner or eat prepackaged meals. She could cook for all of them. She could be there when Neil needed her, even during the long winter nights. They could cuddle beneath warm covers and . . .

Taylor set her grocery sacks down on the counter and let out a little groan of dismay. She was getting way ahead of herself. Neil hadn't asked her to be a mother to his children and it was perfectly obvious that he wasn't looking for another wife. The trip across country must have exhausted her much more than she'd realized. Here she was, standing there daydreaming about the perfect family life with a man she'd met only three hours ago!

THREE

It was six-thirty by Grandma Mac's kitchen clock when Taylor finished assembling the ingredients for the cookies. She walked to the wall phone, took a deep breath, and punched out Neil's number. As she listened to it ring in the house next door, Taylor gave a little smile. She was glad that Neil had no way of knowing that she'd been fantasizing about him.

"Hello?"

"Hi, Neil." Taylor felt her knees shake slightly and she leaned against the counter for support. Neil had the kind of deep voice that had always made her breathless. "I'm ready to bake now. You can send Angela over."

"Do you mind if Michael comes along? Angela's told him all about you and he wants to meet you."

Taylor didn't hesitate. "He's welcome. I'd like to meet him, too."

"Good. By the way, your timing is great."

"My timing?" Taylor frowned slightly.

"We just finished eating. We'll see you in five minutes, okay?"

Taylor felt a very pleasant jolt of surprise. "We? Are you coming, too?"

"Sure, if that's okay with you. Maybe you can teach me the fine points of turning on the oven."

"I'll make out a series of lesson plans." Taylor hung up

the phone and giggled. She felt like she'd just accepted a date with the most popular guy in the class, and she had to remind herself that she was an adult. Neil DiMarco had a very disturbing effect on her. He made her happy and giddy, as if she were poised on the brink of something wonderful. Perhaps it was good that Angela and Michael were coming with him.

Exactly five minutes later, there was a knock on her back door. Taylor opened it and Angela, Michael, and Neil trooped in. They hung their jackets on the hooks by the back door and then Taylor turned to Neil with a question. "Why did you walk all the way around to the back door?"

"We didn't," Michael, a smaller version of his father with the same charming grin, answered her. "We went out the back way and came through the gap in the hedge."

"Did Mrs. Wyler have anything to do with that?"

"Yeah." Michael's grin grew wider. "We didn't think you'd want her to spread all over town that you and Dad were engaged."

"Engaged?"

Michael shrugged. "That's the way her mind works. She thinks we need a new mother."

"Michael's right." Angela nodded solemnly. "It was my zipper's fault."

Taylor's eyebrows rose. "Your zipper?"

"It's true." Neil's eyes were twinkling as he took up the story. "Last winter, the zipper on Angela's parka got stuck and I stapled it together so she could go out to play. Mrs. Wyler's been looking for a new mother for her ever since."

Taylor started to laugh. "You *stapled* it together?"

"Yeah. I tried gaffer's tape, but that pulled loose. And I didn't want to use a bungee cord. The staples worked just fine and it was only for one afternoon. I got her a new parka the next day."

Taylor was still grinning as she turned to Angela. "Next time your zipper gets stuck, bring it over here. I'll teach you how to fix it. I used to have a zipper that got stuck all the time and I learned to do it."

"Thanks, Taylor. Didn't you have a mother either?"

"I had a mother, but she worked long hours." What Taylor said was the truth. Candice had worked long hours, sitting on bar stools and picking up men. "Since she wasn't home much, I had to learn to do a lot of things by myself."

"Like what?" Michael was clearly interested.

"Like cooking, washing my own clothes, and sewing on buttons. Once you know how, it's not that hard. I had a really nice neighbor who taught me to do all that." Taylor decided it was time to change the subject. "Let's get started. Climb up on that stool, Angela. You can be my official stirrer."

The cookie baking went smoothly. Michael measured out the ingredients and put them into the big bowl on the table while Angela stirred. Neil got into the act when the flour was added and it was too stiff for Angela to handle. Then all three of them filled cookie sheets with mounds of dough and Taylor slid them into the oven.

Michael grinned as he took the first pan out of the oven and set it on a rack to cool. "These sure smell good. We haven't had any cookies like these since . . ."

"I know." Taylor spoke up when he hesitated. "Did Grandma Mac bake cookies for you very often?"

"Every week. Angela helped her and she always came home with a shoe box full."

"I brought it back to her when the cookies were gone and she filled it up again. It's right here." Angela pulled open a drawer and took out a foil-lined box. "It's from the slippers you sent her for Christmas."

Taylor blinked back the sudden moisture that welled up in her eyes. She remembered the slippers, a pretty pink velvet pair with rubber soles. Grandma Mac had written to say that she loved them.

"Are those cowboys cool enough to eat yet?"

Neil brought her back to the present with his question, and Taylor saw the sympathy in his eyes. He'd known that she was thinking about Grandma Mac. "Yes, I think so. Why don't you try one and see?"

"Me too." Angela reached for a cookie and nodded. "They're cool enough, Taylor. But be careful of the chocolate part. Grandma Mac said that stays hot for longer."

Taylor poured four glasses of milk and they all sat down to munch cookies. It was a perfect batch, one of the best she'd ever baked, and Taylor was enjoying her second cookie when something beeped. She rose to her feet to take out the pans of cookies, but Neil grabbed her arm.

"It's not the oven timer." He reached into his pocket and pulled out a pager. "I just got paged."

Taylor laughed. "It's a good thing you told me. Your pager and my oven timer sound the same."

"I'd better go back home to return the call." Neil frowned as he glanced down at the number that was displayed. "They wouldn't page me this late unless it was important, and I might need my appointment book."

Angela looked worried. "Do we have to go now, Daddy? We're not finished baking."

"You and Michael can stay, if it's okay with your dad," Taylor offered quickly, glancing at Neil.

"You're sure you don't mind?"

"Not at all. Do you want me to walk them home when we're through?"

Neil shook his head. "I'll come back. It shouldn't take very long. Just save me some of those cookies."

"I'll save you one cookie, Daddy." Angela held up a single finger and grinned at him. "I'm gonna eat all the rest."

"Okay, but I'd better call Doc Swedenberg. If you eat all those cookies, you're going to need your stomach pumped."

"I was just kidding." Angela rolled her eyes at the ceil-

ing. "Why do you always have to take everything so liber-
ally?"

Taylor exchanged an amused glance with Neil and then
she smiled at Angela. "Do you mean *literally?*"

"Maybe." Angela shrugged. "Dad's always saying something that sounds like that."

Neil laughed and ruffled Angela's hair. "Okay, kids. Taylor's in charge. Carry on with the baking and I'll be right
back."

Taylor thought she'd feel nervous when Neil left. She
wasn't used to being around kids. But the conversation
and the laughter went on as they spooned dough onto
Grandma Mac's baking sheets and filled and refilled the
oven.

When there was a brief lull, Taylor asked a question. "I
forgot to ask. What kind of work does your dad do?"

"Daddy does murders." Angela began to grin. "And
he's really good at it, too."

Taylor's eyes widened. She hoped that Angela was just
mispronouncing another word. "Did you say *murders?*"

"Yes, like killing people." Angela climbed up on her
chair again and picked up her empty glass. "Can I have
more milk, Taylor? I'm thirsty."

Taylor nodded and went to the refrigerator to take
out the carton of milk. There had to be some sort of
misunderstanding. Neil couldn't be a killer. She was about
to put the milk carton back into the refrigerator when
she caught a glimpse of Michael's face. He was struggling
not to laugh.

"Okay, what's so funny?" Taylor faced him squarely.

"Nothing." Michael dissolved into gales of laughter.
"We were just teasing you, that's all."

Taylor bit back a grin. "I see. Then your Dad *doesn't* do
murders?"

"That's what's so funny. He does." Michael took a gulp

of his milk and swallowed. "Dad writes murder mysteries for a big publisher in New York."

Taylor laughed. "That's a relief. For a minute there, I thought . . ."

"We know." Michael grinned as he interrupted her. "Dad told Angela to say that whenever anybody asks. A lot of people really fall for it."

"I almost did."

"But you didn't. It did make you nervous, though."

"You're right," Taylor admitted. "Do you always explain right away?"

Michael nodded. "Now, I do. Dad told me I'd better. That was right after Angela did it with Sheriff Kramer."

"Oh, no!" Taylor imagined all sorts of dire consequences. "What did Sheriff Kramer do?"

Angela giggled. "He knocked on the door and had lots of policemen with him."

"But he laughed when Dad explained it and now they're friends," Michael continued the story. "Dad calls to ask him police questions and he even dedicated one of his . . ."

Angela made a shushing noise and held her finger up to her lips. "I think I hear Ollie scratching at the door. Dad must have let him out."

"Can I bring him in?" Michael got up, but he waited for Taylor to decide. "Ollie minds me. I'll just make him sit down and he won't hurt anything."

Angela stared at her hopefully. "Grandma Mac used to always let Ollie come in."

"Okay." Taylor nodded. She knew when she was defeated. If Grandma Mac had let Ollie into her kitchen, she couldn't very well refuse.

Michael opened the door and Ollie barreled in, but when Michael held up his hand, the big dog stopped in his tracks. "If I let Ollie go around and say hello, he'll come right back here and lie down on the rug. You don't mind, do you, Taylor?"

"Not unless he jumps up on the counter and eats all the cookies."

"He won't." Angela giggled. "Come and say hello to me, Ollie."

Taylor watched as Ollie walked to Angela and licked her face. He really was very gentle. Then he moved to Taylor and sat down on his haunches, looking up at her hopefully.

"Hello, Ollie." Taylor bent down to pet him, not realizing that her face was within licking range. Before she knew it, Ollie had given her a wet doggy kiss on her cheek.

"Sorry about that." Michael laughed at her surprised expression.

"It's okay. I don't mind," Taylor reassured him. She'd never before realized how comforting it was to be licked by a dog who obviously thought you were a friend.

"Come on, Ollie." Michael led him over to the rug by the sink. He lowered his hand and gave the sit command, and Ollie sat. "See, Taylor? He's really good."

"Yes, he is. Why don't you get him a dog biscuit? I picked some up at the store. They're in the cupboard, to the left of the coffeepot."

While Ollie munched and watched them, they finished baking the cookies. Taylor filled Angela's box and put the rest in another foil-lined container for the potluck dinner. They were just finishing up the dishes when Neil came through the door.

"Sorry, Taylor." Neil frowned as he saw Ollie. "I guess he got out when I opened our back door. For a big guy, he's pretty sneaky."

"It wasn't a problem. He was perfectly well behaved. Michael just told him to sit and he sat."

"Taylor likes Ollie," Angela informed him. "She even let him lick her face."

Neil glanced at Taylor and laughed. "Did you have a choice?"

"Not really. But I liked it."

"Good. If you're all through baking, I guess we'd better get going. Michael's got school tomorrow and it's getting late."

Taylor glanced at the clock. "You're right. It's almost nine. Is there something wrong, Neil?"

Neil looked a bit startled. "How did you know?"

"Your smile is different. And you look a little upset."

Neil was clearly surprised at her answer. "I thought I was hiding it pretty well, but you're right. My editor just told me that they rescheduled my book tour. It was set for next month, but they want to move it up."

"That's bad?"

"No, it's just inconvenient. I had everything all arranged. The kids told you I wrote, didn't they?"

Taylor nodded. "Angela said you did murders, but Michael explained."

"Taylor didn't fall for it, Dad." Michael looked oddly proud of that fact. "She got a little nervous, but she figured out that we were teasing her. I think it's because she knows you better than anybody else."

Neil glanced at her and Taylor dropped her eyes. She knew what was going through his mind. How could she know him so well when they'd just met?

"We'd better pack up and go home. You two have been in Taylor's hair for long enough." Neil got Angela's jacket from the hook and held it out to her. "It's past bedtime for you, Pumpkin."

Angela shook her head. "I don't want to go, Daddy. I want to stay overnight with Taylor. She's got an extra bedroom. She told me she did."

"Not tonight. You have to get up early and make me some toaster waffles for breakfast. You promised, remember?"

Angela sighed. "I remember. Okay, Daddy. If you can't get along without me, I guess I have to go home."'

"Help Angela with her jacket, will you, son?" Neil exchanged a man-to-man glance with Michael. "I need to take another look at Taylor's phone to make sure it's plugged in right."

While Michael was helping Angela, Neil took Taylor's arm and walked her into the hallway. When they were out of earshot, he turned to her. "I just wanted to say thank you. Angela hasn't warmed up like this to another woman since her mother left."

"When was that?"

"Almost three years ago, right before Angela's second birthday. She's really missed having a mommy. I do everything I can, but it's different."

"Of course it is." Taylor nodded. "And I think you're a great father. She's a very sweet girl and she's welcome to come over to see me any time she wants to."

Neil reached out to touch her hair. It wasn't sensual, just a friendly gesture, but Taylor felt a current of pleasure flow through her. Then he cupped her face in his hand and kissed her lightly on the forehead. "You're a lot like your grandmother and I'm really glad you moved to Two Rivers. It's going to mean a lot to Angela to have you next door."

After they'd left, Taylor sat at the kitchen table with a bemused expression on her face. For a few moments, while Neil and the kids had helped her bake, she had actually felt as if she was a part of a real family.

FOUR

Taylor took one last glance in the mirror and frowned. She was wearing a cream-colored knit dress that had been perfect for a casual evening out in Manhattan, but she wasn't sure it was right for a potluck in Two Rivers. Her bed was strewn with the outfits she'd tried on and discarded: a bottle-green silk dress, a burgundy pantsuit with a shawl collar, a black wool sheath that hugged her figure, and a soft blue suit with a silk blouse in a slightly lighter shade. Nothing seemed to be appropriate and there was no one to advise her.

She'd never been this indecisive before. Taylor sighed and turned away from the mirror. The knit dress would just have to do. She found the perfect scarf, a red and green floral pattern that reminded her of roses and ivy, and draped it around her neck. Once she'd secured it with a plain gold circle pin, she stood back to survey her reflection again. The woman who stared back at her looked anxious and Taylor knew why. First impressions counted for a lot, and she didn't want to get off on the wrong foot. She really wanted her new neighbors to like her.

The grandfather clock in the upstairs hallway was just striking the hour when Taylor went down the stairs. Neil would be here any minute. She pulled out her coat and was just searching for a pair of gloves when her doorbell rang. Taylor closed the closet door—she'd just have to get along without gloves—and hurried to let Neil in.

"Hi. You look . . . very pretty."

Taylor heard the hesitation in his voice and she knew that something was wrong. "My outfit isn't right, is it?"

"It's beautiful. You look great, but you didn't have to get all dressed up. Nobody else does."

Taylor sighed. "And I was afraid I might be too casual. Do you think I'll stick out like a sore thumb?"

"Well . . ."

Neil hesitated again, and Taylor could tell he was uncomfortable. "Please tell me, Neil. I don't have anybody else to ask."

"You'll probably stick out. I think you look beautiful, but most of the women around here don't have much money to spend on clothes."

Taylor caught his meaning immediately. "And this looks too expensive?"

"You got it. It's just a little too stylish for a potluck at the community center."

"Then I'd better change into something else." Taylor nodded quickly. "What will the other women be wearing?"

"Slacks and sweaters."

"If you don't mind waiting a couple of minutes, I'll go up and change."

Neil nodded. "Take your time. These things never start when they're supposed to."

Taylor quickly changed to a pair of gray slacks. She pulled on the red sweater that Grandma Mac had sent her for Christmas one year, and changed to a pair of hard-soled leather moccasins. The whole process took her less than three minutes and when she came back down the stairs, Neil grinned at her.

"Is this better?" Taylor turned around, letting him look at her.

"It's perfect. That's a hand-knit sweater, isn't it?"

"Yes. Grandma Mac made it for me."

"You couldn't have chosen anything better." Neil picked up her coat and held it out for her. "While you were changing I thought about the dress that you were wearing. It'd be perfect at the Cloisters."

"The Cloisters?" Taylor buttoned her coat and picked up her purse.

"It's an old nunnery they converted into a theme restaurant."

Taylor nodded. "It sounds fascinating."

"Absolutely. They have a dress code. Jackets and ties for the men, and dresses for the ladies. It's the kind of place that local couples go for special occasions, like anniversaries and romantic dinners. French cuisine and a great chef. I think you'll like it."

Taylor dropped her eyes. She couldn't help wondering whether Neil was merely telling her about it, or if he was asking her for a date. She took her time about buttoning her coat, but he didn't say any more about it.

"You'll need gloves. It stopped raining, but it's cold out there."

Taylor nodded and grabbed the first pair she could find. They didn't exactly match her coat, but they'd do. "I'd like to read some of your books, Neil. Will you tell me some of the titles?"

"Sure." Neil opened the door and took her arm. "Do you like murder mysteries?"

"I used to. I haven't read any lately, but I'd really like to read yours."

Neil put his arm around her shoulders and walked her to his car. "I'm sure I've got some extra copies in the office. I'll dig out a couple for you."

Taylor was puzzled as she got into Neil's Grand Cherokee and saw that the backseat was empty. "Where are the kids?"

"They're waiting at the house." Neil backed up and

pulled into his own driveway. "Michael said he'd watch for me and bring Angela out. She was having trouble deciding whether she should wear her new red parka or her fake fur jacket."

Taylor nodded solemnly. "She wants to make a fashion statement?"

"I guess so."

"Then it'll be the fur. A girl's never too young for fake fur."

Neil chuckled. "You're probably right, but Angela's starting pretty early. I thought I'd have another couple of years before I had to hire a wardrobe consultant."

"You don't have to hire one. I'm right next door and I'll help. Of course, I'd better research what the fashionable almost-five-year-olds are wearing this year."

Neil reached over to take her hand. "Thanks, Taylor. It's been rough, not having a woman around to advise me."

"You couldn't ask one of the local women?" Taylor's hand tingled where Neil touched it and she wondered how such a simple gesture could send waves of longing through her whole body.

"I tried that with someone I was dating, but it didn't work out."

"What happened?"

"She thought I was asking for more than advice." Neil sighed. "It's partially my fault. I guess I didn't make it clear that I wasn't looking for another wife."

"You don't want to get married again?"

"No. I like my life just the way it is. Marriage would only complicate things. How about you?"

Warning bells went off in Taylor's head. She suspected that Neil would back off if she gave the slightest indication that she might want to get married again. "I tried marriage once and it didn't work. I'd be a fool to go through something like that again!"

"Was it that bad?"

Taylor nodded. "Yes, at the end. Finding out that my husband wanted a divorce was a shock."

"It's always a shock." Neil removed his hand so that he could toot the horn again. "Where are those kids?"

"Here they come." Taylor watched as the front door opened and Michael and Angela came down the steps.

"You're right. It's the fake fur." Neil saluted her. "You're hired as Angela's fashion consultant."

"Thank you. I'll get started right away by telling her that she's too young to wear lipstick."

"Lipstick?" Neil gave Angela a sharp look as he opened the door and she climbed into the backseat. "What's that on your face, Pumpkin?"

"Lipstick, Daddy. I found it in your bathroom. I think Nina left it, or maybe it was . . ."

"Never mind," Neil interrupted her. "Hold still and let Taylor wipe it off. You're too young to wear lipstick."

"I told her to wash her face, but she wouldn't." Michael sounded disgruntled. He mumbled something inaudible about girls and snapped his seat belt.

Angela frowned at him. "But I just wanted to look pretty, like Taylor."

Taylor knew she had to speak up before the disagreement could escalate. "You don't *need* to wear lipstick, Angela. If I had pretty lips like yours, I wouldn't cover them up with lipstick."

"But your lips are pretty and you're wearing lipstick!" Angela wasn't about to give in.

"Do you really think so?"

"Yes, they're very pretty."

"Thank you." Taylor smiled at her. "Then maybe we should both take it off."

Angela thought about it for a moment and then she nodded. "Okay. If you take yours off, I'll take mine off."

"Deal." Taylor pulled a tissue from her purse and wiped

off her lipstick. Then she handed another tissue to Angela. "Your turn."

Angela wiped off her lipstick and smiled at Taylor. "Is that better?"

"Much better. I think you look even prettier without it. And that jacket is stunning. Do you know what it's made of?"

"Fake fur."

"Faux fur." Taylor emphasized the pronunciation. "That's a French word that means 'fake,' but it sounds much classier."

"Faux fur. I like that, Taylor." Angela leaned back to let Michael buckle her seat belt.

Taylor noticed that Neil was chuckling softly as he put the car into gear. As soon as Angela and Michael started talking to each other in the backseat, she leaned closer to him. "What's so funny?"

"My daughter, the master manipulator." Neil grinned at her. "Do you realize that she just got you to ruin your makeup?"

Taylor shrugged. "It doesn't matter. I don't really like to wear it, anyway. It's always struck me as humorous."

"Really?" Neil raised his brows. "Why?"

"Just watch the ads on television. They all say their cosmetics are geared toward the natural look. But if you want to look natural, why wear them at all?"

"Good point. You're a wise lady, Taylor."

"Thanks." Taylor leaned back in her seat and sighed softly. How wise could she be, feeling this way about a man who'd just told her that he didn't want to get married again?

Taylor glanced around her and smiled. The community center was cheerful and bright, even though it was in the basement of the Two Rivers Municipal Building. The walls were painted sunshine yellow, the high basement windows were curtained with blue and white gingham, and the kitchen was equipped with restaurant-style appliances.

The kids had left them right after they'd stepped in the door. Michael had gone with a classmate and Angela had joined a group of girls her age. Neil had led Taylor directly to the kitchen where they gave their contributions to the potluck to April Hennesey, the principal's wife, and introduced her to the ladies who were working in the kitchen. Then he'd taken her out to sit at one of the long tables to wait for everyone else to arrive.

Over the past twenty minutes, Taylor had met a variety of people. Edith Parker had come over to introduce Mrs. Wyler, their nosy neighbor. She'd also met Laura Pringle, who lived in the big green house on the corner, and Sally and Evan Jacobson, who lived directly across the street in the one-story yellow house with a mailbox shaped like a fish. Amy Meyers, the clerk Taylor remembered from Baxter's Grocery Store, had stopped by to say hello, and Nina Langer, a pretty blonde with startling pink lipstick, had come over to greet Neil. Nina had been polite when Neil had introduced them, but Taylor had felt a definite chill. She was almost certain that Nina was the owner of the lipstick that Angela had used.

"Here come the Petersons." Neil motioned toward the couple who had just come in. "They're your neighbors on the other side."

Taylor smiled as the Petersons wove their way through the crowd, heading for their table. Mr. Peterson was built like a former football player with wide shoulders and close-cropped hair. His wife was his physical opposite, a tiny, birdlike woman who looked as if a strong breeze might blow her away.

"Hi. I'm Tom Peterson. And this is my wife, Georgina."

"I'm glad to meet you." Taylor smiled at them both. "I

knocked on your door the other day, but you weren't home."

Georgina nodded. "We just got back in town today. We were visiting my daughter and her husband in Wisconsin. We'll be here for two more weeks and then we leave again, for Florida."

"Do you travel a lot?" Taylor was curious.

"Only in the winter." Tom laughed. "We're snowbirds."

"We head for warmer places when the snow starts to fall." Georgina glanced up at her husband with a smile and he smiled back. "When Tom retired, I made him promise that we'd never have to spend another winter in Minnesota."

Neil turned to Taylor. "Tom and Georgina bought an RV and they drive all over the country."

"Not *all* over," Georgina corrected him. "We only go to the southern states, where it's warm in the winter. We started doing that right after the snowblower incident."

Tom nodded. "When I got my snowblower stuck on the roof of the garage, Georgina made me promise that we'd leave before another winter set in."

"Your snowblower got stuck on top of the *roof*?" Taylor exclaimed.

Neil laughed at her astonished expression. "There was a big snowbank in back of the garage and Tom wheeled his snowblower up there to clear off the roof. It broke down and Tom just left it up there, figuring he'd fix it the next day and finish the job. But during the night we had a big thaw and the snowbank melted before he could wheel it down."

"Is this one of the Minnesota tall tales I've been hearing about?" Taylor turned to Georgina with a grin.

"No, it happened just the way Neil told you. Tom had to climb up there and dismantle it and bring it down in pieces. It took him a whole week to put it back together, and that's when I put my foot down."

Neil nodded. "I was there, Taylor. There's no heat in the garage, so Tom had a tarp spread out in Georgina's kitchen and that's where he worked on it."

"We ate at the café for two solid weeks," Georgina explained. "And that darned snowblower's never worked right since. That was when I decided that I'd had enough winters to last me a lifetime."

Neil smiled at Taylor. "Even though Tom and Georgina bail out every winter, we still love them. And they're always back by the time fishing season opens. Isn't that right, Tom?"

"I wouldn't miss it." Tom nodded quickly and then he turned to Taylor. "Just don't plan to drive anywhere on the opening day of fishing season. They're out on the highway bumper-to-bumper and every car is towing a boat. It's a regular parade. Minnesotans own one boat for every six people. That's the highest boat-to-person ratio in any state."

Taylor smiled at the thought of a neverending parade of boats and cars. "Maybe I should take up fishing, now that I'm living in Minnesota."

"Good idea." Tom winked at Neil. "When we get back, just bring her out to the cabin. I'll teach her to fish off the dock and see how she likes it. Bring the kids, too. Michael likes to fish, and Angela's old enough to dangle a line. We'll make a whole day of it."

"I'll do that. Thanks, Tom."

"Gotta go." Tom waved at someone across the room. "There's Ned Olsen. I have to give him our schedule. He's taking care of our house this year."

When Tom and Georgina had left, Neil pushed back his chair. "Looks like they're ready to serve. Come on, Taylor. I'll show you which hotdish is Edith's. You'd better take some so you can tell her that you liked it."

"Very smart." Taylor nodded. "Is a hotdish the same as a casserole?"

"It's a one-dish meal, baked in the oven.

Taylor nodded and followed Neil to the line that was forming by the buffet table. On the way, they passed by Nina Langer, and Neil gave her a friendly wave. Nina was sitting with a very attractive redhead, and though both of them smiled at Neil, the looks they gave Taylor could have turned water into ice.

Before she had time to worry about it, Angela raced over and took her hand. "They put your cookies in a basket, Taylor. I saw them. They're right down there at the end of the table."

"Good." Taylor smiled down at her and then she happened to glance over at Nina Langer and her friend. They were both staring at her and it wasn't a friendly stare.

FIVE

When Taylor had finished eating, she turned to Neil with a smile. "I never knew there were so many different kinds of pickles."

"Pickled cucumbers, pickled carrots, pickled beans, pickled cauliflower . . ." Neil counted them off on his fingers. "Plus pickled crab apples, pickled peaches, pickled watermelon rind, and pickled meat. The pickling preserves it. My mother used to make pickled pig's feet. They're delicious."

"Pig's feet?" Taylor shuddered slightly. "Do I really want to know about that?"

Neil grinned and shook his head. "Maybe not. You've only been a Minnesotan for two days."

"I didn't eat any tonight, did I?" Taylor glanced down at her empty plate in alarm.

"No. I think you had some headcheese, though."

Taylor shuddered again and decided not to ask what headcheese was. Instead, she got to her feet and picked up her plate. "I think I'll go tell Edith how much I liked her casserole."

"Hotdish," Neil corrected her.

"*Hotdish.* And then I'll poke my head in the kitchen and see if they need any help."

"Good. They can always use an extra pair of hands. Let's

meet back here in twenty minutes or so. If you're not here,
I'll figure somebody handed you a dishtowel."

Taylor found Edith and complimented her on the
chicken hotdish. She remembered her Grandma Mac's
recipe file, each card written out in a different hand-
writing, and asked if Edith would give her the recipe.
Judging by the broad smile on Edith's face as she agreed,
it had been the right thing to do.

The kitchen was crowded, but Taylor managed to find
April Hennesey to ask her if there was anything that she
could do to help with the clean up. April looked surprised
at her offer and said that she had everything under control, but Taylor knew she'd also made points with the principal's wife.

There was only one task left to accomplish before she
could enjoy herself. Taylor pasted a cheerful smile on her
face and headed straight for Nina Langer's table. Her legs
were shaking slightly as she approached. She felt like a
new kid in school, hoping to make friends in a hostile
environment and afraid that her classmates would reject
her.

"Hello, Nina." Taylor put on the friendliest smile she
could muster.

"Hi." Nina smiled, but it was merely a polite gesture.
"Have you meet my friend, Suzanne Voelker?"

"Not yet."

"Suzanne, meet Taylor MacIntyre. She just moved here
from New York."

Taylor smiled at the pretty redhead. "I'm glad to meet
you, Suzanne."

"Same here." Suzanne smiled, but there was a great
deal of curiosity in her glance. "Do you like it here in Two
Rivers?"

Taylor seized the opening she'd been given. "It's wonderful. Everyone is so friendly. I like it a lot better than

Manhattan. Does it really get down to forty below in the winter?"

"Sometimes it gets even colder. You'd better keep your parka handy."

Taylor sighed. "I don't have one yet. I started a list of the things I'll need to buy, but I'm sure I'll forget something important."

"You'd better buy a warm hat," Nina advised. "Get something that covers your head completely. You can freeze your ears in a couple of seconds when it gets that cold outside."

Taylor shivered slightly. "Really?"

"I'm not kidding. When cold weather hits, you've got to protect your skin. It won't *feel* that cold—especially if the sun is shining and there's no wind—but frostbite's nasty and it can happen much quicker than you think."

"Thanks for telling me." Taylor smiled at her.

"Get a thermometer and hang it right outside your kitchen window," Suzanne advised. "And remember to check it every morning before you go out. If it's below thirty-two degrees, just think of your body like a piece of meat that's going in the freezer."

Taylor started to laugh. "I should think of my body like a piece of meat?"

"Well . . . not exactly." Suzanne started to giggle, along with Nina. "I guess that was a bad comparison."

"Oh, I don't know about that." Nina was laughing so hard, her coffee cup sloshed and she had to set it back down on the table. "I've known a few guys with that attitude."

Suzanne glanced around and then pulled out a chair. "Sit down, Taylor. Mrs. Wyler's staring at us."

"Thanks." Taylor slid into the chair. "Is that why all the women are wearing slacks and sweaters, instead of dresses?"

Nina nodded. "Absolutely. Just think about it. If you

wear something with a skirt, all you've got between you and the cold is a thin pair of panty hose. Get some wool slacks and tuck them into your boots."

"Jeans won't work," Suzanne advised. "They're just not warm enough. And forget about fashion. It's not worth it. It's impossible to look like a model when you have to dress up like an Eskimo."

Taylor smiled. The icy atmosphere had thawed the minute they'd started to give her advice. "Thanks for telling me. I didn't really want to ask Neil DiMarco for advice, and he was the only one home when I moved in."

"Neil's always there," Suzanne said. "He's a writer and he works at home. Did Angela do her little act for you?"

Taylor nodded. "Yes, and I almost fell for it. She's really sweet, isn't she?"

"She's a doll." Nina nodded. "And Michael's a good kid, too. It's just too bad that Neil is so freaked about marriage. Those kids need a mother."

Suzanne and Nina exchanged glances and then Suzanne spoke. "Do you have kids of your own, Taylor?"

"No. I guess that's lucky, the way it turned out. My divorce would have been even more of a headache if we'd had kids."

Suzanne rolled her eyes toward the ceiling. "Tell me about it! I've got a son, and the custody thing is a pain. Robby's dad lives in Malibu and it takes me forever to get him settled down after a summer there. They always go off to Disneyland and Knott's Berry Farm, and my ex takes him to screenings of all the new movies. They eat out in fancy restaurants every night and all Robby has to do is look at something and Mark buys it for him."

"That must be tough." Taylor was sympathetic. "How can you complete with something like that?"

"I can't. When Robby comes home to Hamburger Helper and homework, he's impossible for the first week. It's such a contrast. He knows that I don't have extra money to do all the things that his dad does, but he resents it."

"Suzanne teaches math at the high school." Nina smiled at her friend. "She moved back here last year, after her divorce. Her parents live in that big gray house across from the school."

"Do you live with them?" Taylor couldn't imagine any situation that could cause her to move back in with Candice.

"Live with them?" Suzanne rolled her eyes again. "Not on a bet! When I got my first paycheck, I rented a two-bedroom apartment at the Oaks. You probably saw it when you drove into town. It's that big tan apartment building just off the highway. Drop by and see me sometime."

"I'd like to." Taylor smiled. "And you'll have to drop by to see me. I haven't done anything to the house yet, but maybe you can give me some ideas."

Suzanne gave a rueful laugh. "My place would still be a disaster if Nina hadn't come to the rescue. She's an expert at low-cost decorating. Nina can go to a garage sale with twenty dollars and come back with everything you need to fix up a whole room."

"That's because I refuse to pay a penny more than what something's worth and I like knockoffs as much as brand names," Nina explained. "But Taylor probably doesn't need to decorate on the cheap."

"Oh, yes, I do." Taylor nodded quickly. "I don't even have a job yet, and from what I hear, I won't be able to find one in Two Rivers."

"Why?" Nina looked interested.

"I'm a legal secretary. I'll probably have to commute to Minneapolis, and I'm not looking forward to that."

Suzanne looked very sympathetic. "I don't blame you. It's a long, cold trip in the winter. But maybe you can find something else in town. It won't pay as much, but commuting is expensive. You might come out ahead in the long run."

"I'll call you if I hear about anything," Nina offered. "I work at the local paper and part of my job is writing up the want ads. Do you still have your grandmother's phone number?"

Taylor nodded. "Yes, the phone's still in her name. I'd really appreciate it, Nina. I'm here to stay and it's good to know I've got friends in town."

After a few more minutes of conversation, Taylor walked back to the table she shared with Neil. She felt as if she'd accomplished something. Nina and Suzanne were no longer enemies, and they might even turn out to be good friends.

"I saw you talking to Nina and Suzanne." Neil looked a bit worried. "Did they give you a rough time?"

Taylor shook her head. "Not at all. They were friendly."

"Suzanne and Nina were *friendly?*"

"Yes. They gave me all sorts of advice on what to wear in the winter and how to get a local job."

Neil seemed surprised at her answer. "That's good. I wasn't sure how they'd react to you."

"Because they might think that I was competition?"

Neil winced. "Yeah, something like that. I used to date Nina in high school and we went out a couple of times last year."

"And Suzanne?"

"Her, too. Suzanne's son is the same age as Michael."

Taylor just smiled. She wanted to ask whether he was still dating Nina or Suzanne, but it really wasn't any of her business. She'd find out, sooner or later. She was bound to hear, with Mrs. Wyler right across the street.

"Here comes Mary." Neil motioned toward the athletic-looking woman with bleached blond hair who was heading toward their table. "She owns the café."

Mary arrived at their table and gave Taylor a big smile.

"Hi, Taylor. I'm Mary Baxter. I just wanted to tell you that those cookies you brought were incredible. Where did you get them?"

"I made them." Taylor smiled back. "They're called Cowboy Cookies and they're one of Grandma Mac's recipes."

"Bill would have made off with the whole basket if I hadn't slapped his hand. If I had cookies like that at the café, my breakfast crowd would be in heaven."

Neil looked thoughtful. "Do you really think that you could sell them, Mary?"

"Sell them?" Mary looked utterly astounded. "Of course I could sell them! I'd probably go through four or five dozen a day."

Neil was smiling as he turned to Taylor. "How about it, Taylor? Could you make five dozen cookies a day?"

"Of course I could. Why?"

"I was thinking that you might start a cottage industry. You said you weren't looking forward to commuting, and baking cookies is something that you could do at home. I don't know if it would be cost effective. We'll have to figure that out. And you'd have to find more customers in town."

"There's always Bill." Mary jumped into the discussion. "He's got a bakery counter at the grocery store, but it's mostly just bread and rolls. If he sold your cookies at the checkout, most of his customers would buy them. There's Al Cooper, too. I heard him raving about them. Just sit tight and I'll go get him in on this."

When Mary left, Taylor turned to Neil. "Who's Al Cooper?"

"He owns the Bijou. Mary's right, you know. Your cookies would be a big hit with the kids at the matinees."

Before Taylor could do more than nod, she saw Mary drawing a tall, thin man with a full head of coal black hair through the crowd. They were still several tables away when Taylor realized that Al Cooper's startling black hair was obviously dyed. He appeared to be somewhere between sixty and seventy years of age and he was obviously attempting to look like a matinee idol of the thirties. She turned to Neil with a smile. "Would that be Mr. Cooper?"

Neil nodded. "You bet."

"And his hero is Valentino?"

"Smart girl." Neil grinned at her.

The unlikely couple arrived at their table and Mary was the first to speak. "Taylor, this is Al Cooper. He thinks he could sell tons of your cookies on the weekends."

"Mary suggests that I order your cookies for the concession counter at the Bijou. They are very delicious."

Al's voice was surprisingly deep and he had a European accent that she couldn't quite identify. Taylor suspected that his accent was about as real as his hair color, and she made a mental note to ask Neil about it later. "Thank you, Mr. Cooper."

"I shall be delighted to support a fledgling local business." Al nodded and Taylor tried not to stare. He really did resemble an aging Valentino. "When may I anticipate delivery?"

"I'm not sure." Taylor blinked to clear her head. This was all happening very fast.

"We still have to work out the details, Al." Neil reached under the table to squeeze Taylor's hand and she felt a warm tingle. She assumed that he was warning her not to make any commitments yet, and she just nodded.

"Take your time," Mary advised her. "Go over the whole thing with Neil tonight, and let me know when you come to a decision. I really think you could do it, and it's not like you'd be putting anyone else out of business. We used to have a bakery, but it's been closed for almost five years."

Neil glanced around at the crowd of people who were getting into their coats and jackets. "Looks like the party's breaking up. We'll call you, Mary, and let you know what Taylor decides. You, too, Al."

Taylor was thoughtful as she said good-bye to the people she'd met and they collected Angela and Michael. On their drive home, her mind was filled with possibilities. It would be wonderful if she could work at home and support herself in the process. She liked to bake a lot more than she enjoyed typing legal phrases into a computer or standing in line to file papers at a courthouse.

As they pulled up in front of Taylor's house, Angela reached out to tap Neil on the shoulder. "Can Taylor come over and kiss me good night, Daddy?"

"Sure, if she wants to. We need to talk over something anyway." Neil turned to Taylor with a smile. "Why don't you give me a couple of minutes and come over for a nightcap?"

"I'd love to. Ten minutes?"

"That's fine. Just come on in. I'll leave the front door unlocked."

SIX

Taylor headed back down the stairs. She'd said good night to Michael and Angela and now it was time to join Neil. She found him on the couch in the family room, his feet propped up on a leather footstool. The fire in the fireplace was crackling cheerily, Ollie was stretched out near the hearth, and soft music was playing on the stereo. Taylor couldn't help thinking about the cozy domestic scene they made and she spoke without thinking. "You two look like an ad for a mountain resort. All you need are a couple of ski poles propped up in the corner."

"Come and sit down, Taylor." Neil smiled and patted the couch next to him. "I made hot chocolate. It's going to get down below freezing tonight so I laced it with brandy."

Taylor smiled and sat down next to him. "Thanks. I turned up the heat before I left the house, just in case."

"Do you have enough wood for the winter?"

"Wood?" Taylor was alarmed. "Does Grandma Mac have a wood-burning furnace?"

Neil laughed. "Nobody uses those anymore. Your furnace is gas, just like mine. I was talking about the wood for your fireplace."

"I didn't notice any wood. Where would it be?"

"In the woodshed. That's out in back, right next to the garage. I'll show you tomorrow."

Taylor nodded and picked up her mug of hot chocolate. She took a sip and started to smile. "This is wonderful."

"I'm glad you like it." Neil looked pleased. "How about your weather stripping? Does it need to be replaced?"

"I'm not sure. Actually, I don't even know what weather stripping is."

"It's the little strip of foam around the inside of the doors."

As Neil went on to explain all the things she needed to do to weatherize her house, Taylor tried to pay attention. It was difficult to concentrate when Neil was sitting so close to her. The firelight glinted off his hair, turning his eyes an even deeper shade of blue, and throwing the planes of his handsome face into intriguing shadow.

"Taylor?"

Taylor snapped to attention with a jolt. "Yes?"

"I said, I'll help you check your house tomorrow to make sure everything's in shape for the winter."

"I'd appreciate that, Neil. Thank you. When I lived in Manhattan, the super took care of everything."

"What were you thinking about?"

"I was just wondering if I could really start a cookie business."

"I don't see any reason why you couldn't." Neil sat up and grabbed the pen and pad that sat on the coffee table. "I made some notes while you were upstairs with the kids. The way I see it, you have to ask yourself a series of questions. If the answers are right, you've got a real shot at it."

Taylor nodded, trying not to think of his hands and the way his fingers would feel on her skin. "What questions?"

"How many cookies can you bake in a workday? We have to arrive at a reasonable figure so you'll know how many orders you can fill. Say you start at nine, take an hour off for lunch, and bake until four. How many dozen do you think you can make?"

Taylor sighed. "I really don't know, Neil. I'd just have

to try it and see. Last Christmas, I baked cookies for all my friends and it took me all weekend."

"How many friends was that? And how many cookies did you give them?"

Taylor counted them off in her head. "I think there were about a dozen . . . no, thirteen. And I took a tray of cookies to the office. Each friend got three dozen. I put them in tins and I counted the first one to see how many cookies it would take to fill it."

Neil nodded. "That's thirty-six dozen. How many did you take to the office?"

"I'm not sure, but it was a big tray and they were stacked double. It must have been at least six dozen. But those were decorated, so they took longer."

"How much longer?"

"Too much longer." Taylor laughed, remembering how she'd agonized over the frosting. "I had to learn how to use a pastry bag and I ruined about a dozen before I got the hang of it. I'd guess about three hours."

"Okay. And you could have baked another couple of batches in the time it took you to decorate those cookies?"

"Definitely." Taylor nodded quickly. "Especially if they were drop cookies. Those go a lot faster."

Neil looked thoughtful. "That's something I didn't consider. Different types of cookies take longer?"

"Yes. The easiest are the kind you drop on a cookie sheet by the spoonful. They're called drop cookies. You just bake them and they spread out in the oven. Peanut butter cookies have to be pressed down with a fork before they're baked, and my sugar cookies take even more time. They have to be formed into balls, rolled in sugar, and then flattened before they go into the oven."

"The sugar cookies are the most difficult to make?"

"No, I have recipes for some that take even longer. There's one type of Scandinavian cookie dough that has to be spread out in thin circles with a spoon, only two to a cookie sheet. When they come out of the oven, they're rolled into a cone shape before they cool. They're used to hold sweetened whipped cream or ice cream and they're wonderful. And I also make Russian Teacakes. They're formed into balls and baked. Then they're rolled in powdered sugar when they come out of the oven, and again when they're cool. There are Spritz Cookies, too. They're piped onto a cookie sheet. There are others that are cut out in fancy shapes and several kinds that are deep fried instead of baked."

"That's enough." Neil laughed and held up his hand to stop her. "I think you'd better stick to the drop cookies at first. If you get any special orders for the others, you'll just have to charge more to make up for your time."

Taylor nodded. "That's a good idea. If I actually do this, I'll start out with Cowboy Cookies, Oatmeal Raisin Chews, and Coconut Crunch. They're all drop cookies."

"Great." Neil added some figures. "I figure you can make at least twelve dozen drop cookies a day. Does that sound reasonable?"

Taylor thought about it for a moment, and then she shook her head. "Double that. I baked eight dozen Cowboy Cookies last night and that only took a couple of hours."

"But we helped you."

"That's true." Taylor conceded the point with a smile. "Let's split the difference and say that I can make eighteen dozen."

"We'll have to do a test run before we decide. We have to figure out exactly what it costs you, and that won't be easy. You'll have to add up all your supplies, the cost of actually baking the cookies, and the money you'll spend for packaging. And then you'll have to tack on a generous hourly wage for yourself."

Taylor was impressed. "I didn't even think about packaging and Grandma Mac's shoe boxes won't last forever."

"You'll need boxes printed with the name of your business and a telephone number for reorders. I'll hop on the Internet and get the names of some restaurant and bakery suppliers."

"Thanks. What should I do?"

"Take your recipe for Cowboy Cookies and figure out how much of everything you'll need to make eighteen dozen. Don't leave anything out, even if it's inexpensive, or it'll jump up and bite us when we start dealing in bulk."

Taylor nodded. "I'll do it first thing in the morning."

"You should also think of a name for your business— something personal and catchy."

Taylor took another sip of her hot chocolate. It was delicious and it warmed her all the way down to her toes. "I think I'd like to call it Cookies & Kisses."

"That's catchy. What made you think of it?"

Taylor smiled. "That's what Grandma Mac used to write on the box when she sent me cookies."

"You miss her, don't you?"

"Yes, I do. When I moved here, I thought that living in her house would be terribly sad."

"But it's not?" Neil slipped his arm around her shoulders and gave her a little hug.

"No, it's almost as if she's still there. When I go into the kitchen, I think to myself, *This is where she baked cookies.* And when I sit down at the kitchen table I think, *This is where she had her first cup of coffee in the morning.* I never really thought about what her life was like before I moved here, but now I'm living the kind of life she lived. Just walking through her house and seeing all the things she loved and looking out her windows to see what she saw makes me happy. I guess that's kind of silly, but it's true."

"That doesn't sound silly at all." Neil reached out to touch her hair. "I got the same feeling when I moved back home. It was so comforting, I didn't want to change anything. Then I did a little remodeling upstairs and we bought new furniture, but it still has the same warm feeling. It's like all their love just soaked into the house and it's still here."

"That's exactly the way I feel." Taylor leaned closer and touched her lips to his cheek. At first, he seemed startled and he pulled away slightly, but then he pulled her into his arms. Before Taylor had time to hope, or even anticipate, his lips met hers.

His kiss was soft at first, a light touching that made her breath catch in her throat. Then it deepened and Taylor began to tremble. She had no sense of time passing. The moment was perfectly suspended, a dream come true. Her awareness faded, replaced by the reality of the delightful shivers that trembled through her very core, and she responded to him with a fierce and almost frightening need of her own.

Taylor sighed as his fingers trailed over her face, caressing her lightly, almost as if he were tracing a memory. She shuddered as they lingered, warm and gentle on her throat. His hand touched her breast and she gasped in exquisite pleasure, reaching up to wrap her arms tightly around his neck and press her trembling body to his.

The cushions of the couch were soft, but Taylor didn't feel them. The fire crackled, sparks shooting up the chimney, but she didn't hear. Her senses were consumed with the powerful force that had brought them together, her mind spinning crazily and her whole body shaking with an urgent need. She had to be closer, to be one with him.

The touch of his warm hands on her skin left trails of exquisite sensation. She moaned softly, deep in her throat, and her body ignited in a blaze of need. Her fingers played through his hair, touching and caressing in a growing fever, urging him to taste the full depths of her passion. And he did not disappoint her, thrusting hard with his tongue in her mouth, and making her cry out her desire.

There was no stopping, no second thoughts, no

thoughts at all. She was on fire with a fierce longing that knew no boundaries. The leather of the couch caressed her bare skin as his lips found her breasts. And then a new heat rose up in her, igniting a compelling need stronger than she'd ever felt before.

She moaned as his tongue flicked over her nipples, cried out for more as he enveloped one rosy peak in the blazing heat of his mouth. It was too much to bear, too much to resist. She longed to have him inside her, spiraling higher and higher with her until she shattered with bliss.

He heard it first and froze. And then she heard it, too, a growling that made her shiver with something other than passion.

"Ollie?" He raised his head, rolling her to the side and protecting her with his body. "What is it, boy?"

Ollie growled again, deep in his throat, and then they both heard the soft sound of crying, coming from upstairs.

"Angela's having another nightmare." Neil voice was still thick with the passion they'd unleashed as he began to straighten his clothing. "I need to go upstairs."

Taylor nodded, all traces of her desire washed away by the soft sobbing she'd heard. "I'll go with you."

"I'm sorry, Taylor."

Neil kissed her lightly and then he got to his feet. Taylor did the same, wondering whether he was sorry he'd started to make love to her, or whether he regretted having to stop.

When they pushed open Angela's door, they found her covers on the floor. She was curled up into a ball in the center of her bed, shivering uncontrollably and crying in her sleep.

"Hey, Pumpkin." Neil picked up the covers and wrapped them around her, holding her in his arms. "Wake up, honey. You're having another bad dream."

It took a few moments for Angela to wake. When she

did, she still looked frightened. "It was Peaches, Daddy. I tried to run away, but I couldn't."

"There's nothing here now, Pumpkin." Neil brushed back her hair and cuddled her a little closer.

"Are you sure, Daddy?"

Neil looked very serious as he nodded. "I'm positive."

"Not even under my bed?"

"I'll look." Taylor leaned over to lift the dust ruffle and peer under the bed. "The only thing under here is a dust mouse."

Angela gave a shaky smile. "A dust mouse? What's that?"

"It's a little ball of dust that rolls around on the floor every time there's a breeze. Grandma Mac used to call them dust mice."

"And they're cute?"

"They're as cute as they can be. I wouldn't be surprised if all the dust mice got together and chased off the peaches."

"Oh." Angela nodded solemnly. "Will they keep Peaches from coming back?"

"I'm sure they will. They'll probably roll the peaches right down the stairs. You don't have to worry when the dust mice are around."

Angela giggled and then she yawned. "Thanks, Taylor. I feel a lot better now. I think I'll go back to sleep."

"That's a good idea." Neil bent down to kiss her. "Good night, Pumpkin."

Taylor stood next to Neil and they watched as Angela's breathing became deep and even. After she was asleep, they tiptoed out of her room and down the stairs. When they got to the bottom, Neil turned to Taylor. "Dust mice?"

"Why not? They're a lot less frightening than whatever she was dreaming about."

Neil nodded. "I just wish I could figure out what she means by *peaches*. It's not the fruit. Angela loves to eat peaches. I've asked her to describe the peaches in her dream, but she can't seem to find the words."

"How long has she been having these nightmares?"

"They started a few months before her mother left. I asked Melissa, but she said she had no idea what was frightening her."

"It must be very frustrating for you, Neil." Taylor reached out and took his arm. "You want to help, but no one can control what another person dreams."

Neil nodded, and then he looked uncomfortable. "Maybe it's actually a good thing that Angela had one of her nightmares tonight. We were . . . uh . . . I don't think we should have . . ."

"Probably not." Taylor spoke up before Neil could struggle any farther. "After all, we just met. How about going back to the way things were? That'd be fine with me."

Neil looked wary. "Do you think we can?"

"I think so." They could go back to being just friends. She'd already been half in love with him when the evening had started. And there wasn't so much difference between being half in love and being completely in love, was there?

SEVEN

Taylor awoke to the sound of childish laughter. For one brief moment, she wasn't sure where she was. Then her eyes settled on the silver-framed picture of Grandma Mac that sat on the rosewood dresser and she smiled. She was in Grandma Mac's bedroom, snuggled under the pretty patchwork quilt that her grandmother had made. The sun was streaming through the lace curtains at the window, the clock on the old-fashioned vanity read nine-fifteen, and Taylor felt happier than she had in years. She was home and that was a wonderful place to be.

She threw back the covers and reached down for her slippers, pulling them on before the bare soles of her feet could touch the floor. On her first morning here, the icy chill of the linoleum floor had been so unpleasant, she'd decided to keep her slippers right next to the bed.

Thoughts of Neil made her eyes begin to sparkle and a smile turned up the corners of her lips as she remembered the excitement of his kisses. She'd promised they'd go back to the way they were before their passions had gotten out of control, but that didn't mean she couldn't think about him in the privacy of her own bedroom.

Taylor hurried to the bedroom window and pulled the curtains aside, gasping at the sight. Snow had fallen during the night, and the ground in her backyard was covered with a thin blanket of dazzling white. As she watched, a snowball whizzed over the hedge she shared with Neil. She heard his deep laugh and then Michael's shout, accompanied by Angela's infectious giggles. They were playing in the snow—having fun from the sound of it—and Taylor hurried to her closet to get dressed.

Five minutes later, Taylor was ready. She'd found an old pair of wool slacks and a long-sleeved sweatshirt that had seen better days. She didn't have a parka, but the sun was shining and her camel's hair coat would be warm enough. Boots were a problem, and she had to settle for the leather, high-heeled pair that she'd worn on the streets of New York.

As she stepped out, a gust of wind caught the back door and banged it shut. Almost immediately, a parka-clad figure emerged from the hedge. The warmly bundled figure was followed by a large, bounding dog, and Taylor grasped the rail of the stairs as Ollie jumped up to lick her face.

"Down, Ollie." The figure pulled off a green and red ski mask and grinned at her. It was Michael. "Hi, Taylor. We were wondering if you were going to sleep all morning."

Taylor laughed and reached down to pet Ollie. "No way. It sounded like you were having way too much fun. Can I get in on the action?"

"You bet." Michael nodded quickly. "Come on. I'll show you the hole in the hedge."

Taylor ducked through the opening and stepped into Neil's backyard. The first thing she saw was a snowball headed straight for her, and she ducked instinctively. It missed her head by inches, splattering harmlessly against the hedge.

"Whoops. Sorry about that." Neil grinned at her, dusting snow off his mittens. "I was aiming for Michael. Honest!"

Taylor laughed. He sounded like a little boy who'd been caught in the act. "I suppose it just slipped, right?"

"That's exactly what happened." Neil nodded solemnly, but his eyes were twinkling with mischief. "Come and help us, Taylor. We're going to build a snowman."

Angela ran over to take Taylor's hand. "You can help me, Taylor. Ollie and I get to make the head."

"Hold on a second." Neil stared at Taylor's suede leather gloves. "Don't you have any mittens?"

Taylor shook her head. "No, but I can manage with these."

"This snow's pretty wet. You'll ruin them." Neil turned to Michael. "You've got another pair of mittens, don't you, son?"

Michael nodded and reached into his pocket to pull out a second pair of mittens. "Sure. You can use these, Taylor."

"Thanks." Taylor took the mittens and slipped them on over her gloves. "What do you want me to do?"

Neil looked down at her boots and shook his head. "You'll have all you can do to stay on your feet, with those high heels. Don't you have any moonboots?"

"Moonboots?"

"The kind spacemen wear," Angela tried to explain. "You can't fall down if you wear moonboots."

Michael nodded. "She's right. Ernie carries them down at the hardware store, but you'd better get down there today. He always sells out right after the first snow."

"Taylor has to buy girls' moonboots." Angela held out one foot. "They have to be a girl's color, like pink. Only boys wear those ugly blue ones."

Taylor smiled at her. "Since you know all about it, will you help me go shopping for my moonboots?"

"Can I?" Angela turned to Neil. "I could revise her, Daddy."

Neil looked amused. "It's *advise*, Pumpkin. You could advise Taylor."

"That's what I meant. We can all go, can't we, Daddy?"

"Sure, but first we have to build our snowman. Then

we'll have breakfast, and right after that, we'll drive down to the hardware store." Neil took Taylor's arm and led her over to a spot under a big pine tree, where the thick branches had protected the ground from the light snowfall. "I think Taylor had better watch you from here, Pumpkin. We don't want her to slip on the snow."

Angela nodded. "Okay. I'm gonna roll up the head, Taylor. You can tell me when it's big enough. Michael's making the middle and Daddy's gonna make his bottom."

Taylor watched as all three of them picked up loose snow and formed it into balls. She'd never had the chance to make a snowman and she was intrigued. Once the snowballs were formed, they rolled them along in the snow until they got larger and larger, picking up layers of loose snow. Ollie raced through the snow, stopping occasionally to sniff at the balls they were rolling, and once he even knocked Angela off her feet. Taylor expected tears, but Angela was so well padded in her snowpants and parka that she just giggled and got up again.

After several minutes of rolling the balls around, they had cleared little trails in the backyard, crisscrossing in a random pattern. Dry brown grass stuck up from the trails, and Taylor left her spot under the tree, walking down the paths they'd cleared to reach Angela's side.

"I think that's big enough, honey." Taylor tapped her on the shoulder. "The head has to be smaller than the other parts and the snow's almost gone."

Angela nodded and straightened up, dusting the snow off her mittens. Then she called out to her dad, "Taylor says I'm done, Daddy."

"Good job!" Neil glanced at Angela's ball and nodded. "It's nice and round. Remember the one you made last year?"

Angela nodded and turned to Taylor. "It was round in the middle, but it was flat on the top and the bottom. I didn't know that you were supposed to turn it around and around when you rolled it. But that was okay. Daddy said it looked just like a chipmunk with a toothache."

"So you had a snowchipmunk, instead of a snowman?"

Angela grinned. "That's exactly what Daddy said."

"I'm ready here," Neil called out from his spot in the center of the yard. "Bring your torso over, Michael."

Michael nodded and rolled his ball closer. "Coming, Dad. I'll lift it up on top of yours."

"Me next." Angela bent down and rolled her ball to the foot of the snowman. "Is this okay?"

"It's perfect, Pumpkin. Hold on and I'll lift it up for you."

Once the snowman had taken shape, Taylor dashed through the hole in the hedge to get her camera. She snapped a picture of Michael as he draped an old scarf around the neck of the snowman, and another of Angela, when Neil lifted her up to place a straw hat on the top of the snowman's head. She also used the zoom feature to take a picture of Neil's smiling face. If it turned out well, she'd frame it and put it in her bedroom.

"Get the broom, Michael." Neil waited for Michael to dash inside and come out with a broom. He leaned it up against the snowman and stepped back to survey the result. "It doesn't look done yet. What are we missing?"

"Arms, Daddy," Angela answered him.

"You're absolutely right." Neil found two long twigs and stuck them into the opposite sides of the middle ball. "What else?"

Angela glanced at Michael, but he just smiled and let her answer. "His eyes. And his nose."

"Too bad we don't have any coal." Neil smiled at Taylor and explained. "That used to be traditional for the eyes, but nobody has coal-burning furnaces anymore."

"Could you use prunes? I cleaned out Grandma Mac's refrigerator yesterday and I threw out a package of dried-up prunes. They're black, and I think they're just about the right size. I put them in the garbage can if you want to dig them out."

"I'll do it." Michael dashed through the gap in the hedge. He came back a few minutes later, holding up two large prunes and an old carrot. "I got the prunes. And look at what else I found. We can use this old carrot for a nose."

Neil lifted Angela up to place the prunes and the carrot on the snowman's face. After she had finished, they all stood back to look at their creation.

"He's just perfect." Taylor nodded her approval. "He's the best snowman I've ever seen."

Michael grinned. "How many snowmen have you seen?"

"I haven't seen any. But I used to have a picture of one on my calendar, and this looks just like it."

Michael turned to look at their snowman again. "He's the best one we ever made, but I don't think he'll last for long. It's getting warmer."

"Stand right there and I'll take a couple of pictures." Taylor took her camera out of her pocket and snapped several more shots. "I'll get double prints made and you can each have some."

Angela ran over to take her hand. "Did you take pictures while we were making him, Taylor?"

"Yes. I got one of you, putting on his hat. And I took one of Michael when he was tying on the scarf."

"Thanks, Taylor." Neil looked pleased. "Did you take any more?"

Taylor hoped she wasn't blushing as she nodded. "A couple. I don't remember exactly what they were. Is there a one-hour photo place in town?"

"In Two Rivers?" Michael started to laugh. "You're kidding, right?"

Taylor grinned. "I guess I am. Where do you get your film developed?"

"We take it to Foster's Drugs," Neil explained. "Ralph sends it in and it comes back in about a week. There's nothing faster unless you want to drive to Anoka, and that's thirty miles away."

Taylor shook her head. "No, thanks. I can wait a week."

"I'm hungry." Angela tugged at Neil's hand. "Can we have breakfast now?"

Neil smiled down at her. "Sure, Pumpkin. What do you want?"

"Freezer pancakes! Do we have any left, Daddy?"

"I'll have to check. Would you like to join us for breakfast, Taylor?"

"I'd love to, but how about coming over to my house? I'll make the pancakes."

"You've got freezer pancakes?" Angela looked hopeful.

"No, but I've got everything I need to make them from scratch."

"Real pancakes?" Michael's grin lit up his whole face. "Are you talking about the kind you fry on the stove? With maple syrup and butter?"

Taylor nodded. "That's the kind. It won't take long, and you can have juice and coffee while you're waiting."

"Can we, Daddy?" Angela's eyes were shining as she turned to Neil. "We haven't had real pancakes for a long, long time."

Neil nodded, and then he gave Taylor a questioning look. "Are you sure it's not too much trouble?"

"It's no trouble at all. Pancake batter's easy to make. And Angela said she wanted pancakes."

"You're on. But only if you let us pay you back by taking you to the movies tonight. Al Cooper's doing a Frank Capra film festival at the Bijou."

Taylor didn't have to think about it. "It's a deal. I love Frank Capra films. What is Al showing tonight?"

"It's a double feature: *It Happened One Night* and *It's a Wonderful Life.*"

"They're two of my favorites."

"Mine, too. I'm really a sucker for a great romance."

Taylor turned away before he could notice that she was blushing. They'd almost started their own romance, before Angela's nightmare had interrupted them. She reached out to take Angela's hand and smiled down at her. She seemed to be just fine this morning, but she had been very frightened last night. "I bet you don't know this, but Grandma Mac made pancakes for me when I was a little girl."

"She did?"

"Yes, and she made one special pancake that looked just like a heart. Do you want me to try to make one like that for you?"

Angela nodded and kicked up a few flakes of snow as they walked toward the hole in the hedge. "I'd really like to have a heart pancake. But you don't have to worry if it doesn't turn out right. We'll just give your heart to Daddy."

Taylor thought about the old saying about truth coming from the mouths of babes. What Angela had said was perfectly true. She'd already given her heart to Neil. Now she hoped that he'd return the favor and give his heart to her.

EIGHT

"You'd better watch out, Taylor. It's like my great-grandma used to say: 'That man's not the marryin' kind.' "

Taylor's eyebrows shot up in surprise. Suzanne had called her, just to chat, and that's what they'd done for the first few minutes. But it seemed that Suzanne had another agenda in mind. It would be silly to pretend not to know what she meant and Taylor sighed, repeating the same phrase she'd used when she'd run into Nina on the street, and when Mary Baxter had cornered her at the café. "If you're talking about Neil, we're just friends."

"Maybe you are"—Suzanne gave a little laugh—"but I hear you've been spending a lot of time with him. Neil's a great guy—don't get me wrong—but you're bound to be disappointed if you expect him to propose."

Taylor sighed. Several people had told her that it was impossible to keep anything secret in a town the size of Two Rivers, but she hadn't thought that everyone she knew would warn her away from Neil. "I'm not expecting anything, Suzanne."

"Okay, enough said." Suzanne laughed lightly again. "I called to see if you wanted to join us on Friday night. Robby's going over to my parents' house and it's Girls' Night Out."

Taylor started to smile. If she said she'd rather stay home on the chance that Neil would call, Suzanne would be even more convinced that they weren't "just friends." There was no reason why she couldn't accept Suzanne's invitation, and it might dispel some of the gossip that was floating around town about the new romance on Elm Street. "I'd love to come to Girls' Night Out. What is it?"

"It's like a club—a group of local women that get together once a month to do things that the guys don't like to do."

"Like what?" Taylor was curious.

"Sometimes we go to a chick flick or check out a shopping mall. Last month, we just picked up salads from a takeout place and sat around at my apartment, drinking white wine and talking. It's just an excuse to get out of the house for a couple of hours and enjoy ourselves."

Taylor smiled. "It sounds like fun. What are you doing this month?"

"We're driving down to Anoka to do some early Christmas shopping."

"I need to buy a new parka. Would they have something like that in Anoka?"

"Sure. There's a ski shop, if you want a short one, and a couple of the dress shops carry parka coats. I'll show you."

"Thanks." Taylor smiled ruefully, glancing at the dark blue parka that was hanging on a hook by the back door. "I found Grandma Mac's parka, but the sleeves are too short for me. I really need to buy something that fits."

"No problem. Come over to my place around five. It won't be a late night. We usually break up about around ten or ten-thirty."

Taylor was grinning when she hung up the phone. Girls' Night Out sounded pretty tame to her, but it would be good to meet more of the local women. Once her business was up and running, she'd need all the goodwill she could get.

A lot had happened in the past week. Taylor glanced around at the supplies she'd bought. Neil had located a restaurant that was going out of business in an adjoining county and they'd driven over to buy some equipment. She now had two baker's racks on wheels, ten heavy-duty cookie sheets, and a dozen stainless-steel mixing bowls. The inspector from the health department had come to make sure that Grandma Mac's kitchen met the state standards for food preparation, and Taylor had applied for and gotten her small business license.

After much deliberation, Taylor had set her prices and decided on the types of cookies she'd bake. Mary had given her a standing order and so had Bill, for the grocery store. Al Cooper had also come through with a larger order than Taylor had anticipated. He'd done a poll of his customers at the ticket booth, and almost all of them had said they'd buy home-baked cookies if Al had them available at the concession counter.

Neil had done some online research and he'd located a manufacturer that made cardboard boxes. A mistake had been made on one of their orders for a large bakery chain. The boxes had been ordered in pink, but someone had mixed the dye wrong and they'd turned out to be a shade of lavender. Taylor had purchased all of them at a huge discount, and Neil had located a printer to make stick-on labels with the name of her business and her telephone number.

Taylor was very grateful to Neil for his help, but she wished that things were different between them. He hadn't kissed her again, and it was clear that he was serious about their "friends only" decision. He had been very careful not to be alone with her. Whenever he came over, he brought one or both of the kids. Taylor suspected that he didn't entirely trust himself around her and didn't want to be tempted again.

Perhaps it was time for her to make the first move. Taylor had never thought of herself as a seductress, but she was almost certain that she could play the part. She'd seen

Candice in action, and even though her mother was much more blatant than Taylor wanted to be, she'd picked up a few tricks. The first trick was to arrange a time when they could be alone together.

Before she could think of an excuse not to act, Taylor picked up the phone. She punched out Neil's number, her hands trembling slightly. She felt her heart pound as he answered.

"Hi, Neil." Taylor took a deep breath for courage and blurted it out. "Could I see you tonight? I've got a few ideas about the business and I'd really like to run them past you."

Neil sounded friendly as he agreed, and Taylor took another deep breath. "I'm going shopping earlier, but I should be home around ten-thirty. Would you like to come over here? Or should I come there?"

When she hung up the phone, Taylor was smiling. She'd promised to be at Neil's house at eleven to save him the trouble of getting a baby-sitter. That was fine with her. The kids would be asleep, and perhaps he'd make hot chocolate with brandy again. They'd go to the den—it was Neil's favorite room—and she'd do all she could to see that history repeated itself. If Angela didn't have another nightmare and Ollie didn't growl, they might have the opportunity to do what she'd been dreaming about.

Neil hung up the phone and sighed. He hadn't wanted to refuse Taylor when she'd asked for his help, but the evening ahead would be difficult. She was too sweet, too sexy, and much too available. Just looking at her made him imagine her in his bed, her glorious black hair spread out on his pillow and her arms locked around his neck. He wanted her, and he was sure that she wanted him. The way she'd responded to his kisses proved that. There was electricity between them, a growing awareness that made it more and more difficult to keep things on a purely friendly level. Neil sighed again, shaking his head. He couldn't let himself get involved with Taylor. It would be breaking one of his cardinal rules.

He hadn't exactly been a monk since Melissa had left him, but he'd never slept with a local woman. Two Rivers was just too small; everybody knew everything that happened. He'd never made an exception, but no one had ever tempted him as much as Taylor MacIntyre. Somehow he had to be strong enough to resist her or they'd both be headed for big trouble.

Taylor seemed to like living in Two Rivers, but she was used to the excitement of a big city. Their little potluck dinners and community affairs would begin to pale after the novelty wore off. Taylor was used to Broadway shows and dining in fine restaurants, and soon she'd start looking around for more sophisticated amusements. Then he'd be stuck in the same heartbreaking situation he'd had with Melissa. She'd been miserable in Two Rivers and she'd made them all miserable, too. He didn't want to get involved in another relationship that would end up on the rocks and ruin the stable lifestyle he'd managed to salvage for his children.

The kids really liked Taylor. Angela was always begging to go over to Taylor's house, and even Michael had fallen under her spell. She might make a great stepmother for them, but Neil just couldn't take the chance. It would have to be strictly friendship between them. That was the way it had started, and he couldn't allow it to develop into anything deeper, even if both of them wanted more. It was up to him to set the rules for their relationship and keep it on a purely platonic level. He'd make that very clear to Taylor by keeping her at arm's length tonight.

NINE

"Relax, Neil. I don't bite." Taylor sipped her hot chocolate and smiled at him. He looked slightly nervous and she suspected it was because they were sitting in the den again, the scene of their former kisses and near-seduction.

"I know you don't bite." Neil managed a smile. "But maybe it would be better if you did. I was just thinking how pretty you look tonight. I really like that color on you. It reminds me of the pale yellow violets that grow in the woods."

Taylor glanced down at her pale yellow sweater and matching wool slacks. "I like it, too, but it's not very practical. Suzanne talked me into buying it. She said it would be perfect for a special occasion."

"And is this a special occasion?"

"Absolutely. When I was in Anoka, I went into the Fanny Farmer candy shop. Have you ever seen those little chocolate lollipops they make?"

"They used to be my favorites when I was a boy." Neil looked a little wistful. "I haven't thought about them in years."

Taylor laughed. "Then this is your lucky night, because I brought a box over here for the kids. I don't think they'll mind if you have one."

"Thanks, Taylor." Neil looked pleased. "But how does that make tonight a special occasion?"

"When I saw them, it gave me a great idea. Al Cooper was worried about selling chocolate chip cookies at his matinees. He thought the kids might get chocolate on their hands and wipe them on his theatre seats. I came up with the idea of baking my cookies on little sticks, the kind they use for Popsicles. That way the kids could eat them without handling them."

"Cookiepops for the matinees at the Bijou?"

"What do you think?"

"I think it's pure genius. Do you want me to try to find some wooden sticks online?"

"I'd appreciate it." Taylor was grateful. "But first, I'd better see if it works. If I pick up some ice cream on sticks tomorrow, will you and the kids help me eat it?"

Neil laughed. "Of course we will. It's a tough job, but somebody's got to do it."

They sipped their hot chocolate in companionable silence for a moment and then Taylor frowned. Even though Neil had complimented her on her new outfit, he hadn't made any sort of romantic move. "I guess I'd better think about getting back home. I have to organize my pantry tomorrow and make sure I have everything I need."

"You're starting on Monday?"

"Yes. I'll mix up the dough on Sunday and start the baking that night. Mary wants six dozen cookies for Monday morning, and Bill's ordered another six dozen for the store."

"I'll walk you home." Neil got up from his comfortable position on the couch. "And we'll come over on Sunday night to help you. The first day is bound to be rough. You still need to get the kinks out of your routine."

Taylor let him help her into her coat and then she pulled her moonboots on her feet. They walked across his front yard, the fresh snow crunching beneath their boots, and he waited until she'd unlocked her door.

"I'd invite you in, but I suppose you have to get back to the kids." Taylor turned to look up at him.

"Yeah. I can't leave them alone for long. How about tomorrow night? Are you busy?"

"No. I don't have any plans." Taylor held her breath. Was Neil going to ask her out?

"I promised I'd take you to the Cloisters, and you won't have much free time once your business takes off. Shall we do it tomorrow night?"

"That's a wonderful idea. Can you get reservations?"

"It really shouldn't be a problem. And I'll call Mrs. Simmons tomorrow morning to see if she can take care of the kids."

"The kids aren't going with us?" Taylor's heart beat a little faster.

"It's not the type of place for kids. They'd be bored silly if we lingered over wine or coffee. I'll call in a pizza for them and they'll be a lot happier watching tapes at home."

Taylor's spirits rose by leaps and bounds. "What time should I be ready?"

"I'll try to make our reservation for eight. It takes about an hour to drive there, so I'll have to pick you up at seven. Is that too early?"

"No, that's fine." Taylor smiled up at him. "Thanks, Neil. After what you told me about the Cloisters, I'm really looking forward to it."

"Me, too."

Neil reached out and pulled her into his arms, placing a kiss on the side of her cheek. Taylor shivered. The simple brush of his lips against her face sent tremors of passion throughout her body. She wanted to turn so that her lips would meet his, but she didn't. Now that he'd asked her for a real date, she certainly didn't want to scare him off.

* * *

Neil poured himself a snifter of brandy when he got back home and stretched out on the couch, in front of fire. What was it about Taylor that was so seductive? She wasn't overtly sexy, but her femininity came through in hundreds of little ways. It was there in her eyes when she hugged Angela, the sort of look a mother would give to her child. And even with Michael, when she joked and laughed with him, there was a motherly softness and a genuine caring in her voice.

The clothes Taylor wore weren't skimpy or tight. She didn't try to seduce him by wiggling or brushing up against him, like Nina had, and she'd never talked about how lonely she was or how she missed a man's arms around her, the way Suzanne had done. Perhaps it was the absence of these little tricks that appealed to him. Taylor was naturally sexy. And even though she'd never encouraged him to think of her that way, he'd found himself staring at her, wishing he could see what bits of silk and lace lay next to her skin, and picturing how she would look, coming out of the shower in the morning.

Neil glanced at the clock and sighed. It was almost midnight and he wasn't sleepy. If he went to bed, he'd just stare up at the ceiling and wonder what Taylor was doing. He might as well work.

He picked up his brandy and carried it to the office, setting it down on his desk. He switched on his computer and was about to sit down in his chair when he remembered that he'd promised to give Taylor copies of some of his books. He pulled several from the shelves, stacking them on his desk and wondering how she'd like them. Everyone said he was a good writer and he'd won several awards, but Taylor's opinion of his writing meant much more to him than those of the contest judges or the reviewers.

What if she didn't like them? How would he feel if she thought he was a no-talent hack? Neil frowned thought-

fully and straightened the pile of books. Would she tell
him the truth if he asked her?

The moment he considered it, Neil's lips turned up in
a grin. She'd tell him. Taylor wasn't the type to pretend
to like something if she didn't. If she thought that he was
a lousy writer, she'd tell him point-blank and the hell with
the consequences. That meant a lot to him. The other
women in his life had all said they loved his work, but he
wasn't entirely sure they'd meant it. If Taylor said she did,
it would be a genuine compliment.

Neil stuck the books in a bag and shoved them to the
side of his desk. He'd give them to her tomorrow, right
before they left for the Cloisters. And then, after enough
time had passed, he'd take the bull by the horns and ask
for her honest opinion.

Taylor smiled as she read the final paragraph. Neil was
a marvelous writer. She'd dashed into a bookstore in
Anoka and picked up two of his books.

She turned to glance at the clock. She was propped up
in bed, wrapped in her warmest nightgown, and it was
almost one in the morning. She knew she should try to
get some sleep, but Neil's second book was sitting on the
bedside table. Taylor really wanted to read it—it looked
every bit as intriguing as the first—but she'd planned to
get up at seven, and tomorrow was a big day.

Reluctantly, Taylor reached out and snapped off the
light. Then she pulled Grandma Mac's quilt up to cover
her shoulders and snuggled down under its warmth. As
she waited for sleep to take her, she thought about the
book she'd just read. Neil's detective was a small-town sheriff who truly cared about the people in Elsworth Lake, the
fictional town he'd created.

She'd recognized some of the landmarks in the book:
the drugstore where the owner still sold penny candy in

jars and the small theatre that was only open on the weekends. Neils's fictional town had a lot in common with Two
Rivers. The detective, Deputy Thomas Pike, seemed to be
a thinly veiled replica of Neil. Even though Neil's book
was fictional, it was surprisingly autobiographical. It was
there for the reader to see—Neil's love for his children,
his concern for his neighbors, his loneliness and heart-
break over his failed marriage, and his reluctance to get
involved with another woman.

Taylor rolled over and the quilt slid down, exposing her
shoulder to the chilly night air. She pulled it up quickly
and curled into a ball, tucking the quilt more tightly
around her. By reading Neil's book, she thought she understood him much better. Just like his fictional detective,
Neil was lonely. But he was too cautious about risking his
family's happiness to enter into any long-term relation-
ships. It would take time, lots of time, before Neil accepted
that she would be a constant in his life.

TEN

"No more, thank you. I think I've had enough." Taylor shook her head as the waiter appeared to refill her silver wine goblet with mulled wine.

The brown-robed monk, a length of rope knotted around his waist, gave her his most benevolent smile. "Are you certain, Sister? Wine is the fruit of the gods."

"That's true and I'm not driving. But only half a goblet, please."

Neil reached over to take her hand and patted it gently. "Everything in excess. To enjoy the flavor of life, take big bites. Moderation is for monks."

"That's good." The waiter lost his monklike demeanor and grinned at Neil. "Did you just make it up?"

"No, it's on a plaque in the lobby."

"Oh-oh." The waiter slipped out of character again. "I guess I should have known that."

Neil laughed. "Give us a couple more minutes and then we'll both have coffee. You do serve coffee, don't you?"

"Yes, Brother." The waiter managed a pious look. "Cappuccino, of course. It is named after our order and the color of our robes."

"How about espresso?"

"That refers to how fast I'll bring it, Brother."

Taylor was laughing as the waiter walked away. The whole evening had been magical. The cold stone interior of the ancient building had been turned into a warm and cozy enclosure with lovely patterned carpets on the floor and a roaring fire in the hearth. They were sitting at a table quite close to the fire in comfortably padded leather chairs and Taylor felt slightly giddy from the mulled wine and Neil's closeness. The way his hand still clasped hers made her cheeks feel warm.

Neil smiled at her. "It's almost a shame we have to leave. I could sit here all night."

"Me, too. It makes me wish I had a living room like this, with these high-vaulted ceilings and exposed beams. It's spectacular."

"I agree with you, but you'd change your mind when you got your first heating bill."

"I suppose I would." Taylor wished he hadn't mentioned heating bills. Grandma Mac had once mentioned how expensive it was to heat her house in the winter.

"Let's not talk about bills." Neil's words mirrored her thoughts. "Not when we're out enjoying ourselves. I haven't had an entirely adult conversation for ages and it's a real treat."

"Then I guess I'd better not mention Barbie, Barney, or Batman. Have you read any good books lately?"

Neil shook his head. "No, but that reminds me, I've got a bag of books for you in the car."

"Your books?"

"Yes. I don't know if you were serious when you said you wanted to read them, but I rounded up a few copies for you."

"Oh, good!" Taylor was delighted. "The only ones I could find at the bookstore were *Home Again,* and *Out on a Limb.* They told me the others were on back order from the publisher."

"You bought my books?"

"Of course I did." Taylor laughed at his astonished expression. "I finished *Home Again* and I really loved it."

"You're not just saying that?"

Taylor shook her head. "I never would have brought it up if I hadn't liked it. And I like *Out on a Limb,* too. I just finished the part where Deputy Pike has to climb up the big pine tree."

"And you really like my books?"

Neil seemed very anxious and Taylor wondered why. "They're wonderful. Your characters are so real, and I love the setting. That scene in the Bijou, where Mrs. Wyler spills ice cold Coke down Deputy Pike's neck just as Janet Leigh steps into the shower in *Psycho,* has got to be one of the funniest things I've ever read."

"Mrs. *Wyler?*"

"I meant to say *Gladys Smith.* But you were writing about Mrs. Wyler, weren't you?"

Neil looked guilty. "Yes, but you're the only one who's ever caught that. I was very careful to change her hair color and her body type. How did you guess?"

"It was her nervous habit that tipped me off. You know, twiddling her thumbs."

"But Mrs. Wyler doesn't twiddle her thumbs. She winds a piece of hair around her finger."

"Same habit, different action." Taylor grinned at him. "Nobody else noticed?"

"No, not even Mrs. Wyler. She read it when it first came out and asked me how I managed to come up with such a weird character."

"She didn't!" Taylor started to giggle.

"She did. You won't say anything to her, will you?"

"Of course not. It'll be our secret."

"Good." Neil looked very relieved. "Did you recognize anyone else?"

Taylor knew this wasn't the time to mention Deputy Pike and his remarkable resemblance to Neil. "I don't think so. If I do, I won't tell anyone except you."

"Thanks. I wonder why you noticed it and no one else did."

"It could be because I'm new in town. I don't know anyone very well yet, and all I have is a general impression of the neighbors."

"That could be it. Either that, or you're more observant than anyone else in town. I guess I'd better be careful that I don't write *you* into a book."

"Go ahead. I wouldn't mind seeing myself as others see me. Just make me gorgeous, intelligent, and witty, and I won't be upset."

"That won't be difficult. You *are* gorgeous, intelligent, and witty."

Their coffee-bearing monk arrived in time to spare Taylor a reply. She knew she was blushing from Neil's compliment and she felt a warm glow inside. Neil thought she was gorgeous, intelligent, and witty. That was a very good start.

They spoke of other things as they sipped their coffee and shared a raspberry and chocolate torte from the dessert tray. She didn't mention her cookie business and Neil didn't talk about writing. Instead, he told her about growing up in Two Rivers and knowing everyone in town. Then she told him about the law firm where she'd worked, and about her high-rise Manhattan apartment building, where she hadn't known a single one of her neighbors.

They lingered for a long while, sipping coffee and talking. It wasn't until they walked out and got into Neil's car that something happened to startle Taylor out of her mellow mood.

"Your car's warm inside!" Taylor turned to Neil in surprise.

"Yes, it is. When I called for the bill, the valet went out to warm up my car. They always do that in the winter. It's one of those extra touches that makes coming here a pleasure."

Gina Jackson

"It's really nice. I was dreading the thought of getting into an icy car, especially in a skirt."

Neil glanced down at her legs, and Taylor noticed that he had trouble pulling his eyes away. Everyone told her that she had great legs. She'd even been approached by a modeling agency, when she'd first arrived in New York. They'd requested a portfolio of pictures, promising to book her for panty-hose ads, but Taylor hadn't even considered it. She'd figured that it was just another scheme to part a newcomer from her rent money.

"You have really incredible legs." Neil swallowed hard. "But I guess you must have heard that before."

Taylor decided to make a joke of it and laughed. "Yes, I have. But I thought it was in the same category as 'Nice eyes.' "

"What?"

"It's like the guy who's trying to get a date for his sister," Taylor explained. "If he can't think of anything else to say about her, he always says she has nice eyes. When I was in high school 'nice eyes' was the kiss of death."

"But your eyes *are* nice." Neil chuckled. "And so is your hair. I like the way it curls up."

Taylor stared at him in utter confusion. "You actually *like* my hair?"

"Yes. I like everything about you, Taylor. You're a really great person."

"Thank you. I feel the same way about you." Taylor leaned back against the seat as Neil put the car in gear. He'd just paid her a very nice compliment, but she wanted more from him. Anyone could be a really great person. She wanted to be a really great person who was also Neil's lover.

It was past eleven and there was very little traffic on the highway. A lazy snow had started to fall and the white flakes swirled in front of Neil's headlights, dancing up to brush the windshield. It was very still in the warm interior of

Neil's car, just the radio playing softly and the windshield wipers swishing rhythmically. It should have been peaceful, but it wasn't. Taylor was too on edge, too aware of Neil's every movement as she studied his strong hands on the wheel and imagined how it would feel if he pulled her into his arms and stroked her body.

She was lost in the fantasy, shivering slightly at the imagined pleasure, when he pulled up in her driveway. Taylor let go of her delicious dream and turned to smile at him. "I had a wonderful time, Neil. Would you like to come in for some hot chocolate and brandy?"

"Sure. I told Mrs. Simmons it might be a late night and she decided to sleep over."

Taylor waited for Neil to open her door, and then she got out and led the way to her house. What Neil had told her made her heart sing. His baby-sitter was staying overnight, and he really didn't have to go home at all. Had he planned it that way? Or was she assuming too much?

It didn't take long to prepare the hot chocolate. Taylor made it the way Grandma Mac had taught her, with whole milk and cocoa and sugar. When she carried in the mugs, she noticed that Neil had already lit a fire.

"I thought a fire would be nice." Neil took one of the mugs from her. "This smells delicious."

"Thanks." Taylor sat down next to him and for long moments neither of them spoke. But then he turned to her and frowned slightly.

"This decision we made about just being friends won't work anymore, Taylor. Every time I'm with you, I want to touch you. It's driving me crazy."

"Me, too." Taylor looked up to meet his eyes. "I think I'll die if you don't kiss me again."

"Then I'd better save your life." Neil smiled and pulled her into his arms.

As he began to kiss her, a thought flashed through Taylor's mind. This time there would be no distractions, no barking dogs, no nightmares, nothing to keep them apart. But then the thought was gone in a blaze of passion that threatened to consume her.

How could Neil's lips be soft and firm at the same time? It seemed impossible. Instinctively, the tip of Taylor's tongue slipped out to taste them, roving over his mouth and seeking even greater warmth. He made a sound deep in his throat and then his tongue met hers in a dance of desire that knew no bounds, one that left them both breathless and gasping for more.

His hands found the zipper at the back of her dress and slid it down in a soft rustling of fabric. Her hands found his tie to tug it loose and she began to unbutton his shirt. His lips trailed down to kiss the sweet hollow at the base of her throat. Her fingers slipped inside his shirt and stroked the heated expanse of his chest.

He groaned in frustration and she reached out to help him, unclasping her bra and making her breasts naked for him. She shivered slightly in the cool air, and then he was holding her, lifting them up to stand on the rug, their bodies pressed together in an embrace that thrilled them both. She felt a tide of pure warmth flood through her, dissolving her bones and turning her essence to a fiery elixir, consuming them in an inferno that would not be denied.

There was no sense of fumbling as she undressed him, only a burning desire that overcame any awkwardness. And then he was sliding her dress down, past her waist and then her knees, lifting her slightly in his strong arms to set her free.

She had no awareness of details, only the warmth of his fingers on her body, freeing her and making her tremble in the glory of nudity. Their bodies joined then, in an embrace so full of promise and intimacy that her mind began to spin.

And then he was lifting her up in his arms and carrying

her up the stairs to her bedroom with the fluffy soft quilt and the dim light from the small lamp that sat on the nightstand.

They were there, on the top of the quilt, locked in each other's arms. His lips tasted her breasts, the heated peaks of her nipples, until she was so full of longing and passion, she could no longer bear it.

She reached down to touch him, attempting to end the agony of waiting. But he only groaned and clasped her hand, bringing her arms up, over her head, and holding them with one strong hand while he trailed kisses over every inch of her body with his lips and then his tongue.

She cried out, but he would not stop, his lips and tongue seeking the secret places that made her gasp and tremble and moan with delight. And then, when she was certain she couldn't endure another moment of this delicious agony, he thrust inside her and claimed her completely.

"Slow down, darling." His voice was low, ragged with need. "I don't know how much more I can stand. It's been a long time since . . ."

She cut off his protest with her lips, kissing him deeply and drawing him down to her. They felt so right together, all the mysteries solved, all the separate hollows and curves molding together into a complete and glorious whole.

Her hips moved in circles, enticing him, almost escaping in a teasing dance, but drawn back at the very last moment by the power of her need. Her legs lifted, rising up and locking around his back, taking him deeper and deeper inside her until she was robbed of breath. Her lips found his neck, nuzzling and then nipping as passion rose within her.

There was no sense of right or wrong. How could there be? She was one with the man she loved and his passions were hers to take. She delighted in his groans, his gasps for breath, his hard, driving need of her. And then she was whirling up, out of herself. And she was spinning free, caught up in a glorious completion that made her scream and sob with a delight that was as new and as old as time itself.

She heard him cry out as his passions exploded and she held him so tightly, it seemed they would be joined forever, incapable of separation by any mortal means. His fingers stroked her hair. Her hands caressed his back. Their lips met in a soft kiss of gratitude for what they had been given, and then gradually, inevitably, their heartbeats slowed and the madness of passion was tempered by a warm sense of loving and caring.

Long moments passed before she could speak and when she did, it was in a whisper. "I knew it would be like this."

"Yes." His voice was still thick with remembered passion. "So did I. You're wonderful, Taylor."

There was no need for any farther conversation. Taylor knew it and he seemed to know it, too. Instead they embraced, snug and loving, until Neil rolled over and fell back against the pillows, pulling her close to him.

"Are you cold?" His voice was deep in the quiet room.

"Not yet, but we will be." Taylor sat up to grab the coverlet that was folded at the foot of the bed, and spread it over them. Then she snuggled up to his side once more.

She thought they would sleep then, but their love was too new to be satisfied by only one very passionate encounter. Her hands smoothed over the expanse of his chest, caressing and touching until his breathing quickened.

And then he was touching her, his fingers stroking the smooth roundness of her breasts, weighing them in his hands as his thumbs slid over their peaks.

She gasped as desire rose again in a slow, inevitable tide of longing. Her fingers found the part of him that had given her so much pleasure only moments before, and she learned that he wanted her again, as much as she wanted him.

"Glutton." He chuckled, capturing her hand in his. "Didn't you have enough?"

Taylor smiled, her eyes wide with the pleasure she knew was to come. "Never."

Their embrace was softer, their coupling sweeter, the second time they came together. It was languid, like honey flowing from a pitcher, no longer desperate but sweetly certain. They sighed as they caressed and held each other, gently fanning the coals of desire until they burst into flame with an almost magical combustion.

And then they slept, nestled under the coverlet, their arms and legs linked together in comfortable warmth. And Taylor knew that she had never been so happy, or so utterly and completely in love.

ELEVEN

Taylor opened her eyes to sunlight streaming in through the curtains. Winter birds were chirping in the big pine tree outside her bedroom window and the music of their feathered chorus made her smile. She stretched, feeling warm and happy, and then she bounded out of bed, eager to greet the day. It felt almost like Christmas morning and she laughed out loud in delightful anticipation. Neil had given her the best gift of all last night and she could hardly wait to see him again.

She glanced back at the rumpled bedcovers and reached out to pick up the pillow where Neil had rested his head. The faint scent of his cologne lingered and she hugged it tightly. It had happened. It wasn't a dream. Neil had been here in her bed. He'd held her and he'd made love to her.

They'd made love several more times in the night, sleepy, comforting bouts of passion and completion that had left both of them feeling deliciously lethargic. Just as she had fallen asleep, he'd whispered something about getting back home, so he could be there when Mrs. Simmons got up and she wouldn't suspect that he'd spent the night next door.

Taylor smiled as she put Neil's pillow back in place next to hers. The smile was still on her face as she hurried to the bathroom and turned on the shower. As she stepped under the warm stream of water, she began to sing. Her voice sounded good this morning, almost in tune as it bounced off the glass enclosure. Had her fifth-grade music teacher been wrong when she'd asked Taylor to please just mouth the words and refrain from singing at their concerts?

Taylor laughed as she hit a clinker. No, Miss Dearling had been right. She had a terrible voice, but that didn't matter. Neil hadn't chosen her for her singing abilities.

The moment she was dressed, Taylor raced to the kitchen to put on the coffee. She had just poured her first fragrant cup when she heard a knock at her back door.

"Hi, Taylor." Neil smiled at her as she opened the door, but he didn't look very happy. "Can I come in? We have to talk."

With a cold shiver of foreboding, Taylor motioned toward the kitchen table and brought them both coffee. When she'd fortified herself with a sip, she turned to him with real fear in her eyes. "You sound pretty serious. What is it, Neil?"

"About last night . . ." Neil shook his bead and looked down at his cup, refusing to meet her eyes. "I just don't want you to get the wrong idea."

Taylor didn't like the sound of that, but she managed to hide her anxiety. "Maybe you'd better tell me the wrong idea, so I won't get it."

"It was wonderful, Taylor. I mean *really* wonderful. But nothing's changed. I'm not looking for a wife, and I'm concerned that you might expect more of me than I can give."

Taylor nodded quickly. She'd expected something like this. "I understand, Neil. But you don't know me very well if you think I want another husband. I'm not sure if I *ever* want to make that kind of commitment again. I moved here to get away from all that."

"Are you really sure you don't want to get married again?"

"I'm positive." Taylor crossed her fingers under the table, reverting to an old childhood habit. She *did* want to marry Neil; at least her heart did. But her mind told her that it would be a mistake to admit it.

Neil gave a relieved sigh. "I'm really glad you feel that way. What do you think we should do about . . . uh . . . last night?"

"I don't know." Taylor gave him a teasing grin. "It was fun, wasn't it?"

Neil grinned back. "You know it was. But I think we'd better be a little more careful. It'd be too easy to start something that would hurt both of us."

"Are you saying that you're tempted?"

"Of course I'm tempted!" Neil looked shocked. "Sleeping with you was the best thing that's happened to me in a long time."

"But you don't want to do it again?"

"That's part of the problem. I'd like to come over here and sleep with you every night, but it's just not possible. And it wouldn't be good for either one of us."

"You don't think we could keep it casual?"

"I couldn't." Neil leaned forward and met her eyes. "Could you?"

Taylor knew she had to be honest. "No, I don't think I could. I've never slept around. Some of my friends did, but it's just not right for me."

"That's the way I feel, too. And that's part of the reason that we'd better back off. We might even end up married, and then where would we be?"

Taylor thought she knew exactly where they'd be. They'd be living together as a real family, sleeping together every night and sharing their innermost feelings. It sounded like heaven to her, but Neil didn't want to hear that.

Neil sighed, obviously taking her silence for agreement. "I don't want to lose your friendship, Taylor. It means too much to me. And I don't want to lose the closeness between us. Do you think there's any way that we can make it work without the sex?"

"We can try." Taylor tried not to look too doubtful. "I don't know about you, but I'm really going to miss it."

Neil smiled and reached out for her hand, squeezing it hard. "Me, too. It was incredible. I don't think I could ever get enough of you. But I'd better not think of that now."

"Why not?" Taylor felt a thrill rush through her.

"Because if I do, I'll just pick you up and carry you upstairs, and that would be defeating the whole purpose. You've got to help me with this, Taylor."

"I will," Taylor promised and she meant it. "How about breakfast? Maybe a plateful of bacon and eggs will take your mind off your *other* appetites."

Neil smiled at her attempt at lightness. "I'd love to, but I don't have time. They rescheduled my flight and I have to leave for the airport at noon."

"How long will you be gone?" Taylor's smile wavered a bit. She already felt lonely, just knowing that he was leaving.

"A week. Ten cities in seven days. It's going to be a real grind."

Taylor nodded. "How about the kids? Are they going with you?"

"No. Michael has school and Angela's been invited to a birthday party. I asked Mrs. Simmons to come to stay with them while I'm gone. She's done it before and she's completely reliable."

"If there's anything you want me to do for you while you're gone, all you have to do is ask."

"Thanks, but I don't think there's anything, unless . . ." Neil hesitated, frowning slightly. "Actually, there is one thing. I was going to take Angela shopping today, but I won't have time. And Mrs. Simmons doesn't like to drive in the winter unless it's absolutely necessary. Do you think you could help Angela buy a birthday present for the party?"

"Of course I can. We'll drive to the shopping mall in Anoka this afternoon, before I start the baking."

"That's another thing. I know I promised to help you bake tonight, but . . ."

"Don't even think about it." Taylor interrupted what was sure to be an apology. "I've got to learn to do it on my own. It would be nice to have company, though. Do you think Mrs. Simmons would mind if I asked Angela and Michael to come over?"

"Are you kidding? She'd be tickled pink. It'll give her a little time to put her feet up and watch television. Just call when you want them. I'll tell her it's okay to send them over."

Taylor was thoughtful. "Mrs. Simmons shouldn't be driving if she's nervous about it. If the kids have to go somewhere, I'll take them."

"That'd be great." Neil looked relieved. "I'm taking the airport shuttle, so I'll leave my car keys on the kitchen counter. You'd better use the Grand Cherokee while I'm gone."

"But I thought you said my car was fine."

"It is, but mine is safer on the icy roads, and you can load your cookies in the cargo space. It'll be a lot more convenient for making your deliveries."

"Thanks, Neil." Taylor bit back a smile. "But don't you think Mrs. Wyler will get the wrong impression if you let me drive your car while you're gone?"

"Forget Mrs. Wyler. I'll feel a lot better, knowing that you won't break down in a snowbank somewhere."

Neil stood up and so did Taylor. He looked a little uncertain, as if he wanted to say more, but he didn't. He just pulled her into his arms and gave her a friendly hug. "I'll be back next Sunday."

"Just call me if you want to check up on the kids." Taylor smiled up at him. "I'll be here."

"I'll do that. How about Wednesday night?"

"Wednesday's fine. Even if I go somewhere, I'll be home by ten-thirty at the latest."

"Great. I'll run off a copy of my schedule and Michael can bring it over tonight, just in case you need to call me."

"That'd be good." Taylor knew Neil should be going, but he didn't seem to want to leave her.

"Good-bye, Taylor." Neil turned to go, but then he pulled her into his arms again. "You're wonderful, you know?"

Taylor didn't say anything. She just raised her face to his. He kissed her lightly, brushing his lips against hers. And then, even though she could tell that he was making an effort to stop, his kiss grew deeper and more passionate.

"I've got to go." Neil's voice was shaking slightly when he pulled away. "I'll see you when I get back."

Taylor didn't trust her voice. His kiss had affected her more than she wanted to admit. Instead of saying anything at all, she just smiled and gave a little wave as he went out the door.

It was Wednesday afternoon and Taylor sat on a folding chair in Marge Breckner's living room, watching twelve four-year-old girls eat cake and ice cream from pink and white paper plates. Angela was smiling and giggling with the other girls and the party was a lot of fun. Marge, a former kindergarten teacher, had arranged lots of games. Once the cake and ice cream had been eaten, it would be time for Marge's daughter to open her gifts.

Marge made her way through the crowd of mothers and sat down in a chair next to Taylor.

"You're a doll, Taylor." Marge reached out to pat her on the back. "I peeked at the present you brought for Becky and it's the cleverest thing I've ever seen."

Taylor waved the compliment away. "It's just a cookie, Marge."

"But *what* a cookie! It's got to be at least ten inches across and it's all decorated like a birthday cake, with Becky's name and everything. I've never seen anything like it before. Did you make it?"

"Yes. I thought I'd experiment a little. I hope Becky likes chocolate chips."

"Do you know any kid who doesn't?" Marge laughed. "Is Becky's cookie like the Cookiepops that Al's going to sell at the Bijou?"

"They're made from the same recipe. But how did you know about those? They're not going on sale until this weekend."

"Good news travels fast in Two Rivers—almost as fast as bad news. When you've been here longer you'll know that."

"Does everybody in town know about my Cookiepops?" Taylor was surprised.

"Just about. Al's my uncle, and he gave me one of the samples you brought him. It's really clever. I think all the mothers in town ought to get together and write you a thank-you note. You have no idea how many chocolate smears I've washed off Becky's clothes!"

"I can imagine." Taylor glanced at Becky, a charming tomboy who had Marge's red hair. She was wearing a bright yellow dress and she'd already dripped chocolate ice cream down the front.

"You really ought to sell those birthday cookies. Gerry Wilson was in the kitchen when I peeked, and she said she'd like to buy one for her son's next birthday."

Taylor was surprised. "Do you think there'd be a market for them?"

"I don't know why not. Most of us don't have much time for fancy baking. If you took orders for cookies like that, I'm almost sure they'd sell."

"It does sound like a good idea. I'll have to make another one to see how long it takes me and then we'll have to figure out the pricing."

"Who's we?"

Taylor hoped she wasn't blushing. "Neil's been helping me with that."

"So you're partners with him?"

"Oh, no." Taylor shook her head. "It's nothing like that. He's just been really nice about helping me."

Marge glanced over at Angela and smiled. "Looks like you've been nice about helping him, too. Angela used to be so shy I couldn't get a word out of her, but I've heard 'Taylor this,' and 'Taylor that,' all afternoon. And Theresa Luft says Michael's been talking about you at school."

"I hope he's been saying good things." Taylor attempted to make a joke of it.

"He has. He told Hank—he's my oldest—that his dad ought to marry you."

Taylor's winced. "I hope Neil doesn't hear about that. It'll scare him off for sure!"

"You're right—it will." Marge laughed and leaned closer, so they wouldn't be overheard. "Neil's been skittish around women ever since *she* up and left him."

Taylor recognized the disparaging tone in Marge's voice. "You didn't like Neil's former wife?"

"It wasn't just me. Nobody liked Melissa, and God knows we tried to be friendly. Right after Neil moved back home, I called her a couple of times to invite Angela over to play. My husband, Tim, went to school with Neil, so it's not like we're strangers. I told her to just drop Angela off and I'd bring her home again. I'm used to kids, and another one doesn't make any more work. I must have invited her four or five times, but the only time Angela ever came over was once, when Neil brought her."

Taylor bit her tongue. She didn't want to say anything negative about Angela's mother, but it did seem odd that Melissa hadn't accepted any of Marge's invitations.

"Melissa was a model, you know."

"She was?" Taylor filed that away for future reference. Perhaps that was why Neil had seemed so pleased when she admitted that she seldom wore makeup.

"She wouldn't go anywhere unless her face was perfect and every hair was in place. Here in Two Rivers things are casual. It's pretty much come as you are. I don't think Melissa liked that."

"I do." Taylor didn't want Marge to get the wrong impression about her. "I used to have to get dressed up every morning to go to work and living in Two Rivers is like a vacation from all that. Since I moved here, I've only gotten dressed up once."

Marge nodded. "But the Cloisters is a dressy sort of place. It's expected."

"You knew that Neil took me to the Cloisters?"

"Of course I did." Marge laughed at the shocked expression on Taylor's face. "Everybody knows. He's never taken anybody else there, not even Suzanne or Nina. Not that they're jealous. Both of them gave up on Neil a long time ago. Now they're rooting for you."

"Rooting for me? You make it sound like a sporting event."

"Maybe I shouldn't have put it quite that way. But everyone in town likes Neil, and we all want to see him happy. You're not planning to leave Two Rivers, are you?"

"No, I like it here. I admit that I was a little put off by the lack of privacy at first, but I'm getting used to it."

"Lack of privacy?" Marge's forehead wrinkled in a frown. "What do you mean?"

"Everyone in Two Rivers seems to know my private business. You obviously do. You knew that Neil had taken me to the Cloisters."

Marge nodded. "That's true. It's impossible to keep secrets in a small town, and I can see how a newcomer would think that it's simple nosiness. But it really isn't. Nobody's mean or spiteful, not even Mrs. Wyler, and she's just about the worst gossip in Two Rivers. We're just concerned about each other, that's all."

"I know that now." Taylor smiled at her. "It just took some getting used to, that's all."

"And you think you're used to it?"

"I'm really beginning to appreciate it. People wave at me on the street and they all know my name. It's like having a huge family of aunts and uncles and cousins."

"You don't think it's boring here, after coming from New York and all?"

"Boring?" Taylor was astonished. "It's *much* more interesting here! There are all sorts of things to do and it's impossible to feel lonely, the way I did in New York. All I have to do is call someone and invite them over for a cup of coffee. I did that yesterday, with Edith Parker, and she gave me her special chicken hotdish recipe."

Marge smiled and patted Taylor on the back. "You sound just like a small-town girl. If Neil knows what's good for him, he'll put a ring on your finger before somebody else realizes what a find you are."

When the phone rang at eleven that night, Taylor knew exactly who it was. She wanted to snatch it up on the first ring but made herself wait until the second. "Hi, Neil."

"How did you know it was me?"

The connection was perfect and Neil's voice sounded very clear, as if he were calling from next door. "I wasn't expecting any other calls and it's too late for the telephone solicitors."

"How are you?"

Taylor tucked her feet up on the couch and settled back against the deep rose velvet pillows Nina had found on their trip to the thrift store. "I'm fine. How about you?"

"Exhausted." Neil sighed. "They've got me booked on another early morning talk show and I have to be at the studio at six."

"Can I watch it here?"

"No. It's just a local station, but my pub rep is taping it for me. She always takes care of little details like that. If you really want to, we can watch it when I get back."

Taylor fought down a totally unreasonable surge of jealousy. Neil hadn't mentioned that another woman was going on tour with him. But he wouldn't have told her that his pub rep was a woman if he had anything to hide, would he?

"How are the kids?"

"They're fine, Neil. We've settled into a routine. I deliver my cookies early and then I take Michael to school. Angela comes over after she's dressed and I drive her to Becky Breckner's or Suzie Ringstrom's to play. When Michael gets out of school, I bring them both back here and he does his homework while Angela and I mix up the cookie dough. Then they go home for supper and come back to help me bake."

Neil chuckled. "It sounds like you're doing more babysitting than Mrs. Simmons."

"Not really. She has them all night."

Neil's chuckle turned into a laugh. "While they're *sleeping*. That's not exactly a challenge."

"But she cooks their meals and does their laundry. I don't do any of that."

There was another long silence, and when Neil spoke again, his voice was soft. "Thanks, Taylor. I really appreciate all you're doing. And I'm glad Angela's getting out to play. It's good for her to make friends with other girls her age."

"I know. Marge told me she's thinking about starting a preschool for kids Angela's age. You'd let Angela go, wouldn't you?"

"You bet." Neil sounded very definite. "How many kids is she planning to enroll?"

"Just six at first, including Becky. I really think she's going to do it, Neil. She's got the training and she's wonderful with children."

"She certainly is. How was the birthday party?"

"It was great and Angela loved it. I made a giant birthday cookie for Becky and Marge thinks that I should bake them as a special-order item."

"That's a good idea. Have you figured out how much you'd have to charge?"

"Yes." Taylor glanced down at her notebook. She'd known that Neil would ask and she had the answer. "If I limit myself to two colors of frosting, I could do them for four dollars apiece. Do you think anyone would buy them at that price?"

"No."

Taylor was disappointed. She'd really been looking forward to making the birthday cookies. "I guess it won't work then. I really can't do them for any less than four dollars."

"That's not the problem, Taylor. You're pricing them too low. Nobody wants to give a birthday gift that costs less than five bucks. Charge seven. They're worth it, aren't they?"

"Yes, I think they are. But that's pretty expensive for one cookie."

"No, it's not. Most people have a price range in mind when they go shopping. If what they want to buy costs less than they thought it would, they assume that it can't be any good."

"Okay, I'll charge seven. Marge thinks I should start taking orders for Christmas cookies. What do you think?"

"It's a good idea, but don't get in over your head. Do you have anything in mind?"

"I thought I'd bake huge sugar cookies and decorate them with red and green icing. I'm getting pretty good with a pastry bag, and they shouldn't take very long to make."

Neil chuckled. "Don't assume, Taylor. Make one and time yourself. And don't forget to add up the cost of your ingredients. If it works out, charge the same as you do for your birthday cookies."

"That's exactly what I'll do. Is there anything else I'm forgetting?"

"Yes. Make cookies for me on Saturday night. I'm coming home on Sunday and I haven't had a good cookie since I left."

Taylor smiled. "You miss my cookies?"

"You bet I do! And, Taylor . . ."

There was a long pause and Taylor shivered slightly. "Yes, Neil?"

"I miss *you,* too. Probably more than I should."

TWELVE

Taylor felt her heart leap when the airport shuttle pulled up in front of the house next door. She hadn't wanted to intrude on Neil's homecoming with the kids, but she could hardly wait to see him, to touch him, to hug him again. She'd missed him much more than she was willing to admit and he'd said he'd missed her, too.

Neil looked a little tired, but he was smiling as he got out of the shuttle van. Taylor saw Angela and Michael burst out of the house and run to meet him. Angela tugged on Neil's hand and Taylor watched as Neil scooped her up in his arms. He picked up his garment bag with the other hand and grinned at Michael, who was pulling his suitcase up the walk by its strap. Then he turned and looked toward Taylor's house, frowning slightly. Had he expected her to be there to meet him? Taylor wasn't sure, but she wasn't about to stand on ceremony any longer. She dashed to the front door, pulled it open, and called out across the snow-covered lawn.

"Hi, Taylor." Neil began to smile the moment he saw her. "Give me a couple of minutes to lug this stuff inside and settle up with Mrs. Simmons. Then we'll walk over to see you."

Taylor knew she was smiling foolishly, but she didn't care. Neil wanted to see her. "That sounds good. Shall I put on coffee?"

"That would be great. I had a cup on the plane, but it was really awful."

Taylor watched while Neil and the kids went into the house. Then she fairly flew to the kitchen and got out the French roast coffee she'd picked up at the gourmet coffee shop in Anoka. As she ground the beans, she hummed a little tune and it was only after she'd started the coffee that she realized that it was an old Billie Holiday tune *My Man*.

By the time Neil and the kids arrived, the coffee was ready and Taylor had set out a plate of Angela's favorite Cowboy Cookies. She noticed that Neil was eyeing them hungrily, but instead of taking one immediately, he handed her a bulky package. "This is for you. I'm hopeless at gifts, but Lil helped me shop."

Taylor wanted to ask if Lil was the pub rep Neil had mentioned, but she didn't quite dare. Before she could think of a roundabout way to phrase the question, Michael spoke up. "Lil works for Dad's publisher. She's really cool and she sends us great Christmas gifts."

"I got a doll last year." Angela turned to Taylor. "You saw it. It's the big one with all the outfits."

Taylor nodded. She'd admired the doll, which sat in a place of honor on Angela's bed. It was soft and cuddly and the outfits had Velcro fasteners so that even a young child could change the doll's clothing without asking for help. "Lil sounds very nice."

"She is." Michael sounded very certain. "Can we take some cookies and go watch the rest of that tape, Taylor?"

"Sure. It's still in the VCR from last night. Just rewind it when you're through, okay?"

"I will," Michael promised. "Come on, Angela. We can see what Lil picked out for Taylor later."

Neil was waiting for her to open the gift. Taylor smiled, but her heart wasn't in it. He'd asked another woman to pick out her gift. Even if it was perfect, she wished he'd chosen it. She opened the package, carefully loosening the wrap, and her eyes widened in shock as she took the lid off the box and saw the sweatshirt inside. It was the most impractical and ridiculous item of clothing she'd ever seen.

The sweatshirt was black, with a bowl of fruit done in applique on the front. The huge pineapple, done in a bilious shade of yellow, had orange plastic gemstones glued to it at regular intervals. The green spiky leaves were sprinkled with green glitter, and the strawberry, done in eye-popping pink, had rows of fake pink pearls sewn on for its seeds. There was an electric purple plum studded with lavender beads, an apple that was outlined in huge fake rubies, and a green pear that was covered with a combination of lime green and yellow beads. The bowl that held this frightful collection of fruit was made entirely of little round plastic mirrored sequins that would flip up and down and shimmer brightly every time the unlucky recipient moved.

Taylor stared down at Neil's gift in shock. She couldn't believe that another woman had chosen this gift, and there was only one explanation. Lil was jealous and had attempted to sabotage Taylor by sending Neil home with this sweatshirt.

Neil reached out to touch the fabric, sending the mirrors flashing like the sequins on a Sparklette's water truck. "What do you think?"

"I'm speechless," Taylor replied very honestly. "It's a little difficult to take it in, all at once."

"I know. It's pure California, isn't it?"

Neil looked very proud of himself, and Taylor couldn't bear to disappoint him. "It certainly is. I've never seen anything even remotely like it. It's definitely . . . uh . . . one of a kind."

"I knew you'd like it." Neil grinned at her. "Lil wanted

me to get you one with a flower on it, but I told her that you needed something really special."

"So Lil didn't pick this out?"

"No. She said she didn't think it would be right for you, but I knew you'd love it."

"I *do* love it!" Taylor started to grin, touching the sequins and making them shimmer. "It has a very let-it-all-hang-out attitude."

"I told Lil I wanted you to wear it to the Thanksgiving party at the community center, but she didn't think that was a good idea."

"Oh?"

"She said you'd probably want to save it for evenings at home that don't involve food. She checked the label, and it can't be washed or dry-cleaned."

"It'd be a real shame to ruin it the first time I wore it."

"That's why she told me I'd better get another one for the party. She picked it out, and it's under that second layer of tissue paper. Take a look at it and tell me what you think."

Taylor lifted the glittering fruit bowl sweatshirt and placed it carefully on the kitchen table. Then she looked down at the box again and gave a heartfelt sigh of relief. The second sweatshirt was lovely. It had a stylized flower on the front and there were no glitter or sequins in sight.

"Do you like it?"

"It's beautiful, and it's the perfect thing for the party."

"But you like the one I picked out better, don't you?"

"Yes, I do," Taylor answered honestly. A gift that was chosen by a stranger could never be better than a gift from the man she loved. "This sweatshirt is very nice, but the one you picked out is the real winner."

Neil gave a relieved sigh, and then he eyed the plate of cookies again. "Are those what I think they are?"

"Grandma Mac's cowboys," Taylor answered, going

over to the counter to fill his mug with coffee. "Does Lil like cookies?"

"She loves them. I told her about these and she said her mouth was watering just hearing about them."

Taylor nodded and sent up a silent thank you to Lil, the pub rep who had saved her from having to wear the fruit bowl outside the privacy of her home. "I think I should send Lil a box of cowboys to thank her for helping you shop."

"We're all ready, Daddy." Angela stood in the doorway, dressed in a cute outfit that Taylor had found at the mall in Anoka. Angela had outgrown most of her clothing, and she'd taken her shopping on Tuesday morning. Taylor had done a great job as an unpaid fashion consultant, talking Angela out of the frilly lace dresses she'd wanted to buy and suggesting more practical outfits. This one was royal blue, with a bunny motif around the hem of the top.

"Just a second, honey." Neil smiled at her, giving her a thumbs-up sign, and then he turned back to the phone. "Okay, Lil. I'll do it, but I have to be back by December nineteenth. The twenty-first is Angela's birthday and I promised her a big party this year."

Neil didn't miss the unhappy expression that spread over Angela's face as he spoke. She didn't like it when he went on book tours, but this one was important. "You too, Lil. I'll tell Taylor that you loved the cookies and I'll see you at the airport on the fourteenth."

"Do you have to leave again, Daddy?" Angela looked very sad when he hung up the phone.

"Yes, but it's only for five days. I have to give a speech at a big convention in New York."

"Taylor's not going with you, is she?" Angela looked worried.

"No. Taylor will be here, and so will Mrs. Simmons."

"I guess it's okay then." Angela began to smile. "Taylor said the next time you go, I can have a slipper party at her house."

"A *slipper* party?"

"Something like that." Angela shrugged. "It's where all your friends come over and you have sleeping bags and play games."

Neil grinned as he realized what Angela was trying to say. "A *slumber* party?"

"That's the right word. She's going to let us help her make cookies and then we're going to watch *Roger Rabbit* and have a picnic on the rug. We're gonna sleep there, too, in sleeping bags."

"Sounds like fun." Neil wondered whether Taylor knew what she was getting into. A group of four-year-olds wouldn't be easy to handle. "It's very nice of Taylor to have a slumber party for you."

Angela nodded solemnly. "I know. Michael can hardly wait."

"Michael?"

"He's not allowed at my party 'cause it's just for girls. But Taylor's gonna take Michael and his friends to see the Goody balloon. They're gonna ride in it and everything."

For a moment, Neil thought Angela was speaking in a foreign language, but then he realized what she meant. "Are you talking about the Goodyear Blimp?"

"That's it, Daddy." Angela looked very pleased. "I always forget the name. Can I call Taylor now and tell her we're ready to go?"

Neil glanced at the clock on his desktop and nodded. "Tell her we'll pick her up in ten minutes. I just have to change my shirt."

As Angela picked up his phone and punched out the two-digit code for Taylor's house, Neil left the office. He rinsed out his coffee cup, set it in the sink in the kitchen, and then went up the stairs to his room. It seemed that

Taylor had planned all sorts of activities for his kids without consulting him, and that made him uneasy. He was glad that she was taking such an interest in them and the kids were grateful for the attention, but he couldn't seem to shake the feeling that he was losing control of his well-organized life.

Neil pulled off his favorite khaki shirt, a relic from his college days, and took a plaid wool shirt off the hanger. What Angela had told him about the slumber party and the blimp ride had disturbed him. He didn't have any objections to the activities that Taylor had planned for the kids. They were all things that he might do, if he had some extra time. So why was it so unsettling? And why did he feel as if things were going too fast? The kids were happy. Taylor seemed happy. He was the only one who had doubts.

As he buttoned his shirt, Neil thought about the slumber party. He'd never thought to have one for Angela, and even if he had, he couldn't have done it. Men didn't host slumber parties for their daughters. That was something a wife would do.

Neil began to frown as he realized he'd hit on the crux of his problem. Taylor was stepping right into the role of his children's mother, doing all the things for them that Melissa should have done. And instead of being grateful to Taylor for making his children's lives more complete, he was worried that she'd like the role so much, she might want to make it permanent.

Taylor smiled as she picked up their plates. "That was a really good Thanksgiving dinner."

"Yes, it was." Neil smiled up at her. "Where are you going with those?"

"To the kitchen. I promised to help with the pies. Come

on, Angela. I've got an extra apron for you, and Mrs. Hennesey said that you can help with the whipped cream."

"Do I get to squirt it?" Angela grinned as she hopped from her chair.

"Absolutely. I brought cans of whipped cream for Becky and Suzie, too."

There was a flurry of activity in the community center kitchen and Taylor cleared off counter space for the three girls. She located the aprons she'd brought from Grandma Mac's house and tied one around each of them. Then she pulled up chairs for them to stand on and handed each a canister of whipped cream and a paper plate. "Okay, girls. Shake up your cans, but don't press the nozzle yet. We're going to practice one squirt on the paper plates before you start in on the pumpkin pie."

"Like this?" Becky shook her can.

"That's right. Now watch me and do exactly what I do." Taylor pointed the nozzle at her paper plate and pressed it. A nice dollop of whipped cream came out and she nodded. "Okay. You try it now."

All three girls looked very serious as they squirted whipped cream on their plates. Taylor realized that April Hennesey was smiling as she watched them, and she gave the principal's wife a wink before she turned back to her three helpers. "That's just perfect. I'll dish up the pie and give each of you a piece. You squirt on the whipped cream and then Mrs. Hennesey and Mrs. Tolliver will carry it out to the dessert table."

Their little assembly line worked very well, and Taylor could tell the girls were enjoying themselves. They looked very proud that they'd been allowed to work in the kitchen with the grown-ups. When the last piece of pie had been decorated with whipped cream and the girls had run off to the dessert table, Taylor turned to April with a smile. "There goes the next generation of kitchen volunteers."

"I hope so." April smiled back. "You were wonderful

with them, Taylor. You're more of a mother to Angela than Melissa ever was."

"Do you think so?"

"I certainly do. I'll never understand why Neil stuck by her for so long. He should have booted her you-know-what out the door."

Taylor sighed, and then she asked the question that had been plaguing her. "I know this is none of my business, but do you know what happened to break them up?"

"Of course I do. Everybody knows. Melissa hated it here in Two Rivers and she left Neil to run off with another man."

"Where is she now?"

"In Chicago. The last I heard, she was living in a mansion in one of those exclusive suburbs. Her current husband comes from old money."

"And she's happy now?"

April shrugged. "I guess so. Mavis Aiken called her when she was in Chicago for her father-in-law's funeral. Melissa's got a whole staff that she can boss around and they're always flying off on exotic vacations to places that I can't even spell."

"You don't sound very envious."

"I'm not. I like it just fine right here in Two Rivers. I wouldn't mind having someone come in to clean once a week, but that's about it."

"Do you know if they have any children?"

"I think he does, but they're off at college. And as far as I'm concerned, that's all to the good. Melissa never was a good mother, and she'd probably be even worse with stepkids."

"You really don't like her very much, do you?" Taylor couldn't help asking.

"No. When a woman has children, she should accept the responsibility for them. Melissa never did that. She just dumped them with baby-sitters. She's got visitation rights, you know. It was part of the divorce settlement. But she's never been back here to see them."

"Never?" Taylor was shocked. "Do Michael and Angela ever go to visit her?"

"No. And I know for a fact that she doesn't bother to send them birthday and Christmas gifts. She just left and forgot all about them."

"That's . . ." Taylor paused, trying to think of an appropriate word.

"Unnatural and extremely selfish?"

"Exactly. How much trouble would it be to send a package a couple of times a year?"

"Too much, I guess. You've got to understand one thing about Melissa: She's completely self-centered. I don't think she's intentionally cruel, but nothing else matters to her except her own happiness."

When Taylor left the kitchen, she understood Neil's reluctance to start another relationship. He must have been horribly disappointed by Melissa's attitude and saddened by her failure to keep in touch with their children. She wished she could tell him that she was completely different from Melissa, but she reminded herself that Neil wasn't looking for a mother for Angela and Michael. He wasn't looking for a wife either. He just wanted a friend, and that's what she'd be until she could convince him to change his mind.

There were several older boys, huddled in a corner, and Taylor was surprised to see that Michael was hovering on the edges of the group. She'd seen one of the boys before, leaning against the wall outside the local video store. Something about him had made her turn for a second look. He seemed like a typical rebellious teenager, with a gold stud in his pierced earlobe and clothes that were several sizes too large for him, but this particular boy had made her a bit uneasy. She'd asked Mary about him and learned that his name was Keith Powell. Mary swore that he'd been trouble since the day he'd been born.

The expression on Michael's face made Taylor frown. He was staring at Keith Powell in admiration, and she hoped he wasn't starting to fall in with the wrong crowd. These boys were at least two years older than Michael, and Mary had said that Keith and his friends had been involved in a couple of minor shoplifting incidents. She was about to think of some excuse to call Michael and get him away from the boys when he lifted his hand in a casual wave and headed for the dessert table.

Taylor breathed a sigh of relief. Perhaps Michael was just being friendly. Or maybe she was overreacting. There was no need to worry Neil by telling him about it. But as she walked back to Neil's table, Taylor decided to keep an eye on Michael to make certain that he didn't spend too much time with Keith Powell.

Neil had talked to several people while Taylor had been helping out in the kitchen, including Suzanne and Nina. Both of them had been friendly, but Suzanne hadn't reached out to touch him the way she usually did and Nina hadn't given him the sultry look that she usually sent his way.

When Suzanne and Nina had left him for the lure of the dessert table, Neil had thought about their conversation. There was only one way to account for the change in their behavior. It was clear that both of them liked Taylor. The little things they'd said about her proved that. And they obviously thought of them as a couple, because they were treating him exactly the same way they'd treat a friend's husband or boyfriend.

A slow smile slid across Neil's face as he saw Taylor walking toward him. She was wearing the flowered sweatshirt that he'd given her, and she was the most beautiful woman here. There was only one thing wrong with her appearance and that was her expression. She wasn't smiling.

"Hey." Neil reached out and took her hand when Taylor arrived at the table. "You look much too serious. Did something go wrong in the kitchen?"

"No, everything's fine. Did you compliment Angela on her whipped cream?"

"Of course I did. I told her that the pie looked so good, it was almost a shame to eat it."

"What did she say to that?"

"She told me that pie was made to eat and I shouldn't be so silly. And then she ran off to play with Becky and Suzie."

Taylor lifted a forkful of pumpkin pie to her mouth and a blissful expression spread over her face. "This is really great pie. Did you know that Mrs. Wyler made it?"

"Mrs. Wyler made all the pies?" Neil was surprised. He hadn't even known that Mrs. Wyler baked, and he'd been very surprised when she'd shown up at the Thanksgiving party.

"She used to be a pastry chef at a fancy resort before she got married and moved to Two Rivers."

Neil stared at her thoughtfully. "How did you learn that?"

"She told me. I took some cookies over to her while you were gone, and we got to talking about recipes. And then, when I told her that I was in charge of the pie table for the Thanksgiving party, she volunteered to bake enough pumpkin pie for everyone."

"She's never done that before."

"That's because nobody ever asked her. I figured that Mrs. Wyler had too much time on her hands, and that was the reason she was on the phone so much. She just didn't have anything else to do. But that should change, now that Mary's tasted her pumpkin pie."

Neil thought he knew where Taylor was going, but he

decided to ask anyway. "What does Mary have to do with it?"

"Mary really doesn't have time to bake, so she's going to ask Mrs. Wyler to make all the pies for the café. Just wait until you taste her coconut cream. It's pure heaven."

"You've tasted it?"

Taylor chewed and swallowed before she answered. "Of course I have. Angela just adores it and Michael ate three pieces."

Neil started to frown. "But Michael doesn't like coconut cream pie."

"He does now. He agreed to eat one piece, just to be polite, but he changed his mind after the first bite. It think it's because Mrs. Wyler toasts her coconut so it's crunchy instead of soggy."

It seemed that Taylor knew his children's taste in food better than he did, and Neil felt uncomfortable again. What if Taylor moved away? Michael and Angela had come to depend on her, and they'd be heartbroken. And the truth of the matter was, he wasn't exactly immune, either. If Taylor ever left Two Rivers, he'd be heartbroken too.

THIRTEEN

Taylor took the pan of cookies out of the oven and frowned. This just wasn't a good day. Grandma Mac's oven wasn't working right, and she'd almost burned a batch of Christmas sugar cookies. The repairman couldn't come until tomorrow, but Taylor couldn't just sit back and wait. She had orders to fill that she didn't want to cancel at the last minute.

There was a knock on her back door and Taylor hurried to answer it. Had the repairman reconsidered and come out today? When she opened the door and saw Neil standing there, she must have looked disappointed, because he stepped back and began to frown.

"Did I come at a bad time?"

"No. Of course not." Taylor put on a smile and opened the door a little wider. "Come in and have a cup of coffee with me."

Neil slipped off his boots and left them on the rug on the back porch. Then he walked to the coffeepot in his stocking feet, poured himself a cup, and sat down in a chair at the kitchen table. "Something's got you riled. What's wrong?"

"It's my oven. It's gone on the blink and the repairman can't get here until tomorrow." Taylor lifted a cookie off the pan and tipped it over so he could see the bottom.

"Just look at these cookies. They're gooey on top and almost burned on the bottom."

Neil examined a cookie. "It's just your top element, Taylor. I'll give Jim a call. If he's got it in stock, I'll pick it up and put it in for you tonight."

Taylor was almost giddy with relief as Neil walked to the phone and made the call. After a few minutes, he gave her the high sign, and she felt as if the weight of the world had dropped off her shoulders.

"Thanks, Neil." Taylor reached out to take his hand. "How about letting me pay you back by cooking dinner for you tomorrow night?"

Neil gave her a devilish grin. "It's a deal, but you'd better be careful what you promise. I'm not above taking advantage of you."

"It was fun the last time." The words were out of Taylor's mouth before she could stop herself, and she felt her cheeks turning hot. "I'm sorry, Neil. I shouldn't have said that."

Neil stared at her and she stared at him. Tension seemed to crackle between them. Then he pushed back his chair and took her into his arms, his lips clamping tightly over hers.

Taylor sighed, giving in to the blissful feelings that washed over her in a gathering wave. It had been too long. She'd been dreaming of this moment, willing it to happen again, since the morning they'd agreed to cool their relationship.

"We shouldn't be doing this."

His words were thick with longing and Taylor trembled. "No. We shouldn't."

"And we shouldn't be doing this either." He unbuttoned her blouse, his lips trailing kisses down to the valley between her breasts.

"No." Taylor's voice was shaking as her hands reached up, under his shirt. "We shouldn't."

"Then we agree?" He picked her up in his strong arms and walked through the house to the stairs.

"Oh, yes." Taylor sighed, wrapping her arms tightly around his neck so that he could never let her go. "We agree completely."

Taylor felt as if she might faint with pleasure as he climbed the stairs. Dimly, she was aware of the pictures she'd hung on the wall opposite the railing, the colorful prints from an old-fashioned cookbook that Nina had found for her at a thrift shop.

He turned at the top of the stairs and walked through the open doorway, placing her gently on her bed. "You know that this could be a big mistake, don't you?"

Any reply she might have wanted to make was forgotten as he stripped off her slacks, rolling them down from her hips and lifting her to pull them off. And then she was tearing at his clothes, undressing him with only one thought in her mind. She wanted him inside her. She needed him to make love to her now, at this very moment. The hell with the consequences when something felt as right as this did.

"Please, Neil." She was desperate with longing as she reached up to guide him, crying out with delight as he plunged deeply within her, taking her with a force that denied what she'd come to think of as his gentle nature. And there was nothing gentle about her response, straining up against him with a desperate intensity that was born of endless days of deprivation.

The air in the room had been cold. She'd closed the heater vent before she'd come downstairs, but it seemed almost tropical now with the heat of their shared passions. She was on fire. She could feel her skin flush with a fever of wanting, the blaze centered in the secret feminine core of her body.

Her tongue tasted the skin at the base of his throat. She

covered his chest with kisses. He was hot, his body an inferno of desire.

And then they were moving in the familiar patterns of giving and taking, arousal and rapture, climbing to the peak that she'd glimpsed in the distance the first time she'd set eyes on him. They were fellow supplicants filled with one desire, traveling higher and higher into that rarified atmosphere until their breathing grew ragged and their cravings blossomed into a shuddering completion that left them both spent and unable to utter a sound.

It was so quiet and peaceful. They were locked together in the most intimate of embraces for what could have been blissful hours. And then Neil moved, rolling over to his side and gathering her into his arms again.

He reached up to touch her lips with the tip of his finger. "So much for good intentions."

"I know." Taylor smiled. "Would it make you feel better if I told you that I just couldn't help myself?"

"Of course it would, especially if I told you that this thing was bigger than both of us and there was no point in fighting it."

Taylor nodded. "That's a really old line. Is it true?"

"I think it is." Neil sighed and brushed back her hair. "But we don't have time to think about it now. There's something we have to do."

Taylor nodded, loving the teasing light in his eyes. "Pick up the element for my stove?"

"Yes, but not quite yet." Neil rolled over again and ran his fingers down the length of her trembling body. "There's something else we have to do first."

Taylor smiled, reaching up to touch his lips with the tip of her finger. "Again?"

"You read my mind." Neil leaned over to kiss her deeply and then he chuckled. "After that, we'll think about your stove."

FOURTEEN

Taylor filled another cookie sheet and sighed. They were right back to square one again. The night after Neil had repaired her oven had been wonderful. Mrs. Simmons had come in to stay with the kids and Neil had spent the whole night with her. But the very next morning, he'd dropped the bombshell.

As they'd sipped steaming mugs of coffee at her kitchen table, Neil had confessed that he was getting in over his head. If they continued to sleep together, he'd be tempted to ask her to marry him, and he wasn't ready for another wife. They simply had to go back to the way things had been. He'd even told Taylor that she was free to date someone else and he'd understand.

Taylor knew that Neil was running scared. He was afraid he'd get hurt again, as he had with Melissa. But this on-again, off-again affair was driving Taylor crazy. She would have broken it off in a heartbeat if she'd been involved with any other man. But she loved Neil, and she couldn't bring herself to close the door on something so potentially wonderful. They would play it his way, for now.

Several days ago Neil had left for a convention at one of the posh New York hotels. Mrs. Simmons was staying with the kids and Taylor was keeping an eye on things next door. They'd settled back into a routine, the one that Taylor had introduced the last time Neil had left town. Mrs.

Simmons cooked for the kids and did their laundry while Taylor acted as their unofficial parent. It worked out fine for all of them, but Taylor really wished that she could be more than a temporary mother to Angela and Michael.

Angela's slumber party had gone off without a hitch, Michael had received an *A* on the term paper he'd written at Taylor's kitchen table, and Cookies & Kisses was running smoothly. Taylor's orders were increasing by leaps and bounds, and she could hardly wait for Neil to come home so they could talk about expansion.

The stove timer began its rhythmic chime and Taylor hurried over to take two dozen Cowboy Cookies out of the oven. Her oven was working fine now, but it was too small for the volume of orders that were pouring in. Last night she'd worked until one in the morning, and she really needed another oven or two.

An hour passed quickly in Grandma Mac's small kitchen. Taylor juggled bowls of dough, cookie sheets, and cooling racks like a pro. She'd realized that she could double her volume if she had two ovens, but there was no room for another without expensive remodeling and the loss of precious counter space. She needed a bakery with industrial ovens and a full-time assistant to handle the increase in her business.

Mrs. Simmons had offered to help, and she was now handling part of the baking in Neil's kitchen while Michael was in school and Angela was off playing with Becky or Suzie. Taylor ran back and forth between the two houses, delivering cookie dough for Mrs. Simmons to bake and collecting the cookies when they were cool. Taylor had insisted on paying for her time and although Mrs. Simmons had objected at first, she'd finally admitted that she was pleased to have some extra cash right before Christmas.

Taylor couldn't keep up this mad dash between houses forever. She knew that when Neil came home, she'd have to make other arrangements. It wasn't fair to take over his kitchen and disrupt his life. She'd already made an alternative plan, and if things worked out the way she hoped, she'd already have a solution in place when Neil came back from his trip.

The phone rang and Taylor picked up the new cordless phone that sat on the kitchen counter. It was a necessity, since she never knew whether she would be at home or in the kitchen at Neil's house. "Cookies & Kisses. This is Taylor. May I help you?"

At first, Taylor didn't recognize the voice on the other end of the line. When she did, she began to smile. It was Randy Hutchins from Two Rivers Realty, and he had good news. Mrs. Dubinski, the widow of the man who'd owned the town's only bakery, was eager to sell the building.

"When can I see it?" Taylor knew that buying the bakery was a big step. She'd have to get a bank loan, and it would take every drop of her savings. But Randy hadn't thought it would present a problem as long as she used Grandma Mac's house as collateral. "That's great, Randy. I'll meet you there at four."

As Taylor hung up the phone, she frowned slightly. She wished that Neil were here so that she could talk to him about her plan. But Neil was in New York, and she didn't want to bother him there. She'd gather all the facts and wait until he came home to make her final decision.

"It's really big, Taylor." Angela gripped her hand tightly as they walked into the back room of the bakery. "And it doesn't look like a kitchen."

"You're right—it doesn't." Taylor smiled at her. She'd picked up Angela at Becky's house and collected Michael from school. Both of them had wanted to look at the bakery with her.

"Does everything work?" Michael walked over to the

bank of industrial ovens against the wall. "You'd better have Mr. Burkholtz check them out, Taylor."

Taylor nodded, biting back a grin. Michael was definitely his father's son. That was exactly what Neil would have told her. She turned to Randy and asked the most important question. "How much does Mrs. Dubinski want for it?"

"Seventy, but that's just her asking price. The interior needs a lot of work, and I think she'll settle for sixty."

"Sixty dollars?" Angela tugged on Taylor's hand. "I can buy it for you, Taylor. Daddy says I've got sixty-one dollars in my savings account."

Taylor reached down to fluff Angela's hair. "That's very sweet of you, honey, but I couldn't use your savings. And it's not sixty dollars. It's sixty *thousand* dollars. Buildings like this are very expensive."

"That sounds pretty high to me." Michael frowned at Randy. "Joey Murphy's dad just bought a garage and it was only forty. Are you sure you can't bargain her down to that?"

Randy grinned at Taylor. "This kid's got potential as a real estate mogul. He's not even out of high school and he's already smart enough to give me comps."

"Well, can't you?" Michael refused to be put off.

"I don't know." Randy was very serious when he turned back to Michael. "I can try, but this building is more valuable than a garage. The equipment is expensive."

"*If* it works. And there's equipment in a garage, too. Lifts are expensive, and so are tools."

"You've got a point," Randy said. "I'll call Jim and see if he can check out this equipment tomorrow. There's no sense in making an offer until we know what's what. And if I were you, Taylor, I'd call someone to check out the structure and give you an estimate on any improvements you want to make."

Taylor could see the wisdom in that. "Do you know a good contractor?"

"There's Ted Swanson. He's good and he's between jobs right now. I'll give you his number and you can call him. You'd better take the keys, too."

"The keys?" Taylor was surprised. "But I haven't agreed to buy it yet."

Randy shrugged. "That doesn't matter. No one else is interested, and you shouldn't have to run down to my office every time you want to get in."

Randy handed her Ted Swanson's card and a set of keys, and Taylor dropped them into her pocket. She'd never purchased property before, but she was sure that most real estate agents didn't give their prospective clients a set of keys to the property before they'd even made an offer. She reminded herself that this was Two Rivers, where people trusted each other, and turned to Randy with a smile. "How about the bank? Shall I check with them to make sure that I can get a loan?"

"Couldn't hurt. Talk to Ward Sutter over at First National. He wrote the original loan thirty years ago."

"And he's still there?" Taylor was surprised.

"He worked his way up to president. Ward's a good guy; I know him from the Lion's Club. He'll remember the property and give you good advice."

"I'll call him tomorrow and set up an appointment. Do you think he'll need to see any paperwork?"

"Not at this stage. Ward keeps on top of things, and he'll know how your business is doing. And he'll be able to tell you exactly how much this building is worth."

As Taylor drove back to Neil's house, she felt very unsure of herself. Buying property was a big investment and she needed Neil's advice. The only thing that kept her from panicking was the knowledge that he'd promised to call her tomorrow night and come back on Tuesday, in plenty of time to arrange Angela's birthday party.

* * *

Taylor sat in front of Wade Sutter's desk, dressed in one of her best business suits. She'd felt confident when she'd entered his office, but what he'd just told her had taken the wind out of her sails. "I can't use Grandma Mac's house as collateral?"

"I'm afraid not." Wade was a distinguished-looking man with silver hair, and the only thing that kept him from being intimidating was the warmth in his keen brown eyes. "I know she left it to you. There's no problem with that. But until probate closes, it won't officially be yours."

"How long will that take?"

"It could be as soon as six months, but my guess would be closer to a year."

"But I'm living there. Is that illegal?"

"No." Wade smiled to reassure her. "You have the right of occupancy as the executor and the sole beneficiary. But no liens can be made against the property until the title is clear."

"Is it possible for me to get a personal loan until probate is settled?"

"Not on a sum that large. I've been keeping track of your new business and it's doing well. That's a point in your favor. I'd be happy to bend the rules a little and authorize a personal loan for the down payment, but my board of directors would never allow me to finance the entire amount."

It was what Taylor had expected, but she was still disappointed. "So there's no way I can buy the bakery from Mrs. Dubinski?"

"Let me think." Wade put his hands together and made a steeple of his fingers. He was silent for a long moment and then he nodded. "If you could find someone with a good credit rating and available collateral to co-sign for you, the bank would accept that. How about a relative? Or a close friend?"

Taylor thought of Neil, but she couldn't ask him for a

favor like that. And asking Candice was out of the question. Even if her mother agreed, she had a history of credit problems. "I don't think so, Mr. Sutter. But I'll give it some thought and get back to you."

"Do that." Wade stood up and walked around the desk to shake Taylor's hand. "You might talk about nontraditional funding with Randy. He's quite familiar with creative financing."

When Taylor left the bank, she headed straight for Jim Burkholtz's appliance shop to find out what he'd learned about the ovens. The news was good. Only one unit needed repair, and it was a minor problem.

It was five o'clock and already dark when Taylor arrived at the café. She'd agreed to meet Ted Swanson there for dinner, and as she walked in the door, she spotted a ruggedly handsome man wearing jeans and a North Stars hockey shirt, sitting alone in a booth.

Taylor knew he had to be Ted Swanson. Not only did he look the part of a contractor, but he was also drawing something on a tablet of graph paper while he sipped his coffee.

"Mr. Swanson?" Taylor arrived at the booth.

"Ted. And you must be Ms. MacIntyre?"

"Taylor." Taylor slid into the booth and glanced down at his sketch. It looked like the layout of the bakery. "You had a chance to look at the bakery?"

"Yes, I have. The building's basically sound. A couple of the windows need new sills and the back door has to be replaced, but it's in pretty good shape. All it really needs is some cosmetic work."

"Cosmetic work?"

"Paint, new draws on some of the drawers, a couple of new faucets—that sort of thing. You'll need to replace some electrical outlets, but I checked out the wiring and it's sound. There's a couple of ideas I'd like to run past you if you've got the time."

"I've got the time, but I may not have the money." Taylor was embarrassed at having to discuss her finances with someone she'd just met, but it was only fair to tell him that the job might not come through. "I just came from the bank, and they can't give me a loan until probate closes on my grandmother's house. I'll pay you for your time, of course, but unless Randy Hutchins can pull a rabbit out of his hat with the financing, I won't be able to buy the bakery."

Ted gave her a sympathetic look. "Randy's pretty good with the loan companies. Don't give up hope yet. And I won't charge you for looking at the place. It's all a part of the appraisal process."

"Really?" Taylor took heart from his attitude. "Then I really would like to listen to your ideas. Let's have dinner first. I didn't get a break for lunch and I'm starving."

Mary came over to take their order and she grinned at Taylor. "It's a good thing Neil's out of town. He'd have a fit if he saw that you were having dinner with Romeo, here."

"Romeo?" Taylor glanced over at Ted and saw that his face was turning red.

"That's right." Mary winked at Ted. "Dottie and Peggy were fighting again about who got to take your order. The only way I could settle it was to send them both back to the kitchen and come out here myself."

Ted was clearly embarrassed. "Look, Mary, they're both nice girls, but I'm really not . . ."

"I know," Mary interrupted him. "Just do me a favor and keep coming in. They work a lot harder when they're trying to impress you."

Taylor was just wondering whether she should explain about Ted and the bakery when Mary turned to her. "You couldn't do better than this guy, Taylor. He put in some cabinets for me and he did a real good job. He'll have that old bakery spruced up in no time flat."

"You know about the bakery?"

"Of course I do. Mrs. Dubinski called me long distance to see if you were serious about buying it. You are, aren't you?"

"Yes, I am." Taylor remembered what Marge Breckner had told her about how difficult it was to keep secrets in Two Rivers. "I'll make her an offer if Randy can come through with the financing for me."

"Good. You'd be right down the street and that would be nice. And that old bakery's been vacant too long. How about something to eat? You can't make plans on an empty stomach."

"You're right." Taylor smiled at her. "What's good tonight, Mary?"

"Everything. I don't make anything that's *not* good. But if I were you, I'd have the pot roast."

"Then that's what I'll have."

"The same for me," Ted agreed quickly. "And a side of coleslaw with one of your homemade pickles on top."

"You got it. How about you, Taylor. You want any sides?"

"French fries and gravy." Taylor's mouth began to water. Neil had introduced her to his favorite side dish and it was delicious.

Ted waited until Mary had left the booth and then looked down at his drawing. "Let me tell you about the improvements I have in mind. I talked to a friend of mine about your business and she thought you might like to have more than the standard bakery counter in front."

"She did?" Taylor realized that Ted hadn't mentioned his friend's name. Perhaps it was someone he was dating.

"She suggested that you put in tables and serve coffee and cookies in the front. She thought it could be like a little bistro."

"That's a very good idea. And I don't think it would cut into Mary's breakfast business if I only served cookies and coffee. What else did your friend suggest?"

As Ted went on to tell her about other improvements she could make, Taylor began to suspect that she knew who Ted's friend was. Suzanne had called her last night, and when Taylor had said she wanted to buy the bakery, Suzanne had mentioned the very same things. If Ted and Suzanne were dating, why hadn't Suzanne told her? Taylor decided to drive over to Suzanne's apartment, right after she finished her dinner with Ted, and ask her what was going on.

FIFTEEN

"Come on, you two. It's time for food." Taylor grinned as she spotted Ted and Suzanne in the back room of the bakery, standing in the closet that Ted had planned to turn into a walk-in pantry. They seemed to be locked in the same embrace they'd been in when she'd run home to get them all a sandwich. Or perhaps it wasn't the same embrace. Taylor spotted a pile of furniture pads on the floor that appeared suspiciously rumpled. "When are you two going to come out of the closet, anyway?"

"Bad choice of words, Taylor. We're not exactly in the closet." Suzanne gave an embarrassed laugh and pulled away. Her cheeks were pink and her eyes were sparkling.

"It's only until the end of the school year." Ted draped a protective arm around Suzanne's shoulders. "Then we can stop sneaking around."

Taylor understood their problem. Suzanne had explained about the morals clause in her teacher's contract and how it would disqualify her for tenure if she admitted that she was even dating Ted, much less having an affair with him. Ted's divorce wouldn't be final until April, and Suzanne was still on probation as a new teacher. When she received tenure at the end of the school year and when Ted's divorce was final, they could start dating openly.

Taylor had come up with a solution for them. Since Neil had insisted that she was free to date, Taylor was pretending to date Ted. Suzanne, as Taylor's good friend, came along on their dates, and Taylor made herself scarce once they were away from prying eyes. It had worked fine so far. No one suspected that Ted and Suzanne were in love. And as long as they managed to keep their hands off each other in public, no one would.

When Taylor had first mentioned her idea to them, Suzanne had voiced some reservations. Wouldn't Neil be jealous? Taylor had smiled. So what if he was? Perhaps a little touch of jealousy was just what Neil needed. If matters came to a head and Neil insisted that she choose between them, she'd let him in on their secret. But she wasn't about to tip her hand by telling him about it before he asked.

"Any news from Randy?" Ted sat down at the card table Taylor had brought from home and poured three cups of coffee from a Thermos.

"Not yet." Taylor unpacked the sandwiches and passed them around. "He says we might have an answer by the end of next week."

"Do you think it's a good idea to sit here by the window where everyone can see us?" Suzanne looked a little nervous as she took a chair.

"That's part of the plan. I'm with Ted, remember? You're just here to advise me on how we can remodel this place."

"I've already come up with a couple of things," Suzanne said. "I think Ted should build a false frame for this window. It doesn't look cozy enough for a cookie and coffee shop."

"What kind of a frame?" Ted turned to her.

"One with little wooden squares so the window will look like individual panes of glass. It can't weigh very much. Taylor will have to remove it when she cleans the window. But I think it'll add a really homey feel, especially if I make some café-style curtains to cover the bottom half."

Ted thought about it for a minute and nodded. "I'll use

balsa wood. See that beam up there, right over your head?"
Both Taylor and Suzanne looked up at the beam and nodded. "I'll hinge the frame at the top and put a fastener
up there. When you need to wash the window, all you'll
have to do is raise it and hook it in place."

"Great. Let's do it." Taylor was impressed. The idea
made a lot of sense. "What shall I use for a counter?"

"How about a bar? I'm remodeling the Dew Drop Inn
and they're replacing their old one."

Suzanne shook her head. "That place is a dive. Taylor
wouldn't want a bar from there."

"Maybe she would." Ted wasn't so easily discouraged.
"It needs to be refinished, but it's solid mahogany and the
mirror and all the cabinets go with it. It wouldn't take that
much work to sand it down and make it look new again."

Taylor was definitely intrigued. The old mahogany bar
would be a novelty in her cookie and coffee shop, and if
she bought some matching stools, it would provide addi-
tional seating. "How much do they want for it, Ted?"

"Nothing. They're paying me to haul it to the dump. I
could just load it up and bring it over here. What do you
say, Taylor?"

"Sold. The price is right and I can refinish it if you
teach me how."

"No problem." Ted smiled at Suzanne. "Suze and I can
do it for you. We'll work on it at night."

Suzanne nodded, catching his meaning immediately.
"Good idea. We'll do that for you, Taylor. We could probably get it done in a week or so."

Taylor laughed. It would take at least a month if the
sizzling look that Suzanne had given Ted had anything to
do with it. "But what if I can't buy the bakery?"

"No problem," Ted shrugged. "It's free, remember?"

"Heads up." Suzanne glanced out at the sidewalk.
"Here comes Vernon Long. He's on the school board."

Taylor slid a little closer to Ted. "Come on, Ted. It's

time for our act. Just pretend that I'm a giant chocolate cookie."

Ted put his arm around Taylor and they gazed at each other, like lovers who couldn't bear to tear their eyes away. They held that pose until Suzanne tapped Taylor on the arm.

"He's gone. And believe me, he got an eyeful. Are you sure this isn't going to get you in trouble with Neil?"

"I'm sure." Taylor told herself that she was doing the right thing. Her relationship with Neil was going nowhere and jealousy might prompt him into action. But it was a gamble, because it could also have the opposite effect. If Neil thought that she'd found someone new, he might just back off even farther.

Neil hung up the phone and headed straight to the portable bar in his hotel room to pour himself a drink. He'd called Lester Crawley at the post office to find out if the package of toys he'd ordered for Christmas had arrived, and he'd gotten much more than he'd bargained for. Lester had been full of news about the newest couple in town, Taylor and Ted Swanson. It seemed that Taylor wanted to buy the old bakery, and she'd hired Ted as her contractor. Vernon Long had seen them sitting close together at a card table by the front window, staring into each other's eyes.

Neil switched on the television and attempted to watch the eleven o'clock news, but his thoughts weren't on the serial rapist who was stalking New York University or the total ban against smoking that a group of concerned citizens was proposing. Even the ten-second spot on the mystery writers' conference didn't take his attention away from thoughts of Taylor and Ted Swanson.

Neil reminded himself that he'd been the one who'd laid out the ground rules of their relationship. He'd told

Taylor that she could date someone else if she wanted to. But he really hadn't expected Taylor to do it. And he certainly hadn't thought she'd fall in love only a few short days after they'd made their agreement. Neil was so angry, he felt like throwing his glass against the wall. He'd liked Ted Swanson when he'd first met him, but now he hated the guy's guts. Ted was a lowlife, moving in on Taylor when Neil was too far away to do anything about it!

He fumed for several minutes, pacing up and down the carpet in his hotel suite. He told himself that he was just worried about Taylor. She'd admitted that she didn't have a lot of experience with men and Ted might take advantage of that. Painful images floated through Neil's mind. Taylor and Ted in bed, her arms wrapped around his neck. Taylor's lips pressed to Ted's. Taylor's cheeks flushed with passion as Ted . . .

Neil marched to the credenza and picked up the phone. He had to call Taylor and ask her what the hell was going on. He wouldn't use exactly those words, but he would be able to tell if there was a difference in the way she acted toward him. As he put through the call, he reminded himself that Lester loved to gossip and didn't always have his facts straight. It was possible that Taylor had simply hired Ted as a contractor and there was no reason at all to be worried.

"Hi, Neil." Taylor settled back against the pillows and cradled the phone against her cheek. "How's New York?"

As Neil began to tell her about the conference, warning bells pealed in Taylor's head. He sounded stiff and unnatural, not like himself at all. It was clear he really didn't want to talk about the conference. There was something else on his mind. "What is it, Neil? You sound distracted."

"I guess I am." Neil sighed, and Taylor could hear the distress in his voice. "I called Les Crawley earlier. He . . .

uh . . . he mentioned that you were thinking about buying the old bakery building."

"Yes, I am. The bank can't give me a loan, but Randy Hutchins is looking into alternative financing for me." A grin slid over Taylor's face. She knew exactly why Neil sounded so strange. Lester Crawley liked to talk and he'd probably given Neil all the local gossip, including the fact that she'd been spending a lot of time with Ted Swanson.

"I hear you hired a contractor."

Neil's words were clipped, and they confirmed Taylor's suspicions. Neil was definitely jealous. "Randy recommended Ted Swanson and he's agreed to take the job. Of course, it all hinges on whether Randy can come up with a way for me to get the money."

"Are you sure you need to expand? You've only been in business for a little over a month."

"I'm sure. The orders are pouring in and I can't fill them all with one oven." Taylor's grin grew wider. Neil wasn't worried about whether or not she should expand. He was worried about Ted.

"I guess you know best. But how about this contractor? Did you check his references?"

Taylor bit back a giggle. "Of course I did, and he's very highly recommended. He put in some kitchen cabinets for Mary Baxter and she said he was a good worker."

"Mary likes everybody." The tone in Neil's voice dismissed that recommendation.

"I checked with Tim Breckner, too. He worked with Ted on a remodeling job and he told me I couldn't find anyone better."

"Tim said that?"

Neil sounded shocked and Taylor smiled. "Yes, and Marge likes him, too. Tim invited him home one night when they worked late and Marge said Ted was a real doll to compliment her on her overdone pot roast."

"Oh." There was a long pause while Neil thought about

that. "If Tim says he's a good worker, he must be okay. But how about his character? Anybody can be nice for a couple of days, especially if they're getting paid for it. Some of the guys in the building trades are a little flaky."

Taylor raised her eyebrows. "Flaky? What do you mean?"

"I just don't want you to get in any trouble. I've heard that Ted Swanson is a real ladies' man."

"Really?" Taylor had all she could do not to laugh. "I guess that shouldn't surprise me. Ted's a very handsome man. But it's not like I'm about to marry him. I just want him to remodel the bakery for me."

There was a long silence, and then Taylor heard Neil sigh. "Just don't get taken in by anything he says, okay? And get everything in writing. Actually, it might be best if you wait until I come home."

"That's a very good idea," Taylor was quick to agree. "Ted and I are just at the planning stage, and I certainly won't make any big decisions before I talk it over with you."

"Good. Just hold him off until I get back."

"I will," Taylor promised. "We'll just work on the drawings and things like that."

There was another silence and when Neil spoke again, he sounded suspicious. "Are you paying this guy?"

"Not a cent." A smile played over Taylor's face. She knew that Neil wasn't worried about money. "Ted assured me that his estimates are completely free."

"But you said he was already doing drawings. Isn't he going to charge you for that?"

"No, Neil. The drawings are part of the estimate. All I had to do was promise to give him the job if my financing came through."

"What if it doesn't come through?"

"Then we'll both be out of luck." Taylor frowned slightly, hoping that Neil's comment wasn't prophetic.

"Ted's between jobs anyway. He doesn't start in on the Dew Drop Inn until next month. He says that right now his time belongs to me."

There was another long silence and then Neil cleared his throat. "His time is yours, but he's not charging you?"

"That's right. He says it's fun to get into a project at the very beginning because it opens up all sorts of fascinating possibilities."

"Oh?" Neil sounded very suspicious. "Like what?"

"Like expanding the plans to include what Ted sees as my future needs. He thinks that I should turn the front of the bakery into a cookie and coffee shop. And he's already arranged to move the old bar from the Dew Drop Inn to the bakery so that I can use it as a counter. He's bringing the mirror, too."

"Tell him you don't want the mirror, Taylor."

Neil sounded very definite and Taylor was surprised. "Why?"

"Just take my word for it, okay?"

"No." Taylor could be obstinate when the occasion warranted, and this was one of those times. "Tell me why I shouldn't take the mirror."

"Because it's got a life-size nude painted on it, and I don't think that's the sort of image you want for your business."

Taylor started to giggle. "You didn't have to beat around the bush, Neil. Besides, how do *you* know?"

"I went out there when I was a teenager. That nude on the mirror was a big thrill. It's not exactly art, if you know what I mean."

Taylor laughed. "Ted didn't mention it. Maybe he was planning to take off the nude before he brought it to me."

"Maybe."

Neil didn't sound convinced and Taylor grinned. He was definitely jealous. "On the other hand, I might tell Ted to bring it just the way it is and ask Nina to paint on some clothing. She's a very good artist. Then all the old Dew Drop Inn customers would come in to see how I'd managed to cover up the nude."

"What are you going to do about the bar? I seem to remember that it was really scarred up."

"Ted said that won't be a problem. We'll just sand it down and refinish it. It'll take a while, but it's solid mahogany and it'll look great when we're finished."

"We? As in you and Ted?"

"No." Taylor decided to let him off the hook. "We, as in Ted and Suzanne. She wants to learn how to refinish furniture and Ted promised to teach her. She's been helping out a lot, and so has Nina. When will you be back, Neil? We all miss you."

Neil sighed, and when he spoke again, he sounded unhappy. "I'll be back on Tuesday. They booked me on a couple of local talk shows, but I'm canceling. I promised Angela that she could have a big birthday party this year."

"But those talk shows are important, aren't they?"

"Yes, but I can't do them without breaking my promise to Angela. There's no way I can fly home on Friday morning and arrange an instant birthday party for her."

"I'll arrange it for you. Angela will be perfectly satisfied just as long as you get here in time for the party."

"You'd do that for me?"

Neil sounded surprised and Taylor smiled. "Consider it done. All you have to do is find time to shop for Angela's birthday present. And while you're at it, you'd better do your Christmas shopping. That's only a week and a half away."

"I'm way ahead of you. Lil and I hit the stores yesterday and I had everything wrapped. I'm going to be loaded like a pack mule when I get home."

"That's good. How about the kids? They need to go Christmas shopping, don't they?"

There was a long silence and then Neil groaned. "I didn't think about that."

"I'll do it. We'll drive down to the Mall of America this weekend. I've been wanting to go there anyway."

"That'd be perfect." Neil sounded very grateful. "There's an envelope with some cash in my file cabinet. Just take it and use whatever you need for the birthday party and the shopping trip."

"Is it filed under *C,* for *Cash?*"

"No." Neil chuckled. "It's under *M,* for *Money.* It's a big manila envelope; you can't miss it. And, Taylor . . . thank you. I'd really be lost without you."

Taylor didn't make a smart remark. She just smiled and told Neil that she felt the same. After she'd said good night, she snuggled down under the covers and thought about what he'd said. Telling her that he'd be lost without her was the closest that Neil had ever come to any kind of commitment. Perhaps her little scheme to make him jealous was working even better than she'd dared to hope.

SIXTEEN

Everything seemed to be happening at once. Taylor slipped another pan of Christmas cookies into Neil's oven with one hand and grabbed her cordless phone with the other. "Cookies & Kisses. This is Taylor."

Her moonboots were leaving tracks on Neil's kitchen floor, but that was the least of Taylor's worries. She'd wash it tonight after the baking was done. She hurried out the door and raced through the gap in the hedge to her own back door, talking on the phone all the while. "Bear with me, Randy. I'm just leaving Neil's house and running over to mine. I've got cookies in both ovens and I'm going crazy trying to keep up."

When Taylor arrived in her own kitchen, the stove timer was just beginning to ring. She removed two pans of cookies from her oven, stuck in two more, reset the timer, and sank down on a kitchen chair to listen to Randy.

"But you applied to four places, didn't you?" A frown slid across Taylor's face as Randy explained. It seemed that not one of the lending institutions Randy had approached was willing to take a chance on her. "What do we do now?"

Taylor listened as Randy told her to sit tight; there was one more place he wanted to try. She'd just ended her conversation with him when the other cordless phone—the one she'd stuck in the left pocket of her apron—began to ring.

It was Tom Peterson, calling from Florida. "No, Tom, Neil's in New York. I'm actually at my house, but I'm running between both places. What can I do for you?"

Taylor headed out the back door at a gallop, talking to Tom as she dashed back through the gap in the hedge. Marge would be dropping off Angela any minute and she had to be there. "Sure, Tom. I'll go over and run some water through the pipes, no problem. I'll take Michael and Angela with me and we'll flush the toilets, too."

Tom was just telling her not to forget to turn on the outside water tap next to the garage when the cordless phone in her right pocket rang. Taylor answered it, then asked Mary to wait just a moment while she finished her conversation with Tom. The moment Tom said good-bye, Taylor shut off Neil's phone, stuck it back in her left pocket, and retrieved hers.

"Hi, Mary. What can I do for you?" While Mary told her about a big public auction in a neighboring county, Taylor took the Christmas cookies out of Neil's oven and slid them onto a rack. She quickly formed more balls out of dough, rolled them in sugar, and placed them on two cookie sheets. Then she flattened them with a spatula and slipped them into Neil's oven. "Hold on a second. I have to set Neil's timer."

Taylor set the timer and washed her hands at Neil's sink. Then she picked up the phone again and headed for Neil's back door. "I'm on the cordless phone, dashing over to my house. I think I'll actually have four minutes to talk before those cookies come out. What sorts of things will they have at the auction?"

When she got back to her own kitchen, Taylor filled another two cookie sheets while she listened to Mary. A small local bank was merging with a national financial corporation and they had donated their old-fashioned wooden teller's chairs to the public auction. Mary had the flier from the auction at the café, and she thought the teller's chairs would be the perfect height for the bar from the Dew Drop Inn.

"I've never been to a public auction before." Her timer began to beep and Taylor shut it off. She pulled on her oven mitts and opened the door, checking to make sure the cookies were done. "How does it work?"

As Mary explained the system of bidding, Taylor took out the sheets of baked cookies, set them out to cool on her baker's rack, and put in the pans of dough that she had prepared. She reset the timer and then went out her back door again, rushing through the gap in the hedge to Neil's house. "Mrs. Simmons? Oh, that's a long story. I'm bringing the kids in for supper tonight. There'll be six of us. Ted's meeting us there, and so are Suzanne and Nina. I'll tell you all about it then."

After promising Mary that she'd be at the café around five-thirty, Taylor shut off her cordless phone, put it into her right apron pocket, and hurried across Neil's kitchen floor. She had just finished filling two more sheets with dough when she heard Marge pull up in front.

"Hi, Marge." Taylor opened the front door and waved at Marge as she got out of her car with Becky and Angela. "Hi, kids. How about a warm cookie?"

"Cowboys?" Angela looked hopeful.

"Of course. They're out on the rack and they should be cool enough to eat. I'll put some in a basket for you. You can show Becky your new game while Marge and I have a cup of coffee."

Marge followed Taylor to the kitchen and watched as she put some cookies in a basket for the girls. When they had run off, Marge motioned toward the kitchen table. "Sit. You look a little frazzled around the edges. I'll get the coffee if you tell me where it is."

"Thanks." Taylor sank into a chair, but then she popped right up again. "The coffee's at my house. I forgot that I put it on over there. Hold on a second. I'll run over and get the pot."

Marge shook her head. "No, you won't. I'll get it."

"But I have to go anyway. I've got cookies in the oven and they're almost ready to come out."

"I'll do that, too." Marge pushed her right back down again. "How many sheets of cookies do you have to bake before you're through?"

It took Taylor a moment to remember. It seemed that the parade of cookie sheets and dough balls was endless. "I think I have six more pans to bake. Two over at my house and another four here."

"I'll help you. Just sit here and listen for Neil's timer. I'll be back in a couple of minutes."

"Go out the back and slide through the gap in the hedge. My back door's unlocked." Taylor pointed the way. "And don't worry about the phone. I've got both of them in my apron pockets."

"Fine. While I'm gone, I want you to just sit. Will you promise to do that?"

"I promise." Taylor sat obediently. She was exhausted. If Randy didn't find financing for her soon, she would be forced to turn away customers. Baking in two ovens, in two separate locations, was almost impossible. It seemed that everyone wanted her cookies; she just couldn't bake them fast enough.

Taylor closed her eyes for a moment, just to rest them, and thought about Neil. Perhaps things wouldn't have been any easier if he'd been home, but they would have been a lot more pleasant. Even though he'd decided that they shouldn't sleep together again, she missed his smile and his good advice, and just knowing that he was right next door if she needed him.

She must have fallen asleep because it felt as if only seconds had passed before Marge was back with a steaming mug of coffee. Her eyes snapped open and she smiled as she took her first sip. "Mmm. Good!"

"The last two pans are in." Marge glanced toward the stove as Neil's oven timer started to beep. "Stay there, Taylor. I'll get it and shove two more sheets in."

Taylor stayed. She honestly didn't think she could move a muscle. When Marge came back, she favored her with a tired smile. "Thanks, Marge. I think you just saved my life."

"Maybe." Marge laughed. "How about a cookie for energy?"

Taylor winced. "No, thanks. I don't even want to *look* at another cookie, much less taste one."

"Where's Mrs. Simmons? I thought she was helping you."

"She was. But Neil was supposed to come home today and she assumed she'd be going home. She agreed to stay until he got back, but when she told me that she hadn't done the Christmas shopping for her grandchildren yet, I offered to take over for her."

Marge shook her head. "So now you're running a business *and* being a full-time mommy."

"That's right." Taylor was feeling much better, now that her cookie baking was almost finished. "At least we're going down to the café for dinner tonight, so I don't have to cook. All I have to do is the laundry."

Marge raised her eyebrows. "Mrs. Simmons didn't do the laundry before she left?"

"She offered, but I told her I'd do it. That was before I realized that I'd have to do a load every day. Angela's grown out of nearly everything in her closet and she has only two pairs of slacks that are long enough. Neil said to buy anything I needed, so I'm going to pick up some outfits for her when we go to the mall tomorrow."

"The mall?" Marge began to frown. "You're going to the mall the week before Christmas?"

"I have to. The kids haven't done their Christmas shopping, and I have to pick up some party favors. Angela's birthday is only five days away. And that reminds me—does Becky want to go along with us tomorrow? I'm taking Robby Voelker, so Michael has a friend, and Angela should have one, too."

"I guess I'd better put you in for sainthood." Marge just shook her head. "Which mall are you going to?"

"The Mall of America. I've never been there before, and it should be fun. We're leaving at eight, right after I deliver my cookies. We're planning to be there when it opens, and with a little luck, we'll be back before dark."

"How about your cookie baking? Will you have to do that when you get home?"

Taylor nodded. "Yes, but Michael and Robby are helping me, so it shouldn't take very long. Robby's staying with Michael overnight."

"Let me see if I've got this straight." Marge held up her hand and counted off the things that Taylor had mentioned. "You're doing the laundry, getting up at dawn to deliver your cookies, and taking four kids to the Mall of America. When you get back, you're putting in a full day's work while you supervise two rowdy teenagers who don't know a cookie sheet from a skillet and will probably be up all night playing video games. Did I miss anything?"

Taylor laughed. Marge had a real way with words. "Actually, you did. We're all going to the Christmas program at the school tonight, and I have to wash both kitchen floors. And before we go to the school program, I'm driving around to personally deliver the invitations to Angela's party."

"Saint Taylor. It has a nice ring to it. But I think I'll throw a monkey wrench into your plans for that halo."

"How?"

"I've just decided to go to the mall with you. There's no way you should have to handle four kids by yourself, and I still haven't found the right gift for Tim's mother. I'll drive. How's that?"

"Terrific!"

They'd met at the bakery, right after Taylor had dropped Angela and Michael off at the special matinee that Al was running for the children on Sunday afternoon. Since there was no heat, Suzanne, Ted, and Taylor were all huddled in parkas and snow boots.

"She's having a *what?*" Suzanne asked, staring at Taylor in surprise.

"A chocolate pizza party."

"Exactly what is a chocolate pizza?" Ted wanted to know.

"I'm not sure, but I'll come up with something." Taylor smiled. "It should be easy compared to what she really wanted."

"And that was . . . ?" Suzanne prompted her.

"A circus party. I got out of that by explaining that elephants wouldn't fit in the house because of the giant Christmas tree we're buying this afternoon."

"Good thinking." Ted reached out for a cookie from the bag that Taylor had brought. "How do you ever find time to bake?"

"There's always time to bake. I've got it down to a system, now that Michael and Robby are helping me. I'm thinking about hiring them as my assistants if Randy comes through with the financing on this place."

"That would be great." Suzanne smiled. "It would be good for the boys to have a part-time job. Maybe they'd stop wanting to hang around with those losers."

Taylor turned to stare at Suzanne. "Which losers?"

"Keith Powell and his gang. Robby practically worships him."

Ted began to frown. "Is Keith Powell the kid with the gold stud in his ear?"

"That's him. He's been kicked out of school three times this year for fighting, and he hasn't shown up for any of his counseling sessions. His mother seems to think he's just your typical rebellious teenager, but he looks like trouble to me. I really don't want Robby to hook up with that crowd. They ditch school, and I'm almost sure they're the ones who spray-painted graffiti all over the playground."

Taylor was concerned. "But Robby still wants to hang around with him?"

"Of course he does. It's the reason I had to ground him last month. I caught him sneaking off to the old icehouse. Keith has some kind of club in there and Robby wants to join. But you haven't heard the best part."

"What's that?" Taylor and Ted spoke at once.

"The initiation fee. If you want to join the club, you have to give Keith a forty-dollar video game!"

"Forty bucks?" Ted just shook his head. "Where is a kid like Robby supposed to get money like that?"

"Search me. Robby gets five dollars a week for his allowance and he asked me for an advance. He wants to join that stupid club so much, he's willing to give up eight weeks of his allowance!"

Taylor felt uneasy. Did Michael sneak off to the icehouse, too? And did he want to join Keith Powell's club? "Did grounding Robby work?"

"I think so. He swears up and down that he hasn't seen Keith since, but I'm not so sure that I can trust him."

Taylor glanced at her watch and pushed back her chair. "I have to run. You've got the key. Stay here as long as you like."

"But the movie won't be out for another hour." Suzanne turned to her in surprise.

"I know, but I've got a load of wash in the dryer, and I have to hang it up before the permanent press wrinkles."

Taylor went out the door and trudged down the sidewalk toward Neil's house. Soft flakes of snow were falling and she held out her hand to see the icy crystals on the palm of her mitten. No two snowflakes were alike. She'd learned that in grade school. And no two boys were alike either, except that Robby and Michael both thought Keith Powell was some kind of an idol. And she suspected that both of them wanted to join his club.

The back door was unlocked and Taylor took her moonboots off on Neil's back porch, placing them on the boot rug that sat next to the inner door. Then she hurried into Neil's kitchen and made a mad dash to pull the clothes from the dryer before it stopped.

When the clothes had been hung on hangers and the next load of wash was churning around in the machine, Taylor headed for Neil's office. She hadn't wanted to use any cash from his envelope, but she was running low and the bank was already closed for the day.

The envelope was right where he'd told her it would be, but the amount written on the outside of the envelope didn't match the contents. Taylor counted again, to be absolutely certain, but eighty dollars of Neil's money was missing.

Taylor thought about what Suzanne had told her. It cost forty dollars to join Keith's club. Michael and Robby had gone off by themselves at the mall and come back carrying a video store bag. Had Michael taken the money from Neil's envelope to buy them admission to Keith Powell's club?

Fortified by a steaming cup of coffee, Taylor climbed the steps to Michael's room. There was a crumpled video store bag in his wastebasket and she pulled out the paper inside with a sinking heart. It was a receipt for two video games, forty dollars apiece, and Michael had paid cash.

Suzanne wasn't the only one with a problem. She wasn't Michael's mother, but this was something that couldn't wait until Neil came home.

SEVENTEEN

Taylor really didn't want to confront Michael about the missing money, but she told herself she had no choice. She could call Neil and tell him what she suspected, but he was miles away and couldn't do anything about the problem by phone. Neil had trusted her to take care of things while he was away, so it was up to her. After she'd tucked Angela into bed and read her a story, Taylor walked down the hall and knocked on Michael's door.

"Hi, Taylor." Michael was caught up in a video game that involved spiked helmets, futuristic-looking horses, and loud gongs, bangs, and whistles. "Do you want to play Intergalactic Conquistadors?"

"No, thanks. Is that one of your new games?"

Michael swiveled to face her, ignoring the beeping as one of his conquistadors was knocked from his steed. "What new games?"

"The two that you bought at the mall."

"Uh . . . no. This is an old one. How did you know about the new games?"

Taylor decided that beating around the bush would get her nowhere. It was better to just spit it out. "I found the receipt right after I discovered that eighty dollars was missing from the envelope of cash in your dad's filing cabinet."

"Oh." Michael swallowed hard. "I was going to pay it back, Taylor. Honest."

"How?" Taylor sat down on the edge of his bed and regarded him solemnly.

"By shoveling snow. That's where Robby and I went today. We knocked on about a million doors, but we only got one job."

"How much do you get for shoveling someone's sidewalk and driveway?"

"Five bucks. I really thought I could earn it back before Dad got home. That's only sixteen jobs, and Robby and I can do eight a day if we hustle."

"But you only earned five dollars today?"

"Yeah." Michael sighed. "We made a lot of money last year, but now everybody's got snowblowers. Are you going to tell Dad that I borrowed his money?"

Taylor gave him a stern look. "You didn't borrow it, Michael. You stole it. Borrowing means you ask first. And you didn't ask, did you?"

"No." Michael's voice was very small. "But I was going to pay it back, Taylor. I really thought I could."

Michael looked very ashamed of himself and more than a little frightened by what he'd done. Taylor's heart went out to him, but she couldn't afford to be too sympathetic— not if she wanted him to tell the truth about why he'd bought the video games.

"Okay, Michael. You made a bad mistake, but it's not too late to make it right. All you have to do is take the games back, ask for a refund, and get your father's money back."

Michael looked sick. "But I can't. I . . . uh . . . I don't have them anymore."

"Where are they?"

The sick look on Michael's face intensified. "I gave them away. They were a . . . a Christmas present, for a friend."

"Both of them? That's a pretty expensive Christmas present."

"One was from Robby and the other was from me. And

now we can't get them back. You can't just take back a Christmas present."

"Certainly you can." Taylor knew she was almost at the crux of the problem and she couldn't let Michael off the hook quite yet. "You said you gave them to a friend. If you explain that you used your dad's money to buy them and you have to return them for a refund before he gets home, your friend will understand."

"No, he won't. He won't give them back, Taylor. I already talked to him. He said that's my problem, not his."

"That doesn't sound like something a friend would say. Are you sure this person is really your friend?"

Michael shook his head. "I thought he was, but he's not. He just wanted new video games."

"I'm really glad to hear you say that. I don't think that Keith Powell is your friend either."

Michael's eyes widened. "You *know*?"

"Yes. Suzanne told me that Robby wanted to join Keith's club, and I figured that you did, too. And she mentioned that the price of admission was a new forty-dollar video game."

"Keith laughed at us when we told him we wanted the games back." Michael sounded disgusted. "He said he didn't think we'd be dumb enough to buy them, that all the other kids in the club just stole them. They do it all the time—that's how they get all of their video games. But Robby and I don't *steal!*"

"How about the money you took from your dad's envelope? Wasn't that stealing?"

"I didn't think it was if I paid it back, but I guess it was stealing." Michael's cheeks turned a dull red. "I really messed up, Taylor. The worst thing is, now I'm gonna have to call Dad and tell him that I stole eighty dollars from him."

Taylor reached out for his hand and gave it a squeeze. Then she tipped his face up so she could look directly into his eyes. "Tell me the truth, Michael. Do you still want to join Keith's club?"

"No way! Robby and I talked about it, and we decided that Keith is a loser."

"You're right. Have you and Robby learned a lesson from all this?"

Michael nodded. "We decided that Keith and his friends are gonna get in big trouble someday, and we don't want to be anywhere around them."

"Then you're ready to call your dad and tell him what you did?"

Michael looked sick again. "I'm ready. I stole his money, Taylor. I have to admit it."

"Maybe it can wait for a while." Taylor figured it was time to cut Michael a little slack. He'd admitted that he was wrong and was prepared to take the consequences. "There may be a way that you can earn back the money. Are you willing to work hard?"

"Sure, I am. I'd do anything, but nobody wants their sidewalks shoveled."

Taylor smiled. "I need two assistant bakers and I'm willing to consider you and Robby for the job."

"Really?"

Michael gave her such a hopeful look, Taylor wanted to gather him into her arms, hug him, and tell him that everything was going to be okay. But that wasn't what he needed right now and she knew it. "I'm warning you, Michael: I won't be an easy boss. You'll both have to work hard, and you can't eat any of the cookies unless I say it's all right."

"We won't. What do you want us to do, Taylor?"

"I want you to take Mrs. Simmons's place and handle all the baking over here. If you do a good job, I'll pay you each two dollars an hour, and I'll advance you the eighty dollars. You can put the money back in your dad's envelope and work it off."

Michael looked very relieved. "Why are you being so nice about this, Taylor?"

"Because everybody's entitled to one mistake, and I know that you didn't really mean to steal. And because I love you."

"I love you, too." Michael reached out to give her a hug. "And I think that Dad should marry you so you could really be our mom."

After the kids were tucked into bed, Taylor locked up the house and turned off the lights. As she undressed and got into her nightgown, she glanced out the window. She could see her own bedroom window from here and couldn't help wondering whether Neil stood here at night, thinking about her. That might be a bit fanciful for a man who'd made it perfectly clear that he wasn't interested in marrying anyone again, but Taylor still wondered. She knew that when she climbed in bed at night, she thought about Neil and how close they were in their separate bedrooms.

One glance at Neil's alarm clock told Taylor that she had to get to sleep. It was already midnight and she had to get up early to deliver her cookies and bake the crusts for Angela's chocolate pizzas. There were only two days left before the party and she didn't want to leave everything for the last day.

The Christmas tree. Taylor sighed as she thought about it. She'd promised to have the tree in place for the party, and that had to be done tomorrow. She'd take the kids to the Christmas tree lot on the edge of town, pick out the perfect tree, and decorate it tomorrow night. If she organized her day carefully, she could work it all in, especially now that she had two assistant bakers to help her. Perhaps they'd even have a tree-trimming party tomorrow night.

When Taylor climbed into Neil's bed and snuggled

down under the covers, it felt like she was coming home. It was easy to imagine that Neil was in bed with her, his head on the pillow next to hers. They would be a family, living in this cozy house with the kids down the hall, fast asleep.

A smile crossed Taylor's face as she thought about what Michael had told her. He thought that she should be their mom. Angela did, too, Taylor knew that. Now there was only one more person to convince. Somehow she had to make Neil realize that she was the perfect wife for him.

EIGHTEEN

"Don't worry, Taylor. I won't let you fall."

Taylor turned to look at Ted Swanson. He was holding the rickety wooden ladder she'd found in Neil's garage. She picked up the angel she'd found in Grandma Mac's attic and sighed as she gazed up at the top of the Christmas tree. It seemed to be at least three stories high, but of course it wasn't. The high school boy who'd been working at Santa's Hideaway had measured it, and it was precisely twelve feet, three inches tall. Neil's den had a cathedral ceiling and it fit perfectly in the tallest corner. The kids had wanted a giant tree, but now Taylor was wishing they'd settled for something a little shorter.

"Do you want me to do it, Taylor?" Michael looked sympathetic. "I used to be afraid to climb ladders, too."

Taylor shook her head and then took a deep breath. "No, I'll do it. Just make sure nobody wiggles the ladder while I'm up there."

With Christmas music playing softly on Neil's stereo, Taylor began to climb the ladder. She'd never liked heights, but her pride was at stake. The first step was fine and she managed the second with no problem. The third, however, made her knees start to tremble.

Taylor told herself she was being silly. The rungs on the ladder were only twelve inches apart, and that meant she was just three feet in the air. She could jump off right now and she'd be perfectly fine. There was no reason to be so nervous. And even if she did slip and fall, Ted would catch her and keep her from being hurt.

The kids had been excited when she'd asked them if they'd like to have a tree-trimming party. They'd never had any kind of a Christmas party before. Taylor had filled the slow cooker with the ingredients for Sloppy Joes this morning and called everyone to invite them. Suzanne had brought Robby, and Marge and Tim had brought Becky, so that Angela and Michael each had a friend. Taylor had also invited Ted Swanson and Nina, and everyone seemed to be having a good time.

There was only one person who wasn't here, and Taylor missed him a lot. Neil was still in New York. And even though she was happy to be surrounded by her new friends, Taylor couldn't help thinking about how much better this party would be if Neil were here.

Taylor looked up. The top of the tree was still several feet above her. It was a big, bushy pine, and she couldn't attach the angel until she climbed to the top. She forced herself to climb up another rung, and then another. She was almost at the top, and she cautioned herself not to look down.

She climbed until her head was even with the top of the tree. Then she grasped the side of the ladder with one hand and reached out with the other to hang the angel at the very top of the tree. She was just positioning it so its wings weren't crooked when the telephone rang.

"I'll get it!" Michael hollered out, racing for the phone by the leather couch.

Taylor sighed. "If it's for me, tell them I'll call them back. There's no way I'm climbing this ladder twice."

"Okay."

Michael must have picked up the phone, because it stopped ringing. Taylor concentrated on positioning the angel and when she was through, she asked for advice. "Can anybody down there tell if it's straight?"

"It looks straight to me," Marge answered her. "But the back of her robe is caught up on a branch. If you climb up one more rung, you can reach out and flip it loose."

Taylor had just finished freeing the angel's robe when she heard a sharp crack and the rung gave out beneath her feet. She didn't have time to be frightened. It all happened too fast. She just grabbed at the ladder with both hands, but there was nowhere to put her feet and she hung in midair.

"Just let go, Taylor. I'll catch you."

Taylor heard Ted's voice. She wanted to tell him that she wasn't about to let go, but fate intervened as her grip slipped and she fell like a stone.

Robby applauded as she landed in Ted's arms, none the worse for wear. "That was cool, Taylor."

"Thanks." Taylor's voice was shaking. "But I'm not going to apply for stuntwoman school any time in the near future."

Michael was still on the phone and Taylor heard him clearly. "Yeah, Taylor's here. Ted's holding her. Just wait a second and I'll tell him to put her down."

"Thanks, Ted." Taylor smiled at him as Ted set her back on her feet. She was a little shaken, but she wasn't hurt. "Who's on the phone, Michael?"

Michael was wearing a mischievous grin as he walked over and handed her the cordless phone. "It's Dad. He wants to know why Ted was holding you."

Neil frowned as he waited for Taylor to come on the line. He could hear people talking and laughing in the background, and Christmas music was playing. What was Taylor doing? And why was Ted holding her? For the millionth time that day, he wished he were home, instead of in a hotel suite in New York.

"Hi, Neil."

Taylor voice sounded breathless, and that didn't make Neil feel any better. "Hello, Taylor. What's going on?"

"It's a Christmas party. We're trimming the tree and I invited a few friends to join us."

Neil wondered if he should ask, but his curiosity was killing him. "Which friends?"

"Marge and Tim. They brought Becky. And Suzanne and Robby, and Ted and Nina. Mrs. Wyler might drop in later. She's busy baking."

"Oh." Neil was glad he'd asked. At least Taylor wasn't alone with Ted. "Michael said Ted was . . . uh . . . holding you?"

"I fell off your ladder when a rung broke. Ted caught me."

"You're not hurt, are you?" Neil swallowed hard, thinking about Taylor's lovely body lying twisted and broken on the floor.

"Only my pride. But your ladder's in pretty bad shape."

"I can always get another ladder. Are you sure you're not hurt?"

Taylor laughed. "I'm fine. You can see the whole thing on videotape when you get home. Robby said I looked cool when I fell."

"Videotape?" Neil frowned again. "What videotape?"

"The one we're making for you. I asked Nina to bring her camcorder and she's been taping all night. I thought that since you couldn't be here, you'd like to watch a tape of the kids trimming the tree."

Neil swallowed past the lump in his throat. Taylor was really very thoughtful. "I can hardly wait to see it. But what were you doing on my ladder?"

"Putting the angel on top of the tree. We're all set for Angela's birthday party. Suzanne is coming over to help, and Nina's got the decorations all planned out. Marge is going to handle the games and Ted's helping me with Angela's present."

Neil felt a twinge of jealousy that he hoped was completely unfounded. "What present?"

"A playhouse." Taylor lowered her voice. "Ted's building it in my living room and it's almost finished."

"Your living room? That sounds awfully inconvenient."

"Not really. He's been working really hard on it, Neil. Most nights he doesn't quit until one or two in the morning."

Neil tried to push back his jealous feelings, but he was finding it difficult. Taylor had practically admitted that Ted had been at her house every night. "Have you been staying up that late?"

"No. I gave Ted a key and he let's himself in and out. I've been getting plenty of sleep, Neil. I don't know what it is, but I just can't seem to keep my eyes open once I get the kids in bed."

"What kids?"

"Your kids." There was a long pause, and then Taylor sighed. "I'm sorry, Neil. I guess I forgot to tell you. Mrs. Simmons had to go home and I've been staying at your house. I hope you don't mind, but it was easier than bringing Michael and Angela over to my place . . . Maybe I should have asked first, but I've been using your oven for my baking."

"No problem." Neil felt a surge of very welcome relief. Ted was working late at Taylor's house, but Taylor wasn't there. "I guess I was just lucky when I called you the other night and caught you at home."

"I wasn't home. My cordless phone works just fine over here. I found that out the first day, when I was running back and forth to bake."

"Running back and forth?" Neil was completely confused. "You're baking at both houses?"

"I have to. I really need two ovens, and I'm not sure even two is enough. Just wait until you come home and see how many orders I've filled."

Neil listened as Taylor told him about her mad dash from her kitchen to his, and how she'd ended up hiring Michael and Robby to help her bake. When she was finished, he began to frown. "I think you were right when you looked at the bakery. If your orders have increased that much, you need a bigger place. Did you find out any more about the financing?"

"Yes, but the news isn't good. Four places have already turned me down."

"Why? You're showing a profit, aren't you?"

"Of course I am. But they say I haven't been in business long enough to develop a track record. Randy's trying with one last lender, but he hasn't heard back from them yet."

She sounded sad and Neil began to frown. "Don't give up yet. There's got to be some way you can get a loan. When I get back we'll talk about it."

"Okay. You'll be here in time for the party, won't you, Neil?"

"You bet."

Neil said good-bye and hung up the phone. He was glad he'd called Taylor, but now he felt even lonelier. There was a party at his house—the first party since he'd moved back to Two Rivers—and he really wished that he could be there to enjoy it with Taylor.

NINETEEN

"It's my birthday, Daddy!"

Taylor watched as Angela, dressed in her very best party dress, threw herself into Neil's arms. Neil dropped his baggage to pick her up and Michael retrieved it and carried it to the side, where no one would trip over it.

"Happy birthday, Pumpkin."

Taylor and Neil shared a smile over Angela's head. It was the kind of bonding smile that made Taylor feel warm all over.

"Hey, Dad. Did you have a good trip?" Michael walked over to pat Neil on the back and Taylor grinned. He'd decided that he was too old for hugs.

"Yes, except for missing you guys. What did you do while I was gone?"

Taylor listened as Angela told him all about their exciting trip to the Mall of America and how she and Becky had stood in line to see Santa. Michael took up the story at that point and told Neil about the Christmas tree farm and how they'd tied their tree on top of the Grand Cherokee.

"It sounds like you had a good time."

"We did," Michael said. "And we ate real food while you were gone. Taylor cooked and we sat at the kitchen table just like a family."

"She made meatloaf, and smashed potatoes, and we

even had drumsticks," Angela said. "Taylor's a four-day chef."

Michael laughed and interpreted for his dad. "She means *gourmet chef*. I wish you could have been at the tree-trimming party, Dad. It was fun, except for when Taylor fell off the ladder. And that was okay since she didn't get hurt. Come and see our Christmas tree. It's really cool."

"Okay. Just let me take my bags upstairs and then you can show me." Neil set Angela down and pointed to one of his suitcases. "Can you take the big one for me, Michael? You can carry that green box, Angela."

Angela nodded and skipped over to get the box. "Is it a present for me, Daddy?"

"Yes, but it's a *Christmas* present. I got you something else for your birthday. When your party's over, we'll put this under the tree." Neil turned to Taylor with a smile. "I'll just put my things upstairs and be with you in a minute."

Taylor was really glad that Neil was home. She wished she could throw her arms around him and hug him. "Go ahead. I've got some last-minute things to do in the kitchen."

By the time Taylor had finished setting out the party dishes, Neil was back. He walked over to hug her and Taylor felt happier than she'd been in days. "Would you like to take a peek at Angela's chocolate pizzas?"

"Definitely. You told me about them on the phone, but I just couldn't visualize a chocolate pizza."

"They're in here." Taylor opened the refrigerator door so that he could see the six chocolate pizzas that were arranged on the shelves.

"They look great." Neil grinned. "What's the stuff that looks like cheese on top?"

"Grated white chocolate. The tomato sauce is strawberry pie filling and the sausages are pieces of macaroons that I dipped in melted chocolate."

"What are those things that look like green pepper rings on the top?"

"Pieces of green apple fruit rolls. It was Ted's idea. Where are the kids?"

"They're putting my presents under the tree. I caved in when they begged. I think Angela wants everyone to see how many presents she's getting."

"She's really excited about Christmas." Taylor smiled as she remembered the countless questions about Christmas that Angela had asked. "When are you planning to open your presents?"

"On Christmas Eve. I tried to wait until Christmas Day last year, but Michael convinced me that all his friends opened their presents on Christmas Eve."

"Doesn't that make Christmas Day kind of boring?"

Neil sighed. "It does at our house. Most of Michael's friends go to their grandparents on Christmas Day. They have a big dinner and get more presents over there. Michael didn't say anything last year, but I know he was lonely on Christmas Day."

"Then we should plan something special for this year." Taylor made up her mind. "Let's have a big Christmas dinner together, and I'll wait until Christmas Day to give Michael and Angela my presents. That'll give them something to look forward to."

"That's a really good idea, but nothing's open on Christmas Day. We'd probably have to drive to a fast-food place in Anoka."

"You don't eat fast food on Christmas unless you're desperate." Taylor shook her head. "I'll cook if you let me use your oven. It's impossible to make a Christmas turkey with all the trimmings if you only have one oven. Maybe we could even invite some other people who don't have anywhere else to go."

"Like who? Ted Swanson?"

Taylor bit back a smile at the question. Neil was definitely jealous. "Ted's driving to Hibbing to see his family. I was thinking of Mrs. Wyler. She doesn't have any relatives in town."

"We can invite Mrs. Wyler." Neil looked relieved, and Taylor suspected he was glad that Ted wouldn't be in town over the holidays. "Anyone else?"

Taylor thought about the people she knew. "Suzanne and Robby are going to her parents, and Marge and Tim always spend Christmas Day with his mother. Nina's going to her parents, and the Petersons won't be back until the spring thaw. How about Mary and Bill? Do they have any relatives in town?"

"Not that I know of. I'll call Bill and ask. And there's always the Tollivers. They don't have anyone."

"We could invite Lester Crawley." Taylor waited for Neil's reaction. She knew that Lester was the one who'd told Neil that she was spending time with Ted.

"Lester? I don't know, Taylor. He's got a big mouth. If Lester knows that we're spending Christmas together, he'll spread the news all over . . ."

Neil stopped in midsentence and Taylor held her breath. Would Neil *want* to counter Lester's gossip with new gossip about the two of them?

"Sure." Neil flashed her a grin that looked perfectly guileless. It might have fooled Taylor if she hadn't known better. "Let's invite Lester. Maybe he'll hit it off with Mrs. Wyler and they can go off in a corner and compare stories."

"Thanks for all your help." Taylor said good-bye to Marge and Becky at the door. They'd been the last guests to leave. Angela's party had been a wonderful success. The games had been fun, the chocolate pizza had produced squeals and a spontaneous burst of applause from the adults, and Angela had loved all her gifts.

Neil came up behind her and slipped an arm around her shoulders. "You've worked really hard, Taylor. Why don't I take you and the kids out to supper."

"Supper?" The thought of food made Taylor laugh. "After potato chips, submarine sandwiches, chocolate pizza, and ice cream, do you really think the kids will want any supper?"

Neil grinned as he shook his head. "I guess not. I just thought it would be good for you to get out for a while."

"Maybe it would, but I don't really have time. I still have a ton of Christmas cookies to bake. Do you mind if I use your oven tonight? It would make everything a lot easier."

"Just think of it as your second oven. It's not like I'm going to be using it. And I'll help you bake. Michael and Robby can handle things over here and I'll pitch in at your house. Did you hear anything from Randy while I was gone?"

"Not a thing." Taylor shook her head. "He said he should hear something from Prime Lending right after Christmas. They're my last hope."

Neil reached out to give her a little hug. "Don't worry about it now, honey. If it falls through, we'll put our heads together and come up with something else."

"Okay." Taylor leaned a little closer and returned his hug. It was good to know that Neil was on her side, and he'd called her "honey." Did that mean that her attempt to make him jealous was making him think twice about their relationship?

"Thanks for offering to cook Christmas dinner." Neil's arms tightened around her. "It'll mean a lot to the kids to have a real family Christmas."

"It'll mean a lot to me, too. You're the only real family I've got."

"I'm not going to put your present under the tree. It's really special and I want to give it to you when we're alone.

How about Christmas night after everyone leaves and the kids are in bed?"

"All right." Taylor smiled at him. "But now my curiosity is killing me. Give me a hint."

Neil shook his head. "You remind me of Angela. She always asks for hints."

"Come on, Neil. Suspense isn't good for me. If I get distracted, I might mistake the salt for the sugar in the Cowboy Cookies."

Neil laughed. "We can't have that! Okay, one hint and that's all. Your present came from Tiffany's, and you're just going to have to wait until Christmas night to find out what it is."

"Fair enough." Taylor's eyes began to sparkle. She reminded herself that Tiffany's sold all kinds of jewelry, but she couldn't help hoping that her Christmas present was an engagement ring.

TWENTY

Taylor groaned as the alarm clock went off. Her first instinct was to turn it off and go back to sleep, but then she remembered what day it was. It was Christmas morning, and she had to get up to put the turkey into the oven.

It was impossible to think about cooking until she'd had her first cup of coffee. Taylor slipped into her warm robe, pulled on her slippers, and hurried down to the kitchen to see if she'd set her new automatic coffeemaker correctly. The kids had bought two when they'd gone to the mall, one for her and one for their dad.

The last of the coffee was just dripping down into the glass carafe and Taylor quickly poured herself a cup.

The turkey was thawed and waiting for her attention. Taylor lifted it out of the bottom of the refrigerator, slit the plastic wrapping with a kitchen knife, and reached inside to take out the bag that contained the giblets. She'd cook them up for Ollie as a special treat. Then she removed the long, skinny neck, dropped it into a plastic bag, and returned it to the refrigerator. It would go in the soup pot tomorrow, along with the carcass and any meat that remained on the bird after Neil had carved it.

After washing the turkey, inside and out, drying it, and salting the cavity, Taylor plunked it into Grandma Mac's biggest roaster and seasoned the outside. She stuffed the liver and gizzard back into the cavity, removed one rack to make room for the large roaster in the oven, and turned the oven on to the temperature that Grandma Mac's cookbook recommended. She gulped her second cup of coffee as she chopped up onions and celery and sauteed them. Neil had told her that Minnesotans called it "dressing" instead of "stuffing," and she made a mental note to remember that when she carried it to the table.

The stuffing/dressing went into the slow cooker. Taylor plugged it in, switched it to low, and gave a satisfied smile. Her work here was finished. She'd prepare the rest of the meal at Neil's house.

It was ten minutes to seven when Taylor rushed upstairs to take a shower. She dressed in a casual outfit, slacks and a washable sweater, and hung the dress she'd wear for the party on the back of her bedroom door. When she'd finished her cooking chores, she'd come back here to change.

At eight-thirty Taylor knocked softly on Neil's back door. It was opened almost immediately by Angela, who was still in her pajamas and robe.

"Merry Christmas, Taylor." Angela gave her a wide, happy smile. "Daddy said we could put on the music when you got here."

"Hi, Taylor. She's talking about Christmas music. I didn't have the stomach for it when Angela got up at six." Neil was standing at the coffeemaker, looking bleary-eyed. When the kids had gone off to bed, they'd worked in Neil's kitchen. There had been potatoes to peel and store in a bowl of salted water in Neil's refrigerator, cranberry sauce to make, and several pies to bake. It had been past midnight when they'd finally settled down on the couch with a Christmas toddy, and neither one of them had gotten much sleep.

"Go sit down, Neil. I'll make the coffee." Taylor walked to the coffeemaker, filled the filter with coffee, poured in the water, and switched it on. She reset the clock—Neil had managed to set it for P.M. instead of A.M.—and then she carried the box she'd brought to the table. "We're having doughnuts for breakfast."

"Chocolate?" Angela looked hopeful.

"Of course. I've got some maple bars for Michael and your daddy's favorite apple fritters."

Neil smiled as Taylor brought him the first cup of coffee from the pot. "I don't know how you can function this early in the morning."

"It's because she's a morning person and you're not." Michael came into the kitchen, his hair wet from the shower. He was dressed for the morning in blue jeans and a polo shirt. "Don't worry, Taylor. I'm going to change before the company gets here."

Taylor laughed. "I wasn't worried. I'm going to change, too."

"So am I," Angela piped up. "I can wear my best dress, can't I, Taylor?"

"Of course you can, and I'll fix your hair with bows. Do you want some juice?"

Angela nodded, and Taylor took the container of orange juice out of Neil's refrigerator. She poured juice for the kids and got a cup of coffee for herself. Then she sat down and stared at the array of doughnuts in the box. "I'll take the French cream if nobody else wants it."

"Take it. You're entitled." Neil reached out for the apple fritter. "How did you get these, anyway? Nothing's open."

"I drove up to the doughnut shop in Anoka. They're open until noon today. The girl at the counter told me that they sell a lot of doughnuts because nobody wants to cook breakfast on Christmas morning."

Neil bit into his apple fritter, a blissful expression sliding across his face. "I guess you *are* a morning person."

"Dad's a night person. He likes to work late at night,

when there are no distractions." Michael turned to Neil. "Isn't that right, Dad?"

"That's right, son."

"And you like to get up early." Michael turned back to Taylor again. "One of you is always awake when we need you. That's why you make such an ideal couple. Your schedules coincide with the needs of a growing family."

Taylor was startled and she looked over to meet Neil's eyes. He didn't look upset and she was a bit surprised. As she watched, Neil reached out to cuff Michael gently on the shoulder.

"That's very smart. How did you come up with that?"

"I called the Love Lady." Michael mentioned the name of a popular local radio show. "I told her about both of you, and she said that you were perfect together."

Taylor's mouth dropped open. Everyone in town listened to the Love Lady show. "You didn't tell her our names, did you?"

"Of course not." Michael looked offended. "I'd never do anything to embarrass you, Taylor. I called you 'Lucy' and I called Dad 'Ricky,' just like on that old TV show."

Taylor was relieved. "Thanks, Michael. I should have known you wouldn't use our real names."

"Yeah. And the only other thing I said about you was that you lived next door to us in Two Rivers and you had a cookie business."

Taylor rinsed the last dish, handed it to Neil to stick into the dishwasher, and sighed. "We're finished."

"Good." Neil came up behind her and put his arms around her waist. "I think everyone had a good time, don't you?"

"They said they did. And we don't have many leftovers, so the food must have been good."

"It was. Let's go into the den, Taylor. I want to give you your Christmas present."

Taylor snuggled against him and smiled. "I've got a present for you, too."

"I thought I already got mine." Neil sounded surprised.

"That was from the kids." Taylor remembered how delighted Neil had been when he'd unwrapped the coffee-maker with the built-in timer. "I helped them pick it out, but they used their own money."

"How about the metal frame ladder? That was from you, wasn't it?"

"Yes, but it wasn't really a Christmas present. It was a replacement for the one I broke. Your real present is still under the tree, way in back."

"And my present for you is in my desk. Why don't you pour us a glass of wine while I get it? We'll open them by the tree."

Taylor poured them both glasses of wine and carried them into the den. She retrieved his present and placed it on the coffee table, and then she sat down on the couch to admire the lights on the huge Christmas tree.

"This is for you." Neil walked in and handed her the present.

Taylor's hopes rose as she accepted the small box. There was a gold Tiffany's seal on the package and it was small enough to be a ring box. Taylor's hopes soared. Had Neil finally realized that he wanted her for his wife?

"Open yours first." Taylor handed him the present she'd wrapped. "I really hope you like it."

Taylor held her breath as Neil opened the present. His reaction was even better than she'd hoped. He looked truly delighted to receive the videos to complete his Frank Capra collection and he pulled her into his arms.

They kissed for long moments, and Taylor felt a familiar heat begin to rise in her body. Neil loved her—she was sure of it. He couldn't kiss her this way if he didn't. She could tell he wanted her every bit as much as she wanted him, and only a low woof from Ollie, who'd been sleeping on the rug at the foot of the Christmas tree, roused them from their embrace.

"What is it, boy?" Neil pulled away to look at Ollie. His legs were twitching and he was whimpering, low in his throat. Then his legs started to move, as if he were running, and his whimpers grew louder and more distressed.

"What's wrong with Ollie?" Taylor stared at the golden retriever in alarm. "Is he sick?"

Neil walked over to wake Ollie, who looked dazed when he opened his eyes. He licked Neil's hand, his tail thumping happily against the rug, and then he rolled over and went back to sleep. "It was just a doggy dream. He has those once in a while. He was probably chasing a rabbit in his sleep."

"I'm glad it's nothing serious." Taylor was relieved. "Everyone was slipping him tidbits from the table, and I thought he might have gotten something that wasn't good for him."

"The only thing he shouldn't have is chocolate. If he eats too much, it's really bad for him. Other than that, Ollie can eat anything we eat. He's got a cast-iron stomach."

"I know. While you were gone, Mrs. Simmons caught Angela feeding him a whole box of Froot Loops. We took him to the vet, but he said not to worry."

Neil looked very surprised. "You took Ollie to the vet?"

"Yes. Angela went with me."

"Where did you take him?"

"To Dr. Sobania in Anoka. I found the number in the back of your phone book. He seems like a nice man, and he was very good with Angela. After he explained that all that sugar would upset Ollie's stomach, she promised us that she'd never feed him more than three spoonfuls of Froot Loops again." Taylor realized that Neil was frowning.

"What's the matter? Didn't you want me to take Ollie to Dr. Sobania?"

Neil shook his head. "It's not that. I'm glad you took him. I'm just wondering how you managed to drag him into the office."

"We didn't have to drag him. I just told him that he had to go and he walked right in."

"You just *told* him he had to go?"

Taylor nodded. "Angela and I explained it to him. We promised him that if he was a good boy, we'd buy him a hamburger on the way home."

"And he just trotted right in the door?"

"Yes." Taylor didn't understand why Neil looked so amazed. "He was really very good."

Neil just shook his head in amazement. "The last time I took Ollie in for his shots, I had to drag him through the door. He hates to go to the vet."

"He does? Well, he didn't give me a speck of trouble. He never does. You should have seen how good he was when I took him along to deliver my cookies. He hopped right in your car and sat in the back to guard the cookies."

Neil's mouth dropped open. "You left Ollie alone with your cookies and he didn't eat any?"

"That's right. I told him he'd get a dog biscuit if he guarded them for me."

Neil looked bemused. "I think you must be a sorceress, Taylor. Michael's more responsible, Angela's stopped arguing about bedtime, and Ollie's going off to the vet without a whimper. Not only that: Mrs. Wyler's quit gossiping. Is there anyone in Two Rivers that you haven't bewitched?"

"You." The answer popped out and Taylor winced. She wished she could call her answer back, but it was too late.

"You're wrong about that, Taylor. I've fallen under your spell, too." Neil smiled at her, and Taylor began to tremble. Was he going to take her into his arms and kiss her again? A long moment passed, and then he looked down at the present she'd given him, deliberately breaking the connection between them. "I've looked all over for these tapes. What did you do? Conjure them up out of thin air?"

Taylor's voice was a bit unsteady when she answered him. "The big video store at the mall ordered them for me. I hope you don't mind, but I went through all the tapes on your shelves to make sure I didn't order any duplicates."

"You can go through my tapes any time you want. Open your present, Taylor. I can hardly wait to see how you like it."

Taylor slit the tape with her fingernail and carefully peeled back the paper. When she uncovered a small velvet jewelry box, her hands began to tremble. She opened the lid, praying that what she wanted most in the world was inside, and tried not to show her disappointment when she saw that it was a necklace made of small gold hearts with rubies in the centers.

"Do you like it?"

Neil sounded anxious, and Taylor turned to him with a smile. "I love it. It's just beautiful, Neil."

"Let me put it on for you."

Neil removed the necklace from the box and clasped it around her neck. His fingers were warm on her skin and Taylor sighed. She told herself that she had no right to be disappointed. The necklace was beautiful, and it was obviously very expensive, but she couldn't help wishing that Neil had spent his money on an engagement ring instead.

TWENTY-ONE

Neil had worked hard for the past six days. He'd finished the outline for his next book and sent it off to his editor. Now there was nothing to do but wait for a response. As he glanced at the calendar on his office wall, he was surprised to see that it was New Year's Eve. He usually did something with the kids on New Year's Eve, but he'd been so busy, he hadn't planned a thing.

"Michael?" Neil stuck his head out of the office and called for his son. But Michael didn't answer, and Neil remembered that he'd gone to the ice rink with Robby, to try out his new hockey skates. Angela wasn't home either. Marge had picked her up early this morning so that she could spend the day with Becky. The new furniture for Marge's preschool was being delivered, and Angela and Becky were eager to see it before Buttons 'n' Bows opened, the second week in January.

Neil was about to call Taylor to see if she had any plans for the day when he remembered that she was tied up with Suzanne and Nina, planning a baby shower for one of Nina's cousins. He was alone, and now that he finally had some free time, there was no one to spend it with.

Neil prowled through the house with a frown on his face. He felt as if all his friends had deserted him. Perhaps a walk through the snow might help to relieve the boredom. He slipped into his parka and whistled for Ollie, rousing him from a nap on the leather couch in the den and hooking him up to his leash. Then he pulled on his gloves and went out the front door, feeling better the minute he stepped out into the white, sunny world outside.

The air was brisk, and Neil let Ollie sniff at the bushes to his heart's content. As they turned the corner and passed the old bakery, Neil glanced inside. It really would be a perfect place for Taylor. She'd shown him the drawings, and converting the front room into a cookie and coffee shop was a great idea. He'd thought about offering to co-sign her loan, but he'd decided to wait to see if she could get other financing. He wasn't sure he wanted to mix business with pleasure, and his relationship with Taylor was definitely pleasure.

As Neil stared in the big plate glass window, he could almost see the improvements that Suzanne and Nina had suggested. The bar from the Dew Drop Inn would look great on the far wall, and he could imagine Taylor, smiling and happy, pouring coffee and serving her cookies. She'd told him that if she bought the bakery, she'd hire Michael and Robby to work for her full time over the summer. They were already working part-time, and Neil was pleased with how responsible both boys were becoming. Some of the local teenagers had too much time on their hands, and jobs in Two Rivers were scarce. If Michael and Robby worked for Taylor, they'd stay out of trouble, and it would give them a small weekly paycheck and a sense of real accomplishment.

Ollie tugged on the leash and Neil realized that he'd been standing there daydreaming for several minutes. He gave Ollie a pat and then he walked on, heading down the street toward the café. Ollie was always welcome there. Mary was crazy about him. She let him sit under Neil's booth and she always gave him some kind of treat while Neil ate apple pie and drank coffee.

"Hi, Neil." Mary came over to greet him as he hung

his parka on the row of coat hooks on the back wall. "And how's my favorite boy?"

Ollie licked Mary's hand as she reached down to pet him and Neil grinned at the eager expression on Ollie's face. "He's fine, but I have a real apple pie deficiency. I was hoping you might be able to do something about that."

"Coming right up." Mary motioned him toward a vacant booth. "You boys go and sit down. I'll be right there."

Neil had just gotten settled when Mary came over with his coffee and apple pie. She had another dish on her tray—something that smelled like roast beef—and Neil raised his eyebrows in a question.

"Beef ends. When I make roast beef sandwiches, I save them for him." Mary put the dish on the floor and Ollie looked up at her with pure adoration. "Go ahead, Ollie. They're for you."

Neil grinned as Ollie began to scarf up the beef. "You spoil him, Mary. Every time I snap on his leash, he wants to come down here."

"He's always welcome—you know that." Mary slid into the other side of the booth. "I need to talk to you, Neil."

Neil noticed that Mary looked worried. "Sure. What is it?"

"It's Taylor. What's going on, Neil? Are you going to dither around until Ted Swanson gets the jump on you?"

Neil winced. Mary didn't pull her punches. "Taylor says that Ted's just a friend."

"Maybe that's Taylor's impression, but I'm pretty sure Ted's got other ideas. My niece works at the Anoka Jewel Mart. She called to tell me that Ted was in there this morning, asking about engagement rings."

Neil put down his fork and stared at Mary. The apple pie he'd been eating had lost all of its appeal. "Did he buy one?"

"Not yet. But he picked one out, and Pam said he promised to come in next week to arrange for the financing."

Neil's stomach lurched, and it had nothing to do with the fact that he hadn't eaten breakfast. "Then you think he's gearing up to ask Taylor to marry him?"

"What else can I think? When you were away, they spent almost every day together, and I know he's not dating anyone else. I heard he was working on some kind of project over at her house."

Neil nodded. "He built Angela's playhouse in Taylor's living room. But Taylor wasn't there. She stayed at my house with the kids."

"Well that's something, at least." Mary didn't sound entirely convinced. "All the same, I wouldn't wait around much longer to make your move."

Neil dug in his heels mentally. Mary was known to exaggerate, and this might be one of those times. "Did Ted say that the ring was for Taylor?"

"No. Pam tried to find out, but Ted wouldn't say. The only thing he told her was that he hadn't proposed yet. Forewarned is forearmed, and I thought you should know about it right away."

"Thanks for telling me, Mary. If you hear any more . . ."

"I'll call you right away." Mary reached out to pat his hand. "It's not too late, Neil. Taylor would never lie to you. If she told you that Ted was just a friend, it's true. But that doesn't mean you should let any grass grow under your feet. If I were you, I'd get things settled between you now. Taylor's right for you and she's a perfect mother for the kids. I can't blame you for being cautious, but Taylor's different from Melissa. She's one of us. And if you dawdle around much longer, you could end up losing her."

Neil stared at Mary in alarm. "Wait a second, Mary. You mean you think that Taylor might actually marry a man she doesn't love?"

"It's been known to happen. Taylor likes Ted. That's as

plain as the nose on your face. And it's not that unusual when you think about it. Ted's a real nice guy, and he'd make a good husband for her."

"But Taylor doesn't want to get married again. She told me that."

Mary shot him a pitying glance. "It's pretty clear you don't understand the workings of the female mind."

"What's *that* supposed to mean?"

"Maybe that's what Taylor says. She might even believe it. But Ted can be mighty persuasive, and she hasn't had any other offers." Mary paused and gave him a sharp look. "Has she?"

"No, not that I know of." This conversation was making Neil very uncomfortable, and he almost wished that he hadn't taken Ollie for a walk.

"Just between you and me, I think Taylor should get another offer from someone she already loves." Mary slid out of the booth and stood up. She put her hands flat on the table and stared him right in the eye. "Don't blow it, Neil. If you do, you're going to regret it for the rest of your life."

Taylor stomped the snow off her boots at the back door and left them on the rug by the door. The red light on her answering machine was blinking and she hesitated, her finger poised over the message button. If someone had called in to place a large order, she'd have to turn it down. Even with Michael and Robby helping her, she was limited by having only two ovens. But perhaps this message wasn't from a customer. Neil had promised to call her with an update on the box manufacturers he'd contacted on the web.

She took a deep breath and pressed the button. The recorded machine voice told her she had "one messages." This was supposed to be the age of technology. Why couldn't someone build an answering machine that was capable of differentiating between one message and multiple messages? But her minor irritation vanished completely when she heard Randy Hutchin's voice.

Hi, Taylor. It's Randy. I heard from Prime Lending and I'm at the office. Call me.

Taylor's fingers were shaking as she punched out Randy's number. Was it good news or bad? She was tired of running back and forth between Neil's kitchen and her own. It was massively inconvenient and she didn't know what she was going to do if Randy told her that she couldn't buy the bakery.

Neil had just logged online when the doorbell rang. He logged off again with a sigh and got up to answer the door. It was Lester Crawley and he looked upset. "What's wrong, Lester?"

"This came for you from a Chicago lawyer. You got to sign for it."

"Sure." Neil signed his name and took the letter. "Thanks, Lester."

Lester nodded, but he didn't seem in any hurry to get back to the post office. "Melissa lives in Chicago, doesn't she?"

Neil nodded and glanced down at the return address. Lester was right; his registered letter was from a Chicago law firm.

"She's not making trouble for you, is she, Neil?"

Neil had been wondering the same thing, but he put on a smile for Lester's benefit. "It's probably just business."

"That's good." Lester looked very relieved. "I'd better get going then. Inez is holding down the fort for me, and she's never been good at reading the scale. I don't want her overcharging folks on their postage."

"Right. Thanks, Lester." Neil waited until Lester had climbed back into his car and then glanced down at the letter again. Despite what he'd told Lester, he didn't have any business dealings in Chicago. The only person he knew there was Melissa.

Neil told himself not to panic as he carried the letter into the kitchen. He got a fresh cup of coffee, sat down at the table, and slit open the envelope with a table knife. Despite his resolve, his hands were shaking slightly as pulled out the papers inside.

"Damn!" Neil slammed his fist on the table. It had only taken a glance to see why the papers had been sent by registered letter. Neil picked them back up to read them carefully, but nothing had changed. He was being sued. By Melissa.

Neil felt like tearing up the papers, but that wouldn't do any good. They had been filed with the court. Melissa had left the kids without a backward glance. She hadn't even bothered to say good-bye. In the three years since she'd left, she'd never called to check on them or sent them a birthday or Christmas card. And now it seemed the mother of his children had experienced a change of heart. The legal document he'd just read had informed him that Melissa was initiating a custody suit.

Taylor dropped into a chair. This was undoubtedly the worst day of her life. She'd just talked to Randy, and Prime Lending had turned her down. There was work to do, dough to mix, and cookies to bake, but Taylor just sat there staring at the snow that fell outside her window. Prime Lending would finance a loan for her when she had clear title to Grandma Mac's house, but Taylor couldn't wait that long. And once probate had been settled, she wouldn't need to deal with Prime Lending. She could get a regular loan at a much better rate from Ward Sutter at First National.

She felt like crying, but she wouldn't allow herself the luxury of tears. There was work to do and she had to do it. Taylor got to her feet and began to assemble the ingredients for the cookies she had to bake that night. There was no way she'd disappoint her customers.

Taylor had just dumped the chocolate chips into her bowl of Cowboy Cookie dough when there was a knock on her back door. Taylor washed her hands and went to open it. But it wasn't Michael or Angela, as she'd expected. It was Neil, and he looked every bit as upset as she felt.

"What's wrong, Neil?" Taylor took his parka and led him over to the table, getting him settled with a cup of coffee. "You look like death warmed over."

Neil nodded. "So do you. Did Prime Lending turn you down for the loan?"

"Yes." Taylor poured herself a cup of coffee and sat down in the opposite chair. "Randy tried everywhere, but no one is willing to take a chance on a business that doesn't have a two-year track record."

Neil looked very sympathetic. "I'm sorry, Taylor. Just give me a couple of days to make some calls and maybe I can come up with something."

"Thanks, Neil." Taylor put her own troubles on hold for the moment. "Tell me what's wrong with you."

"I guess this isn't my day either. I just got a registered letter from Melissa's lawyer. She's suing me for custody of Angela and Michael."

Taylor stared at him in shock. "What possible reason could she have?"

"She claims that I travel too much. I'm not home to provide a loving, stable home for Michael and Angela."

"That's ridiculous!" Taylor's voice was shaking with anger. "What kind of life would *she* provide?"

"A good one, according to her lawyer. Her husband

makes enough money so that Melissa doesn't have to work, and she's decided to be a full-time, stay-at-home mom."

Taylor shook her head. "That's ridiculous. You've got to fight it, Neil. It's like Mary always says: Leopards don't change their spots."

"I know. I don't doubt her intentions, Taylor. She's not an evil person. I'm sure she thinks she'll be a good mother."

"But you know she won't be," Taylor prompted him.

"Unfortunately, that's true. Once the novelty of having the kids wears off, she'll hire someone to take care of them and go off to do whatever rich wives do. But how can I prove that?"

Taylor reached out to take his hand. It was cold, and she warmed it between hers. "Did you call your lawyer?"

"Yes, but he doesn't think I've got a prayer. Melissa's right, in a way. I *do* travel a lot."

"I know, but Michael and Angela are either with Mrs. Simmons or with me. It's not like you're going off and leaving them alone. And you're a great father, Neil."

"Thanks." Neil looked up at her and Taylor could see the misery in his eyes. "But the judge doesn't know me and the custody hearing is going to be held in Chicago. Melissa has a good case on paper. She's married, and if the kids went to live with her, they'd have a father *and* a mother."

Taylor just nodded. The perfect solution to Neil's dilemma had already occurred to her, but there was no way she'd suggest it. She got up and walked around the table to hug him. "It's not over yet, not by a long shot. Just let me make a couple of calls. I still have connections at the law firm where I used to work, and one of their lawyers might be able to think of something you could do. Just wait right here and I'll be back."

Taylor used the phone in her bedroom to make the call. She didn't want Neil to overhear what she was going to say. She talked to two lawyers, and when she hung up, she squared her shoulders and walked back downstairs to tell Neil what she'd learned. Both lawyers had agreed that if Neil married her, it might tip the scale in his favor. They'd also had several other suggestions and she could hardly wait to tell Neil about them.

"I talked to two lawyers and they had some ideas." Taylor saw that Neil's knuckles were white as he gripped his coffee mug. "They said your lawyer should request a change of venue. If the custody hearing is held here, your lawyer can call witnesses to describe Michael and Angela's life in Two Rivers. You can also call Mrs. Simmons to verify that she takes care of the children when you travel. And you can call me too.

"They're right," Neil agreed. "My lawyer is already doing that. What else did they suggest?"

Taylor hesitated, but this wasn't the time for tact. "They said that if you got remarried, it would weaken Melissa's case. Then the scales would be even."

"That's what my lawyer said. But I can't do it, Taylor. It wouldn't be fair to ask someone to marry me as a favor. What else did they say?"

Taylor had the urge to bop him over the head with her coffee mug. Didn't he know that all he had to do was ask her and she'd jump at the chance? But it wouldn't be right to extort a proposal out of Neil. "They suggested that you hire a private detective to see if there's anything unsuitable about Melissa's lifestyle in Chicago."

"Yes. I'll do that." Neil looked a little sick as he said the words. "I don't like the idea of prying into her private life, but this is war. Anything else?"

"They said you should start gathering letters from members of the community about what a good father you are. Some judges are impressed by that kind of paperwork."

"I'll do it, but Melissa's got a good lawyer. She'll probably have as many letters as I do."

"She can't, and that's the beauty of this strategy. Since Melissa and her husband don't have any children together, she won't be able to get anyone in Chicago to swear that she's a good mother."

"That's very smart." Neil looked impressed. "What else?"

"That's about it for right now. They promised to think about it overnight and give me a call tomorrow with any other suggestions they can come up with."

"Okay." Neil got up from the table.

"I just want you to know that I'll do anything I can to help, Neil. It looks like we're both going to have a rotten New Year's Eve."

"You said it!" Neil was about to open the door when he turned and stared at her. Then he walked back to the table and took her hand. "Taylor?"

"Yes, Neil?"

"You have plans, don't you?"

"For New Year's Eve?" Taylor felt her pulse quicken as Neil nodded. "Not really. I was just going to open a split of champagne, turn on the television, and watch the ball drop in Times Square."

"That doesn't sound like much fun. I'm not sure if I'd be good company, but would you like to do something with me?"

"Sure. We can be lousy company together. What did you have in mind?"

"I'll think of something and get back to you. And, Taylor? Thanks for everything. You're . . . well . . . you're the best friend I've ever had."

When Neil left, Taylor sat back down at the table. It was obvious that Neil thought of her only as a friend. He still hadn't asked her to marry him, not even when he was faced with the possibility of losing custody of Michael and Angela. A lump of sadness rose in her throat and then she was sobbing, her tears falling in splotches on the yellow

Formica surface of Grandma Mac's table. She cried until her throat was scratchy and her eyes were swollen. And then she stood up, took a deep calming breath, and marched back to the counter to mix up the rest of her cookie dough.

TWENTY-TWO

"Dad? I'm home!"

"In here, Michael."

"You won't believe what Mr. Jessup taught me at the rink! Now I can do a back . . ." Michael stopped in mid-boast and stared at Neil. "You look awful, Dad. Are you sick?"

"No. It's just . . . uh . . . never mind, Michael. I just have a personal problem."

"So you won't tell me." Michael sighed and flopped down in the captain's chair by Neil's desk. "That's really not fair, Dad. I'm practically grown up and I thought we were buddies."

"We are."

"Then wouldn't it help if you talked about it? Taylor says I'm a really good listener. We tell each other our problems and it helps a lot."

Neil just stared at his son. Somehow, when he'd been out of town, or perhaps when his back had been turned for an instant, Michael had grown up.

"Why are you looking at me like that?" Michael cocked his head to the side. "Don't you believe that I know how to listen?"

"I'm sure you do. I was just wondering when you'd grown up on me."

"It wasn't that long ago." Michael grinned. "So give, Dad. What's wrong?"

Neil wavered. He'd have to tell Michael about it sooner or later, and Melissa's court action affected the kids every bit as much as it affected him. "I guess you're old enough to hear it, son. It's your mother. She's petitioning the court for full custody of Angela and you."

"That's crazy!" Michael shook his head. "She doesn't want us. She never did. She can't win, can she, Dad?"

"I don't know. I'm doing everything in my power to see that she doesn't, but my lawyer says that she has a good case."

"How can she?" Michael was outraged. "She left us without even saying good-bye!"

Neil reached out to take Michael's hand. "I know. But she's remarried now, and her husband makes enough money so that she can afford to stay home and take care of you."

"But she wasn't working when she was married to you and she didn't stay home then. She could have, but she didn't."

"She says she will now, and a judge might believe her. He might also think that you should live with her because you'd have two parents instead of just one."

Neil watched a myriad of expressions cross Michael's face. There was disbelief, anger, and then a deep concern. "We can't tell Angela. She's too young to understand, and she'd just worry."

"You're right, son." Neil nodded. "The only person I told was Taylor."

"What did she say."

"She said she'd do anything she could to help."

"That's good. You said that the judge might give us to her because she was married, right?"

Neil winced. He thought he knew the path that Mi-

chael's thoughts were taking, but it would be best to let
him talk. "That's right."

"Then why don't you get married? Taylor loves us and
she'd marry you if you asked her. And she said she'd do
anything she could to help."

Neil shook his head. "I can't ask Taylor to marry me.
She has her own life and she might want to marry someone
else."

"But she doesn't."

"How do you know that?" Neil decided that Michael
was old enough to know all the facts. "I went down to the
café this morning and Mary told me that Ted Swanson was
at the Jewel Mart in Anoka, looking at engagement rings.
She thinks Ted is going to ask Taylor to marry him."

Michael stared at him for a moment and then he started
to laugh. "Ted? And Taylor? No way, Dad! Taylor likes Ted,
but she wouldn't marry him. They're just friends."

"Are you sure?"

"Positive. Why don't you just ask her to marry you, Dad?
The worst she can do is say no."

"It wouldn't be fair, Michael. I'd be asking Taylor for a
big favor and I'd be giving her nothing in return."

"I guess you're right." Michael sighed, obviously disappointed. He was silent for a moment, and then he looked
thoughtful. "Do you have good credit?"

Neil was surprised at the abrupt change in subject. "Yes,
I do. Why?"

"Then you could give Taylor a favor in return. She
needs to buy the bakery and nobody will loan her the
money."

"Lend," Neil corrected him automatically.

"Okay, nobody'll *lend* her the money. But if she married
you, the bank would give her the money. Come on, Dad.
All you have to do is point that out to her. If you got married, you'd be doing each other favors, and there's nothing
wrong with that."

Neil sighed. "That's not the right way to look at marriage, Michael. People don't marry so that they can do each other favors. People marry for love."

"I know, but this is an unusual situation."

"That's true, Michael. But I still don't think it's fair to Taylor to . . ."

"Do you want us to live with *her?*" Michael interrupted him.

"Of course I don't! But . . ."

"Then just do it, Dad." Michael got up and walked around the desk to give him a hug. "You've got to think about us. We love you and we want to stay with you."

Neil hugged Michael back. "Okay, son. I'll ask Taylor."

"I still don't know how you managed to get reservations at the last minute." Taylor gazed out at the glittering city lights below. They were seated in the Sky Room of the Minneapolis Towers, a new luxury hotel. The dining room was on the twenty-third floor and they had a choice spot by the wraparound windows.

As the waiter served their appetizer—tiny potato pancakes topped with sour cream and two kinds of caviar—Taylor glanced at Neil over the rim of her champagne flute. He was staring at her, looking anxious. She could see it in the depths of his blue eyes. She waited until the waiter had left them and then reached across the small table to take his head. "Are you thinking about the custody case?"

"Yes, but I'd like to forget it for now. You look beautiful, Taylor."

"Thank you." Taylor smiled. She'd worn her best dress—a red silk with a plunging neckline.

Neil had ordered for both of them and Taylor felt as if she were in heaven as she ate crispy duck with cranberry sauce, tender baby asparagus, and individual chocolate souffles for dessert. That was followed by coffee flamed with brandy and topped with whipped cream. By the time they'd finished, Taylor wondered if she dared to take a deep breath.

"That was a totally incredible dinner." Taylor smiled across the table at Neil. "I'm so full, I don't think I can move. We may have to sit here for hours."

"We can do that. They're open all night, and there's a big New Year's Eve party at midnight. But I did make other plans."

"Oh?" Taylor's breath caught in her throat as he reached out to take her hand. She hoped he was going to ask her to stay with him tonight.

"I know this isn't fair to you, Taylor, but I have to ask you a question."

"Of course." Neil looked very serious and she could tell that what he was about to ask her was very important to him. "What is it, Neil?"

Neil took a deep breath and then he squeezed her hand hard. "Will you fly to Las Vegas and marry me tonight?"

TWENTY-THREE

Taylor removed the last of her clothing from her closet and added it to the pile she'd made on her bed. This wasn't the way she'd planned to start her marriage with Neil, but she *was* Mrs. Neil DiMarco. They'd been married at the Silver Bells Wedding Chapel in Las Vegas, going straight there in a taxi from the airport. She even had an engagement and wedding ring; Neil had brought along his mother's set.

Neil had explained everything on the flight: how Michael had convinced him that it was the right thing to do and how sorry he was to involve her in his problems. He'd assured her that it would be a marriage in name only and once the custody battle was over, they would get a quiet divorce and resume their separate lives.

Taylor was convinced that she'd done the right thing. Neil needed a wife to retain full custody of Angela and Michael and he'd asked her, not someone else. Perhaps that meant that he was beginning to love her the way she loved him.

"I'm ready for another load." Michael stood in the doorway, grinning from ear to ear. "You want me to take those clothes on the bed, Taylor?"

"They're ready to go. When you come back, I'll have the dresser emptied out."

"Where are you putting Taylor's clothes, Michael?" Neil looked up from the box he'd been packing.

"In the bedroom. I just shoved yours over to make room. Yours are on the right side and Taylor's are on the left."

Neil looked uneasy. "I thought I told you to put them in the guest closet."

"You did, but what if the judge sends somebody out to look at our house? They'll think it's kind of funny if Taylor's clothes are in the guest room."

Neil stared at his son for a moment. "I didn't think about that. I guess I'd better go back over and clear out some dresser drawers."

"Good idea." Michael beamed at his dad. "Go ahead. I've got this covered."

After Neil had left, Taylor turned to Michael. "I smell a rat, Michael. I think you'd better tell me exactly what you're trying to do."

"I'm just being careful, that's all." Michael looked the soul of innocence. "If anybody finds out that you married Dad for the wrong reason, we'll have to go live with *her.*"

"Okay. But I can't shake the feeling that you have something up your sleeve. What is it?"

"Well . . ." Michael shifted from foot to foot. "I was hoping that Dad would get used to being married to you if you're in the same room and all."

"That's what I thought. Don't get your hopes up, Michael. Your father's a very stubborn man."

"You said it!" Michael laughed. "But you love him anyway, don't you, Taylor?"

Taylor took a deep breath. She'd always been truthful with Michael and this wasn't the time to start lying. "Yes, I do. But that doesn't do much good because I don't think he loves me."

"Sure he does. He just won't admit it. That's his stubborn side coming out. But you can work on him if you're living with us. It'll all turn out right in the end, you'll see."

As Michael picked up the armload of clothing and left, Taylor stared after him with an amused expression. His explanation about why she should share Neil's closet had been brilliant. She just hoped that she could come up with an equally brilliant reason to share Neil's bed.

Neil straightened up and massaged his aching back. He'd emptied out half of his dresser drawers and now he was waiting for Michael to bring over Taylor's things. He walked to the closet and shook his head as he saw all Taylor's clothing hanging neatly on the left side. It certainly *looked* as if they were man and wife. He really didn't think that the judge would send anyone out to look at the house, but it couldn't hurt to be prepared.

Without really thinking about what he was doing, Neil reached out to touch one of Taylor's dresses. It was silk and it felt almost as smooth as her skin. A faint perfume clung to the material—Taylor's own special scent. It reminded him of violets and conjured up delightful images of Taylor lying naked in his bed.

What were they going to do about sleeping arrangements? Neil swallowed hard. He wanted to take Taylor to his bed and make love to her. After all, she *was* his wife. But when she'd agreed to marry him, he'd promised her that it would be a business arrangement. He'd agreed to co-sign the loan for the bakery and make up the alimony payments that she'd be forfeiting by marrying again. She'd agreed to do her part by pretending that their marriage was real and helping him retain custody of Angela and Michael. They hadn't discussed making love, but the way he felt right now, they'd better reach some sort of agreement about that soon.

"Here's another box, Dad." Michael walked into the

room and set the box on the floor. "Taylor said she'll put it away. She's got a new set of sheets she's going to put on the bed."

"*This* bed?" The words were out before Neil had time to consider them.

"I guess so." Michael shrugged. "She's going to be sleeping in here, isn't she?"

"I . . . uh . . . that's something we'll have to discuss." Neil frowned. Michael was growing up too fast to suit him.

"We'd better talk about Angela, Dad." Michael looked very serious as he sat down on the bed. "I think she's too young to understand the reason why you married Taylor. If you tell her it's just a business arrangement, she'll probably tell Becky and all the other kids at preschool."

Neil knew Michael was right. Angela was too young to understand.

"If Angela tells, we're sunk with the judge. I think we'd be a lot better off pretending that this is the real thing."

"You're right, son."

"So Taylor had better sleep in here with you. Angela knows that married people sleep in the same room. She's going to blab it all over if Taylor stays in the guest room."

Neil sighed. This was getting a lot more complicated than he'd thought it would be.

"Taylor understands. She'll go along with it." Michael stood up and headed for the door. "Don't worry, Dad. You and Taylor are smart. You'll figure out some way to work it all out."

"This is not going to work, Taylor."

"I know." Taylor was in bed, the covers pulled up to her chin, watching Neil as he slipped into his robe. "You don't like pajamas, right?"

"I hate them. But that's not all of it, Taylor. Maybe I'd better go down to my office and work for a while."

Taylor knew better than to argue. She could see that Neil had made up his mind. But even though she did her best to control them, the tears slipped out and rolled down her cheeks.

"What's wrong?" Neil crossed the floor in an instant and took her into his arms. "You're not sorry you married me, are you?"

Taylor took a deep breath and hoped her voice wouldn't shake. Just being in Neil's arms again made her long for him desperately. "No. I'm glad we got married, but . . ."

"But what?"

"This isn't exactly the way I hoped my wedding night would be."

Neil groaned and then he reached out to stroke her hair. "I know. It's not exactly what I had in mind either. Just looking at you in my bed . . . well . . . it's hard to take."

"Should we amend our agreement?" Taylor held her breath, hoping that Neil would reconsider. He'd insisted that they keep their distance when they were in private and she'd reluctantly agreed.

"We can't."

Neil's voice was thick with passion and Taylor heard it. He was having doubts, too. She let the sheet slip down slightly and was instantly rewarded as his arms tightened around her. "Could we make an exception, just for tonight?"

"Do you think we should?"

Taylor turned her head so her lips met his in a kiss of longing. And then she whispered, "Yes, Neil. I definitely think we should."

When the alarm clock sounded at seven the next morning, Taylor woke up with a smile on her face. She reached over to shut it off and then rolled back to the center of the bed, reaching out for the man she loved. Her fingers encountered a tangled sheet, still slightly warm from her husband's body. Neil was up. She could hear him downstairs, clanking around in the kitchen.

Taylor jumped out of bed and slipped into the velvet robe that was hanging from a hook on the back of the door. It was Neil's, but that didn't matter. They were married now. She located her slippers, pulled them on, and ran lightly down the stairs. Neil was sitting at the table reading his newspaper and sipping a cup of coffee.

"Good morning, Taylor."

Neil smiled up at her, but she could see the wariness in his eyes. Taylor sighed. It seemed that last night's loving embraces had been the exception, rather than the rule. She had won a battle, but there was still a war to fight. And she intended to fight it with every feminine wile she possessed.

"Good morning, Neil." Taylor walked over to the refrigerator and took out the eggs and bacon she'd brought over from Grandma Mac's refrigerator. "Sunny side up, over easy, or scrambled?"

Neil stared at her with an expression very close to adoration. "You're making breakfast?"

"Of course I am." Taylor put strips of bacon in the frying pan and got out another, for the eggs. "You didn't answer my question. How do you like your eggs?"

"Over easy, unless that's too hard to do."

"No problem. How about the kids? Are they up yet?"

"Michael's in the shower and Angela's getting dressed. They should be down in a couple of minutes."

"Okay." Taylor put another frying pan on the stove and took a package of cheese out of the refrigerator. "I'll start their breakfast. They like their eggs scrambled with cheese. Michael prefers his toast just this side of being charred, but Angela wants it lightly golden. And both of them love apple jelly."

"Why do you know more about my kids than I do?"

Taylor laughed at Neil's obvious surprise. "When I stayed here with them, I fixed breakfast every morning. I don't know more about them than you do. I just know what they like to eat for breakfast."

"Hi, Taylor." Michael came into the kitchen and grinned as he saw her at the stove. "Are you making breakfast?"

"Are scrambled eggs with cheese all right?"

"You bet." Michael went to get the apple jelly out of the refrigerator and set it on the counter. "I can make the toast."

"Thanks, Michael."

"Is it cheesy eggs, Taylor?" Angela ran into the kitchen and looked very pleased when Taylor nodded. She hurried to the table to kiss Neil on the cheek and then she went straight to the counter. "I'll put on the jelly."

Taylor got out the kitchen stool so that Angela could stand on it and handed her a plate for the toast. Then she noticed that Neil was watching them, looking a bit surprised. "They always help me with breakfast. It goes faster that way."

"That's good." A smile twitched at the corners of Neil's lips as he watched Angela spoon out a huge gob of jelly and drop it on a piece of toast. "No jelly for me, Pumpkin. I'll just take butter."

Angela turned around on her stool to face him. "Are you sure, Daddy? It's really good for you. It's got lots of violins."

"That's *vitamins.*"

Both Taylor and Michael spoke at once, and then all three of them started to laugh. Taylor was the first to recover, and she left the stove for a moment to give Angela a hug. "You did that on purpose, didn't you, Angel Fuzz?"

"Well . . . maybe." Angela giggled. "It always makes you laugh and moms should laugh. It makes kids feel good."

"It makes moms feel good, too." Taylor gave her another hug and then she went back to the stove to flip over the bacon.

When Neil's breakfast was ready, Taylor carried it over to the table and set it down in front of him. "Here you go, lord and master. Eggs, just the way you like them."

"Aren't you glad you married her, Daddy?" Angela jumped down from her perch on the stool and carried the plate of toast to the table. "Now we've got a mom to cook us real food for breakfast."

Neil began eating, but Taylor noticed that he looked worried. She knew exactly what he was thinking and it concerned her, too. Angela was so happy to have a mother. How would she feel once the court case had been decided and their marriage was over?

TWENTY-FOUR

They'd been married for a week and Neil felt like an impostor as they said good-bye to their guests. They'd just hosted a huge dinner party for four couples and their kids. Marge and Tim had come with Becky, Barb and Ray Ringstrom had brought Suzie, Jim and Patsy Burkholtz had brought their son Gary, and Suzanne had arrived with Robby. Ted Swanson had joined them, too. Taylor had explained that she'd invited him to even out the numbers, but Neil still had his suspicions. He'd watched Ted carefully during the evening. He had been friendly and polite to Taylor, nothing more. But there was still the matter of the engagement ring and the installments that Ted was making.

On their flight to Las Vegas, Neil had told Taylor that she could let Ted in on the reason for their marriage. She'd assured him that it wasn't necessary, but Neil suspected she'd changed her mind. It was clear that Ted knew all about their marriage of convenience and was helping them maintain the myth. And though he appreciated Ted's cooperation, it galled Neil to entertain the man who would probably be Taylor's next husband.

Just as soon as the last car had pulled away, Neil shut the door and turned to Angela and Michael. "Time for bed, kids."

"Okay." Michael nodded. "Come on, Angel Fuzz. To-morrow's the big day."

Neil exchanged an amused glance with Taylor. Michael was now calling Angela the nickname Taylor had given her. Both kids were really excited about Taylor's expansion. Neil and Taylor were meeting with Randy early to-morrow morning to sign all the paperwork, and by the time school was out, the old Two Rivers Bakery would belong to Taylor.

Once Taylor had gone upstairs with the kids, Neil sat down in the den. His marriage to Taylor was working out well, much better than he'd expected. There was only one problem: He couldn't seem to keep his hands off her. After their first passionate night, Neil had done his best to avoid any physical contact with her. He knew that one sexy glance from her incredible violet-blue eyes would make his resolve crumble. He'd tried, but he couldn't seem to control his urge to step up behind her and hug her when she was in the kitchen, or slip his arm around her shoulders when they were watching a movie with the kids. It had been six days since they'd slept together and he was going crazy.

They'd agreed that they would operate on different schedules. Taylor went to bed shortly after the kids were tucked in, and he spent the night working in his office. After Taylor got up, Neil crawled into his bed, still warm from her body, and slept. He guessed it was working, but it was taking a heavy toll on his work. It was impossible to concentrate, knowing that Taylor was upstairs in his bed. There had been several nights when he'd just given up and watched old movies until dawn. Part of his problem was that Taylor wanted him every bit as much as he wanted her. Was he being a fool for not taking advantage of the fact that they were married?

Neil sighed and flopped down on the leather couch. Ollie jumped up to lick his hand, but that didn't make

Neil feel much better. Ollie would pad upstairs once Taylor went to bed. Even his dog had abandoned him in the middle of the night. Ollie had taken to sleeping upstairs with Taylor, occupying the spot that should have been Neil's.

There was no point in denying what he knew now—that he'd been a fool not to propose to Taylor sooner. He loved her and wanted her as his real wife. Now it was too late. He'd blown it, and it was completely his fault. It was so crazy no one would believe it if he wrote it into the plot of one of his books. He was in love with his new wife, but he couldn't have her. He'd promised Taylor that they would quietly divorce right after the custody hearing was over.

"Neil? They're in bed and they're waiting for you."

Her quiet voice roused him from his unhappy thoughts and Neil got up to climb the stairs. He tucked Michael in, tousled his hair, and gave him a hug. "Good night, son."

" 'Night, Dad." Michael gave a contented smile. "I never knew how much fun it would be to invite people over, just like a real family."

Neil smiled back. It was pretty obvious that Michael had missed having a mother who liked to entertain his friends. "Yes. It was a lot of fun."

"We'll do it again, won't we, Dad?"

"Sure." Neil flicked off the light and went down the hall to Angela's room.

"Look at my book, Daddy." Angela smiled up at him. "It's *Green Eggs and Ham,* and Mommy promised to make it for me for breakfast. She taught me to read the first page. Do you want me to say it to you?"

"I'd like that, Pumpkin." Neil smiled and tried not to look as upset as he felt. Angela had called Taylor "Mommy." Should he point out that Taylor wasn't actually her mother? Or should he just pretend he hadn't noticed?

"How was that, Daddy?" Angela closed the book when

she was through and handed it to him. "Taylor's going to teach me the next page tomorrow."

"That's wonderful. You read very well, Pumpkin." Neil was slightly relieved. At least she'd used Taylor's name, not calling her "Mommy" again. He wouldn't say anything now—it would only upset Angela—but he would discuss it with Taylor.

"You'd better get some sleep, Pumpkin." Neil leaned down to kiss Angela's cheek and gave her a big hug. Then he turned off the lamp, made sure her nightlight was working, and tiptoed out. As he walked down the hall to his bedroom, he remembered what Angela had said about green eggs and ham for breakfast. He had to ask Taylor exactly how she intended to make green eggs and ham for his precocious daughter.

Neil heard the shower running when he went into his bedroom. What if Taylor thought she was alone and came out of the bathroom naked? He had to warn her that he was here so that she'd put on a robe or a flannel night-gown—anything that would cover her lovely body. He walked to the bathroom, pulled open the door, and called out. "I'm here, Taylor. I need to talk to you."

"Okay. I'll be out in a minute."

Despite his best intentions, Neil eyes were drawn to the figure outlined behind the frosted glass doors. Taylor was washing her hair, her arms raised above her head, her breasts firm and lovely beneath the spray. The sight of her made Neil groan deep in his throat. He didn't want to stop looking, she was so damn beautiful, but he knew he wouldn't be able to control himself if he didn't make an exit fast.

Swearing softly, Neil tore his eyes away and left the bathroom. His knees felt weak and he sat down hard on the edge of the bed. No, he shouldn't sit on the bed. Just being there, just knowing that she wouldn't resist if he pulled her down on the mattress and explored every inch of her body with his hands and his mouth, was an agony. He rose to his feet and walked across the room to one of the wing chairs that she'd placed by the window. He had to calm down and stop thinking of her this way. She was only a friend, a temporary wife who'd leave him the minute the court case was decided. Sex didn't enter into it. Not one bit. He'd always prided himself on his ability to control himself, and he'd managed very well until now. It was odd that every shred of his self-control seemed to vanish when Taylor was around.

Taylor rinsed her hair, flipped off the water, and wrapped a towel around her head. Then she slid back the glass door and stepped out of the shower. Neil had sounded serious, and she hoped that nothing was wrong.

She reached for her warm chenille robe, but it wasn't there. She'd put in a load of clothes, right before their company had arrived, and it was still in the washer, along with her long flannel nightgown. All she had was the lacy peignoir set that Suzanne and Nina had given her as a wedding present.

A smile spread slowly across Taylor's face. She'd been trying to cooperate with Neil, deliberately wearing nightwear that covered her completely even though he didn't come to bed until she was up and dressed. Perhaps it was time to let him see exactly what he was missing.

Taylor slipped into the lacy confection. It was so sheer, it was almost indecent, and that didn't upset her in the least. She put on the filmy robe that was a part of the set and stared at her reflection in the mirror. It would be a real blow to her feminine pride if Neil was able to resist her.

When Taylor entered the room, Neil's reaction was even better than she'd hoped. He looked as if he wanted to jump up from the wing chair and ravish her on the spot.

* * *

Neil just stared at the vision before him. *My God she is beautiful!* He swallowed convulsively, told himself that he had to keep himself under control, and took a deep breath. Even breathing was difficult with Taylor so near. "I need to talk to you, Taylor."

"Yes?"

She sat down in the opposite chair and Neil almost groaned. He could see right through that silky, lacy thing she was wearing, and that wasn't going to make this conversation any easier. "When I went in to tuck Angela in, she called you 'Mommy.' "

"I know." Taylor didn't seem at all surprised. "I explained that I'm not her mother, but she still says it once in a while. I didn't want to make an issue of it, Neil. I thought it would be better if we just tried to ignore it."

Neil didn't dare look at her, so he stared down at her feet. But even her feet were sexy, especially when he recalled how she'd thrown her legs around his back and locked her feet together, taking him even more deeply into her sweet warmth. "You're probably right. There's . . . uh . . . just one other thing."

"Yes, Neil?"

She raised her lovely violet eyes to his and Neil felt like panting. He could smell the scent of her perfume and it almost drove him wild. He forced himself to concentrate. What was the other thing he'd wanted to discuss with her? It was impossible to think when she was so close since he could just reach out and touch her. "Uh . . . it's . . . the green eggs and ham. That's it. Angela said you promised to make green eggs and ham for her."

"That's true. I did."

Taylor laughed, and it was nearly his undoing. He wanted to throw her down on the floor, rip that lacy thing off her body, and turn that sexy laugh of hers into a scream of pleasure. He remembered the little moans and sighs she'd given when he'd kissed her lips and her breasts. And that joyous cry she'd given when he'd covered her body with his.

This wasn't getting him anywhere. What were they talking about? Neil blinked, swallowed again, and tried not to think of the warm, sweet flesh that was only inches from his hands. "Uh . . . how are you planning to make green eggs and ham?"

"I'll just use green food coloring."

"Oh." The words barely registered in Neil's mind. He knew he should leave the bedroom now that his questions had been answered, but he didn't think that he could get up.

"Don't worry, Neil. I won't make any green eggs for you if you don't want them."

She was smiling at him now, her eyes sparkling. Her lips looked ripe and full and he hungered to taste them. He knew he shouldn't, but he wanted some excuse to touch her, to feel her warm skin under that frothy lace and thin silk. He wanted to run his fingers over her, to loosen that flimsy little ribbon above her breasts, to cup her warm flesh in his hands and . . .

"This floor is so cold." She shivered slightly and tucked her feet up under her.

"You're right. Maybe we should put in wall-to-wall carpeting." Neil was surprised he'd been capable of speech. The filmy covering of lace and silk had pulled tightly against her and his eyes were glued to her curves of sweet flesh.

"Would you carry me to bed, Neil?"

She held out her arms, and Neil groaned as he got up from his chair and picked her up in his arms. Her warm body nestled against his and he shuddered at the heated, feminine feel of her. As he carried her across the floor and put her down on the bed, he knew he was at the breaking point.

"Uh . . . Taylor . . . I've got to get back to work." He gave it his best try, but her fingers were laced around the back of his neck and she didn't release him.

"You didn't tell me if you enjoyed our first dinner party. Did you have a good time?"

"Yes. It was wonderful." His lips were only inches from hers and Neil could feel the warmth radiating from her body. If he didn't kiss her soon, he'd burst. But he couldn't kiss her. If he kissed her, he'd never stop, and they'd wind up in bed again.

"Do you like my nightgown, Neil? The girls bought it for me as a wedding present."

"It's . . . uh . . . very nice." *Nice?* Neil almost laughed. As a writer, he should have been able to come up with a better word. He was about to straighten up and go back downstairs when she pulled him down and kissed him.

"Neil." The way she breathed his name made him think of rumpled sheets and soft pillows and the sweet liquid warmth that was his for the taking. She smiled the sexiest smile he'd ever seen. "I was beginning to think that you didn't want me."

"Never think that." The last of Neil's resistance crumpled and he happily gave up the fight.

TWENTY-FIVE

It was Valentine's Day and they'd been married for six weeks. Taylor filled the gleaming coffee urn she'd bought and turned on the switch. It was eight-thirty in the morning and the coffee would be ready in time for her first customers when she opened at nine.

Now that the front room of the bakery had been converted into a cookie and coffee shop, Taylor, Angela, Michael, and Ollie left the house at ten minutes to seven. Taylor dropped Michael off at the bakery. He seemed proud that she'd given him his own key and that she trusted him to unlock the door, switch on the lights, and turn on the ovens. Then Taylor drove Angela and Ollie to Marge's preschool. Marge had decided that she needed a resident dog, and Ollie had been officially invited to attend Buttons 'n' Bows with Angela.

By the time Taylor got back to the bakery, Suzanne and Robby were there. She chatted with Suzanne for a few minutes, supervising the boys while they baked the morning cookies, and then Suzanne left. Michael and Robby helped out until it was time for them to walk to school.

At two in the afternoon, Neil walked down to join her at the bakery. He spent an hour with her, helping in any way he could. Sometimes he mixed dough for her or waited on the customers. At ten after three, Robby and Michael came in and settled down at a table in the front to do their homework. They usually brought several friends with them, and Neil was their unofficial tutor. Then Neil watched the shop while Taylor and the boys went in the back to bake the dozens of cookies she needed for her regular orders. When they were through for the day, Neil dropped Taylor off at the house so she could start dinner. Then he picked up Angela and Ollie from preschool and took Robby home.

Taylor sighed as the aroma of fresh coffee began to fill the air. They were the perfect example of a normal, hard-working Two Rivers family. Neil pretended to love her whenever anyone was around and no one, not even Nina or Suzanne, suspected they'd agreed to split up once his custody case was decided.

She'd never dreamed that this kind of half-marriage could be so frustrating. Neil hadn't made love to her since the time she'd worn her wedding peignoir set, and Taylor hadn't tried to seduce him again. It was clear that he wanted her, but she couldn't bear to see him acting so ashamed and guilty on the mornings after they'd made love. She still wanted him to make love to her—she'd never stop wanting that—but she had decided that Neil had to conquer his personal demons first.

Michael poked his head around the swinging door that led to the workroom. "Do you want me to get another bag of flour out of the storeroom before I go to school?"

"Do we need it?"

"Yeah. The one you're using is almost empty. I'll bring it out and set it on the counter. Robby's bringing you more sugar. You're getting low on that, too."

"Thanks, Michael. When you've done that, you'd better get a move on. I don't want either of you to be late for school."

"We won't be late, Mrs. DiMarco," Robby called out. "It only takes us five minutes to walk it from here."

Taylor smiled. Robby had called her "Mrs. DiMarco,"

and it still sounded strange and wonderful to her. She just wished she felt more like Neil's wife. She did feel like a mother. Even though she hadn't given birth to Michael or Angela, she knew they thought of her as their mom. If only Neil would think of her as his wife.

When the boys had left, Taylor picked up a towel and wiped down the bar. The antique bar from the Dew Drop Inn looked wonderful. Suzanne and Ted had done a great job refinishing it. And the stools she'd purchased, thanks to Mary's tip about the auction, matched it perfectly. Even the mirror behind the bar was magnificent. Nina had painted a lovely turn-of-the-century dress on the curvaceous nude, and everyone who'd come in for her grand opening had complimented her on the clever way she'd salvaged the mirror. Of course, none of her male customers had admitted to seeing the mirror in its former state, but Taylor wasn't fooled. Neil had told her that almost every boy who'd ever attended Two Rivers High School had driven out to the Dew Drop Inn to stare at the nude. He'd called it a rite of passage, and Taylor didn't think he'd been exaggerating.

There was a knock on the front door and Taylor glanced up. Nina was standing there, shivering in the cold, and she ran to unlock the door. "Hi, Nina. The coffee's almost ready. Do you want a cup?"

"I could use one." Nina slipped out of her boots and left them on the slatted boot rack by the door. She hung her parka on the large, old-fashioned coat tree that Taylor had found in an antique store, shoved her feet into the shoes she'd brought with her, and hopped up on a stool. "It smells divine in here!"

"Vanilla and chocolate," Taylor said. "There's no way I can go wrong with that combination. How about a Cowboy Cookie for breakfast?"

"Great." Nina accepted the cookie Taylor brought her and took a bite. A blissful expression spread across her face, and she took a sip of steaming coffee from one of the new white mugs with Cookies & Kisses silk-screened on the side. "This is a lot better than a bowl of cold cereal, but I'd better watch it. If I keep on scarfing up your cookies, I'm going to gain weight."

"With your metabolism?" Taylor laughed, but she was envious. Nina was a junk-food junkie. She continually snacked on high-calorie foods but never gained an ounce.

"It'll catch up with me sooner or later. That's what my mother always says." Nina held out her hand for another cookie and grinned. "But until then, I intend to keep right on eating your cookies for breakfast, along with all your other regulars."

Taylor nodded. She did have regulars, the same group of people who stopped in every morning. Some of them had their cookies and coffee here, while others ordered theirs to go. Her new place was doing a brisk business, her volume increasing every day. Just last night, she'd talked to Neil about the possibility of hiring an assistant.

"I'm thinking about switching jobs." Nina took another sip of her coffee. "I think I've gone as far as I can at the paper. It's a dead end."

"Why is that?" An intriguing idea popped into Taylor's head, but she waited for Nina's explanation.

"The only other person on the payroll is Wes Garvey. He's the printer, and I wouldn't want his job. And Morrie doesn't need an assistant editor."

"Do you want to be the assistant editor?"

"Not really. I like Wes and Morrie. They're great guys, but most of the time I'm bored to tears. I've been with the paper for almost ten years and it's getting stale."

"Do you think Morrie could replace you?"

"In a heartbeat." Nina laughed. "I just sort of fell into the job when Morrie's wife got pregnant and decided to stay home with the baby. Now that he's in school, I think she might like to come back to her old job."

"What kind of work would you like to do?"

Nina held out her mug for a refill. "Something with people. I'm tired of sitting in my little cubicle typing letters and answering the phone. You know me, Taylor. I'm a friendly person. Being stuck behind a desk isn't what I had in mind for myself."

"If you don't mind my asking, what are you earning at the paper?"

"Two hundred a week. I know I could earn more somewhere else, but I really don't need a lot of money. My parents won't take any rent for the apartment over their garage and I don't have many expenses."

Taylor began to smile. "How would you like to work for me?"

"For you?" Nina looked surprised. "What would I do?"

Taylor was ready for that question. She'd thought about it for the past week. "You'd be my assistant. You'd wait on customers and help me mix up the dough. You could even decorate some of the fancy cookies, if you wanted to try your hand at it."

"I accept." Nina stuck out her hand and waited for Taylor to shake it. "I love this place and I'd really like to work here."

Taylor just stared at Nina. "But I haven't even told you what I could pay you."

"It doesn't matter. I'm so bored at the paper, I'd work here for free."

"Some businesswoman you are!" Taylor laughed. "If I realized that you were so desperate, I would have hired you last week. I'll meet your salary at the paper. That's really no problem. And you can have all the free cookies you can eat."

Nina smiled back at her. "That last incentive really clinches it. When do you want me to start?"

"Yesterday."

Nina slid off her stool and headed for the coatrack. "I'll

go talk to Morrie's wife right now and see when she wants to go back to work."

After Nina had left, Taylor opened her shop for business. The early morning crowd trooped in, and she didn't have time to draw a deep breath until ten-thirty. She was just wiping down the counter, wondering whether she'd have time to dash into the back to mix up more dough, when the bell tinkled and a man bearing a huge bouquet of red roses came in.

"Are you Mrs. DiMarco?"

Taylor nodded, staring at the massive bouquet in awe.

"These are for you." The man, who was wearing a jacket with Anoka Floral embroidered above the pocket, handed her the bouquet. "It sure smells good in here."

Taylor had been about to open the cash register to give him a tip, but he seemed fascinated by the big glass jars of cookies that were displayed behind the bar. "Would you like a tip, or would you rather have cookies?"

"Cookies." The man was obviously pleased as Taylor filled one of her Cookies & Kisses takeout bags for him.

"Here you go." Taylor handed him the bag. "I put in some chocolate chip, some oatmeal raisin, and some sugar cookies."

When the door had closed behind him, Taylor glanced down at the lovely bouquet. The card said: *Happy Valentine's Day—We love you.* It was signed with Michael and Angela's names. It was very sweet of them to send her flowers, but Taylor wished that Neil had added his name to the card.

When all of her customers had left, Taylor took advantage of the lull to dash in the back and add the final touches to the Valentine's Day cookie she'd made for Neil and the kids. It was a giant chocolate fudge cookie shaped like a heart and decorated with pink frosting.

"Taylor?"

Taylor was surprised as the back door opened and a familiar voice hailed her. Neil was there on the doorstep, stomping the snow off his boots. "Hi, Neil. What are you doing here so early?"

"I woke up and didn't feel like writing today, so I came down to help out."

Taylor wondered why her knees always trembled when he smiled at her. "Are you hungry?"

"Not really. I polished off that ham you made last night. You weren't saving it for anything, were you?"

"No." Taylor crossed her fingers as she told the little white lie. She'd planned to make a scalloped potato casserole tonight with chunks of ham and onion mixed in, but it didn't matter. She'd just fix something else for their supper.

"So how is it going?"

Neil walked closer and Taylor's breath caught in her throat. He was so very handsome and she loved him so much. "Business is booming today. I'm selling cookies just as fast as I can bake them. Even the man who delivered my bouquet wanted cookies instead of a tip."

"It came already?" Neil looked surprised. "I just called in the order this morning. Michael wanted me to do it last night, but they were closed."

Taylor smiled. "That was very sweet of them, Neil. Was it your idea? Or theirs?"

"Theirs. Actually, it was Angela's. Some of the kids in preschool were talking about giving their mothers flowers for Valentine's Day, and she asked me if you could have some."

"It was very sweet of her." Taylor was pleased. In the past week she'd noticed that Angela was calling her Mommy quite frequently, and just yesterday she'd overheard Angela telling a group of ladies at one of the tables that her mommy baked better cookies than any of the other mommies.

"You look tired." Neil sounded concerned. "You're

working too hard, Taylor. I think it's time you hired some help."

Taylor grinned at him. "I did. Something wonderful happened this morning. Nina told me that she wanted to change jobs. I probably should have discussed it with you first, but I thought she'd be perfect as my assistant and hired her on the spot."

"You hired Nina?" Neil looked pleased. "That was a good move, Taylor. Nina's great with people, and she'll bring in a lot of business. She'll have every guy in town coming in here to flirt with her."

"I know. I think it's going to work out just fine. She's going to start as soon as she can, and then I'll have more time for you and the kids. I don't want anyone saying that I'm too busy to be a good wife and mother."

"They'd never say that. They couldn't, because it's just not true. You're the best mother the kids could have."

"Thanks." Taylor's smile faltered slightly when he didn't mention what a good wife she was. Of course, she wasn't really supposed to be a real wife. He'd made that perfectly clear.

"Uh . . . Taylor?"

Taylor stared at Neil closely. He looked hesitant, not at all like his usual confident self. "What, Neil?"

"This is for you." Neil drew a large package from behind his back and thrust it into her arms. "I'm not very good at wrapping presents. I hope you don't mind."

"I don't mind at all." Taylor looked down at the package. It was covered with more tape than paper and the red bow on top was definitely lopsided.

"It's for Valentine's Day. I wanted to get you something and I picked it out all by myself."

Taylor had all she could do not to laugh. Neil sounded like a little boy presenting his favorite little girl with a gift. "It's not alive, is it?"

"What?"

Taylor could see that she'd thrown him completely off-balance by her question. "You're wearing the same expression my first boyfriend did when he gave me his pet frog."

"It's not alive." Neil grinned at her. "Open it, Taylor. I can hardly wait to see if you like it."

Taylor slit the tape with her fingernail. It wasn't easy, since there seemed to be several layers of it crisscrossed and piled on top of one another. She managed to loosen the paper enough to pull the box out and opened the lid. There was something fuzzy and pink inside.

"I hope it fits. I had to special-order it."

Taylor bit back a grin as she took the fuzzy pink garment out of the box and held it up. It was a blanket sleeper, the same design they made for toddlers, in an adult size. It had attached booties with rubber soles on the bottom and a long zipper up the front.

"The carpet installer can't come for two weeks, and I thought you needed something to tide you over. We're getting wall-to-wall carpeting in the bedroom, but you have to look at the samples and pick out the color you want."

"Thank you." Taylor wrapped her arms around his neck and gave him a big hug. "I can hardly wait to go home and put on my blanket sleeper."

It wasn't until the bell tinkled and Neil went out to wait on the customers who'd come in, that Taylor remembered what had happened the night they'd discussed wall-to-wall carpeting for the bedroom. She loved Neil's gift, but it would cover her from head to toe and it certainly wasn't sexy. Was Neil simply being kind and thoughtful, buying her the blanket sleeper so she wouldn't be cold? Or was this his way of telling her that he refused to be tempted to sleep with her again?

TWENTY-SIX

"I'll handle everything for you, Taylor. Don't worry."

Nina reached out to squeeze her arm and Taylor gave her a shaky smile. It was the first week in April and the custody hearing was set for this afternoon. "I know you will, Nina. I'm just nervous, that's all."

"You don't have to be nervous. The judge would have to be blind, deaf, and dumb not to let you and Neil have the kids. Practically everybody in town wrote letters."

"I know. Neil's lawyer called last night and told us that he had over five hundred testimonials. Make sure you tell everyone how much we appreciate their support."

"I will. What are you wearing?"

That question made Taylor smile, even though the butterflies were churning in her stomach. "Suzanne called last night to discuss that with me. She suggested that I walk into the courtroom in a housedress with some of those pink foam rollers in my hair."

Nina started to laugh, but then she stopped and gave Taylor a sharp look. "You're not going to do it, are you?"

"Of course not. Suzanne was just kidding around. I'm wearing a perfectly tasteful skirt and jacket. And I thought I'd put on the pin that Angela made for me in preschool."

"That's a great touch," Nina said. "The judge will know right away that she gave it to you."

Taylor gave one last look around and then headed for

the door. Neil and the kids were waiting for her at home and she had to get dressed.

"It's going to turn out right, Taylor. Just try to relax and be yourself. You're a wonderful mother to the kids and a perfect wife for Neil."

"Thanks, Nina." As Taylor walked out the door, she realized that Nina was half right. She knew she was a good mother for Michael and Angela, but she certainly wasn't a perfect wife for Neil. He wouldn't let her be his real wife, even though that was what she wanted.

In the several minutes it took her to walk the block and a half to the house, Taylor greeted three of their neighbors. She couldn't help wondering what their reactions would be when she moved back into her own house after the custody case was settled. Would they feel betrayed at the way she'd pretended to be Neil's loving wife? Or would they understand that she'd had only Michael and Angela's best interests at heart?

The private detective Neil had hired to investigate Melissa's life in Chicago had learned that Melissa was heavily involved in charity work and that she'd agreed to be a guest speaker at week-long conferences in Los Angeles, Washington D.C., and Seattle. This was important because it effectively canceled out her objection to Neil's book tours.

When Taylor turned up the walkway to the house, Neil opened the door. It was obvious that he'd been watching for her. "We've got a problem. I told Angela why we were going to court and she got so upset, she spilled juice on her dress. I said it was okay, that you'd take care of it the minute you got home, but she won't stop crying."

"No problem." Taylor smiled to reassure him and hurried into the house. They were due at the courthouse in less than an hour and she didn't want Angela to look as though she'd been crying.

"I'm sorry, Mommy." Angela was sitting at the kitchen

table, tears running down her cheeks. "I didn't mean to spill. Honest, I didn't."

Taylor put her arms around Angela. "It doesn't matter, Angel Fuzz. That's not the dress I want you to wear."

"It's not?" Angela's tears stopped flowing and she blinked in surprise. "Daddy said it was."

"I know, but I changed my mind. I think we should wear the same color so the judge can tell we're a family. What do you think?"

"That's a really good idea." Angela looked very relieved. "Then I can be your little girl and you can be my mommy."

Taylor held out her hand. "Let's go upstairs and get ready. I'd like to wear that pretty pin you made for me in preschool."

"Okay." Angela began to smile. "But some of the pink macaroni came off."

"We'll glue it back on. I've got a little tube of glue in my room."

As they went up the stairs, Angela still looked a little worried. "The judge won't be mean, will he, Mommy?"

"Everybody I talked to says he's very nice. Do you know that he has a granddaughter your age?"

"What's her name?"

"Trudi Ambrose. Maybe you'll get to talk to him in his chambers and you can ask him about her."

"What's a *chambers*, Mommy?"

"It's just like an office, with a desk and chairs. He'll probably have lots of big books, just like Daddy has in his office."

"I want to see his chambers. Will Michael go, too?"

"I think so." They stepped into Angela's room and Taylor went straight to the closet. "Which dress would you like to wear? The green one or the blue one?"

Angela thought about it for a moment and then she made up her mind. "The green one."

"That's a very good choice." Taylor took it off the

hanger and helped Angela put it on. When she was dressed, Taylor smiled at her. "You look very pretty and now you can help me. I'll wear my green suit and I'll put your pin on the collar, where everyone can see it."

It didn't take Taylor long to dress in her green suit and repair the pin. It was a daisy with macaroni petals that Angela had painted pink. While no one would mistake it for fine jewelry, it was Taylor's favorite pin.

"I'm almost ready." Taylor ran a brush through her hair and secured it with a gold barrette; then they started down the stairs. But before they got to the bottom step, Angela tugged on her hand.

"The judge won't make us go away, will he, Mommy?"

Taylor sighed. It was the question she'd been dreading. She'd thought that she should prepare Angela, if the judge decided in Melissa's favor, but that seemed cruel and heartless. "If Judge Ambrose is as fair as everyone says he is, he'll do the right thing. Just answer all of his questions and tell him the truth. Michael will do exactly the same thing, and then the judge will know that you belong with your daddy and me."

"Okay. Can we stop at Sammy's for pizza on the way home?"

"Maybe. That depends on what time it is."

Taylor breathed a sigh of relief as they all went out to the car. Angela didn't seem worried any longer, and now she was looking forward to talking to the judge. Neil backed out the driveway, and then they were on their way. He looked tense and Taylor reached out to squeeze his hand.

"Thanks, Taylor." Neil spoke in a low voice so the kids wouldn't hear him. "I'm really glad you're here with me. It would be hell going through this alone."

"Don't worry, Neil. Everything's going to turn out just fine." Taylor gave him a shaky smile. One of her former coworkers in New York had been fond of repeating her grandmother's favorite saying: "From your lips to God's ears." And she hoped that it would be prophetic.

When Taylor and Neil entered the courthouse they found a crowd of friends waiting for them in the lobby. Marge and Tim were there, and they'd brought Becky and Suzie Ringstrom with them.

"Barb's filling in for me at the preschool." Marge answered the question before Taylor had time to ask. "We thought the judge should see that Angela and Michael have friends in Two Rivers. Suzanne's here, too, and she brought Robby. She got a substitute and took the afternoon off. And Jim and Patsy Burkholtz are already inside with Gary. We thought there might be a problem with taking the boys out of school, but Stu Hennesey offered to bus in their whole class if we thought it would help."

Taylor reached out and hugged Marge. "Thank you for coming. It really means a lot to us."

When they walked into the courtroom Taylor got an even bigger surprise. The large room was filled to overflowing with their friends and neighbors.

"They must have closed down the whole town." Neil was clearly astonished. "Did you ask all of them to come?"

"No, I didn't mention it to anyone. You have lots of good friends."

"They're your friends, too." Neil led the way to a table in front where his lawyer, Kyle Murphy, was waiting for them.

"Let's take our seats." Kyle smiled at Michael. "I want you to sit right next to your dad."

Michael sat down and Kyle turned to Angela. "You can take this chair right next to your brother, Angela. And we'll put Taylor on the other side."

"I don't want to sit there." Angela looked worried. "Can't I sit on Mommy's lap?"

"That's fine, Angela. But could you sit in your own chair until the judge comes in? I want him to see that pretty pin you made for her. When you think he's seen it, you can climb up in her lap."

Angela smiled at him, happy with this arrangement, and then her eyes widened. "How did you know I made Mommy's pin?"

"Because my daughter made one, too. Hers is blue, and my wife wears it all the time."

Angela nodded, and then she glanced at the other table, where Melissa was sitting with her new husband and her lawyer. "Is that the lady that says she's my mommy?"

"Yes." Kyle scribbled a note. "Don't you remember her, Angela?"

Angela looked over at the other table again and shook her head. Then Melissa moved forward slightly, giving Angela her first glimpse of her husband, Peter Cheswick. Angela gasped and grabbed Taylor's hand. "It's *Peaches*, Mommy! Don't let him get me!"

"I won't." Taylor held Angela tightly. She was trembling so hard, her teeth were chattering. "It's all right, Angel Fuzz. Just tell me exactly where Peaches is."

"He's right next to the lady that's pretending to be my mommy. That's *Peaches!*"

Taylor's mind whirled. Peaches was Peter Cheswick, and it made sense, now that she thought about it. She could understand how "Pete Cheswick" could be translated to "Peaches" in a toddler's mind.

Peter Cheswick was obviously the source of Angela's nightmares. Taylor turned to Kyle with a frown. "Angela still has nightmares about someone she calls Peaches. Peaches is Peter Cheswick, and Neil told me her nightmares started a few months before Melissa left."

"I see." Kyle looked very solemn as he reached out to pat Angela's hand. "Don't worry, honey. Your mommy and

I will protect you. But I need your help, Angela. Can you tell me why you're so afraid of him?"

"I don't remember."

Angela's voice was small and frightened, and Taylor hugged her. "Try to remember, Angel Fuzz. It's really important."

"Really?" Angela sighed when Taylor nodded. "I'll try, Mommy. I think it was bedtime and . . . and I needed a drink of water. And Daddy always got it for me."

Taylor held her closer. "That's very good, Angela. What happened next?"

"I called for Daddy, but he didn't come. And I went to his room. I know I did. But Daddy wasn't there. It was Mommy and . . . and *Peaches!*"

"Peter Cheswick was in your daddy's bed?" Kyle spoke very softly.

"Yes, and he got really mad at me. He spanked me hard and then he put me in my room and I couldn't get out. And he said that if I told Daddy, he'd spank me again!"

Michael had been listening to their conversation and he tapped Kyle's arm. "Angela's right. I remember that morning. She was crying and I went to her room. The door was locked, but the key was in the lock, so I let her out. She was really scared, but she was too little to tell me what happened. She just kept saying 'Peaches' and crying."

"Did you tell your mother about it?" Kyle asked.

"Yeah, but she said that Angela must have locked the door by herself. She was lying, though. I know that now. Angela couldn't have locked herself in, not when the key was on the outside of the door. Peter Cheswick must have done it so she wouldn't bother them."

"Okay." Kyle patted Michael on the back and then he turned back to Taylor. "We need to have a conference in the judge's chambers. Just stay right here with the kids and let me handle it. We've got a really good chance of getting this whole lousy case dismissed."

While the lawyers were conferring with the judge in his chambers, Taylor explained it all to Neil. He wanted to slug Peter Cheswick for what he'd done to Angela, and Taylor barely managed to restrain him.

The meeting in the judge's chambers was brief. Within five minutes, the lawyers came back into the courtroom. A moment later, the judge came out to make an announcement. Melissa and her husband had withdrawn their petition for custody. The judge also announced that he'd never received so many testimonials from neighbors and friends in a custody case.

Angela waited until they were standing outside, surrounded by their friends, on the courtroom steps. "We won, didn't we, Mommy?"

"Yes, we won." Taylor was so happy, she picked Angela up and kissed her smiling face.

Angela laughed as Taylor set her down again, and then she tugged on Neil's sleeve. "I'm hungry, Daddy. Can we go to Sammy's to get a pizza?"

"We can do better than that, Pumpkin." Neil motioned to all of their friends. "We'll meet you all down at Cookies & Kisses. We'll bring in pizzas and have a victory party."

Taylor was smiling as she stood there, Neil's arm around her waist. She'd hoped that there would be a celebration after the hearing, and she'd baked Cowboy Cookies for the occasion. But as she accepted their friends' congratulations, Taylor felt a deep sorrow welling up inside her. It was over. The custody case had been decided. Now that Michael and Angela were home to stay, Neil no longer needed her to be his wife.

TWENTY-SEVEN

Neil opened another box of pizza and set it on the counter. All their friends and neighbors were there, packing the front room of Cookies & Kisses to overflowing. Taylor had propped open the swinging door to the bakery and there were even people in back, sitting on stools around the stainless steel work island.

Everything had turned out all right in the end. Neil doubted that Melissa would ever reopen the custody issue, and his family was secure. This was due, in no small part, to Taylor. She was a perfect mother for the kids and he knew she loved them. And for brief moments, during the past few weeks, he'd thought that she might just love him, too.

Neil frowned. He'd been wrong about that. Taylor cared for him—that was obvious—but there was definitely a fly in the ointment. Taylor and Ted Swanson were standing by one of the ovens, laughing and talking. There was an easy familiarity between them that made Neil's blood boil. Taylor was his wife, and damned if Ted wasn't trying to pick her up, right here in front of all their friends. Ted's hand was on Taylor's arm, and they sure looked like a couple to Neil.

He couldn't stand to watch them any longer. Neil turned away and walked into the front room. It was his own fault for dragging his feet. He should have told Taylor that he loved her months ago, before she'd even met Ted.

"Hi, Neil." Mary Baxter reached out and took his arm. "I'm so happy for you."

Neil nodded and put on a smile. "Thanks for everything, Mary. I know you organized that letter-writing campaign."

"It was nothing." Mary waved away his thanks. "Where's Ted?"

"I saw him in back a minute ago. He was talking to Taylor."

Mary pulled him away to a quiet corner, and then she leaned close so that they wouldn't be overheard. "I think he's going to do it today."

"Do what?"

"Propose. My cousin called to say he picked up the ring this morning. He told her that he'd been planning to wait, but he changed his mind. That sure sounds like a proposal-in-the-making to me."

Neil's smile faltered. "Did he tell your cousin the name of the woman?"

"No. She asked, but he wouldn't say. I just love a good mystery, don't you?"

"Uh . . . sure. Sure, I do."

"I've been keeping my eye on him, but the only women I've seen him with are Nina and Suzanne. They hang around together all the time, so that doesn't count. And you say he's with Taylor now?"

Neil nodded. He didn't trust his voice.

"That doesn't count either. Taylor's *your* wife. Did you see him with any other women?"

Neil cleared his throat. "I saw him talking to Jenny Hoffman."

"Jenny?" Mary looked horrified. "I hope it's not her! That giggle of hers would drive a man crazy in ten seconds flat. Help me keep an eye on him, will you, Neil?"

"I'll do that." Neil made his way toward the swinging

door. You bet he'd keep an eye on Ted! And if Ted made one move toward Taylor, he'd . . .

Neil stopped in his tracks and began to frown. He couldn't do anything. He'd promised to give Taylor a quiet divorce, and soon she'd be free to choose any husband she wanted.

"What's the matter, Neil?"

Neil turned and bumped into Suzanne. She was staring up at him, looking puzzled, and he quickly put his smile back in place. "Hi, Suzanne. Nothing's wrong. I guess I'm still reeling over everything that's happened."

"I can understand that. You must be very happy."

"Yes. Yes, I am."

"Hold on a second." Suzanne walked over to one of the tables and poured him a glass of champagne. She handed it to him, poured one for herself, and touched the rim of her glass to his. "A toast to the future."

Neil took a sip. "Who brought the champagne?"

"Ted. He said he thought we should celebrate all the wonderful things that happened today."

Neil's eyes narrowed. "Like what?"

"Like winning the custody case. And everything else, too."

Neil noticed that Suzanne looked very happy. Her eyes were sparkling, her cheeks were rosy, and she looked as if she knew a delicious secret. Was it possible that Ted had already proposed to Taylor and Suzanne knew about it?

"I've got to run, Neil." Suzanne stood on her tiptoes and placed a kiss on Neil's cheek. "Congratulations. This really is a wonderful day."

She walked away and Neil didn't call her back. He didn't want to ask her what she knew. What he wanted to do was drag Taylor home and keep her with him for the rest of her life.

* * *

Taylor had known it was coming, but she hadn't thought it would be quite this soon. Neil had told her that he wanted to talk to her once the kids were in bed, and he'd asked her to come down to the den right after she'd taken her evening shower.

She stepped out of the shower and sighed as she gazed at the lovely peignoir set that was still hanging behind the bathroom door. It had worked the last time she'd worn it, but she wouldn't resort to that kind of trickery again. Neil knew that if he wanted her, all he had to do was ask.

Taylor toweled herself off and put on a flannel nightgown. Perhaps if she cooperated with Neil, if she let him know that she was willing to continue with their platonic marriage, he wouldn't want to get a divorce right away.

She sighed as she padded across the new carpeting toward the door. She loved their bedroom, but soon she'd be moving and sleeping in her own bed again. She wouldn't be here to wake Angela and Michael in the mornings, to smile at them over their breakfast, or to make sure they remembered to take their vitamins and brush their teeth. Neil would be the one to tuck them in at night and wake them up in the morning. She'd still see them; Taylor knew that. Michael would still be working at the bakery and Angela would still come in to visit when preschool was out for the day, but it wouldn't be the same. She wouldn't be their mother anymore.

Taylor grabbed a tissue out of the box on the dresser and dabbed at her eyes. She should be celebrating, not crying. Neil had won the custody case. Neil and the kids were safe. But now he was preparing to cast her aside, to throw her out of the only real home she'd ever known. She'd be on the fringes of his happy family, a friend to the children, a friend to him, but nothing more. She loved Angela and Michael. And she loved Neil, too. It just wasn't fair.

Neil didn't love her. She simply had to accept it. He didn't want her as his real wife or the mother of his children. He wanted to go back to his old way of doing things, to the freedom he'd had as a single parent. She had to harden her heart and stiffen her backbone. Her pride was at stake. Neil didn't want her and she had to pretend that she didn't want him either.

Neil had just finished lighting a fire in the fireplace when Taylor came into the den. She looked so sweet in her flannel nightgown, he wanted to pull her into his arms and kiss her. He had no idea how she'd managed it, but she looked even more seductive than she had in her revealing lace nightgown.

It was an effort, but Neil managed to control himself. He couldn't let his emotions run away with him. Taylor wasn't his any longer. She'd never been his. She was Ted's fiancée, and somehow he had to keep his distance. "How about some coffee with chocolate and brandy?"

"I'd love some." She smiled at him, and it almost broke his heart. "Do you want some help in the kitchen?"

"No, I'll get it. Just stay here and enjoy the fire."

Neil kept the smile on his face until he reached the kitchen. Then he began to scowl. He owed Taylor a lot and he couldn't fault her for accepting Ted's proposal. Though he didn't want to admit it, Ted did seem like a decent guy. As he filled two mugs with cold coffee and put them in the microwave to heat, Neil wondered if he should come right out and ask her. *Tell me the truth, Taylor,* he could say. *Did Ted propose to you?* But what if she lied to him and said no? She might not want to tell him until their divorce was final, and he didn't want to force her to lie.

Neil watched the cups go around and around on the carousel, but he really didn't see them. He knew he was being a coward by not asking Taylor, but he didn't want her to confirm his worst fear. He'd much rather stick his head in the sand like an ostrich, ignoring the threat that Ted presented, and forget all about his promise to divorce Taylor.

What would happen if he told Taylor that he loved her, that he'd loved her for months, and he didn't want their marriage to end? She'd have to make a choice. She could divorce him and marry Ted, or she could stay right here, married to him.

Neil sighed. He couldn't do that. He loved Taylor and he had to keep the promise he'd made to her, even though it was breaking his heart. A line from an old Laurel and Hardy movie popped into his head. *Here's another fine mess you've gotten us into, Ollie.* And Ollie was another problem. He had grown very attached to Taylor and was used to sleeping right next to her to on the pillow. The loyal dog Neil had raised from a puppy would probably leave him when Taylor did.

The microwave beeped and Neil took out the mugs of coffee. He stirred in instant cocoa mix, poured in a generous measure of brandy, and sighed. He didn't think Michael would be all that upset when they broke up. He'd still see Taylor every day, and his life wouldn't change that much. There might be a problem with Angela, but now that she was in preschool, she was already spending more time away from Taylor. He'd ask Taylor if she'd come to stay with the kids when he was gone. He was sure she would, at least until she had children of her own. And Taylor would probably want to have children with Ted.

That thought rankled so much, Neil almost knocked over the mugs. Visions of Ted and Taylor in bed together made him want to go out and smash something. He had to stop thinking about it. It was driving him crazy. And he couldn't let Taylor know that he wanted to fall on his knees and beg her to please stay with him.

TWENTY-EIGHT

Taylor pulled on her oldest pair of jeans and a sweatshirt. Today was even worse than she'd thought it would be. She hadn't slept well. Every time she'd closed her eyes and tried to rest, she'd thought about Neil and the kids and she'd started to cry.

As she brushed her hair, Taylor blinked back even more tears. Her eyes were puffy, her complexion was blotchy, and she felt every bit as bad as she looked. Thank goodness it was Sunday and she didn't have to go to work. There was no way she could pretend to be cheerful for a crowd of customers at Cookies & Kisses. Today marked the end of her marriage to Neil—the day that she would leave her happy home and move back into Grandma Mac's house.

Taylor forced a smile and went down the stairs. She didn't want to cry in front of the kids. She headed straight for the kitchen and poured herself a cup of coffee from the pot. Then she opened the refrigerator, took out the eggs, and got out the frying pans. She'd pretend it was just another normal day. It was the only way she'd be able to cope.

Taylor hadn't told anyone about the pending divorce, and she didn't think Neil had either. It wouldn't be final for several months, and it would probably take the neighbors a while to realize that they had split up and were living in separate houses again. Everyone was used to seeing them racing back and forth between the two houses, so no one would think twice about it. The only real difference was that Taylor would now be sleeping in Grandma Mac's house and Neil would be sleeping in his.

Angela didn't seem to be having a problem with their new living arrangements. Perhaps she was too young to understand. Taylor had promised to stay with the kids whenever Neil had to leave on a tour, and that aspect of their lives was unchanged. For the first few weeks, Taylor had agreed to tuck the kids in at night and come over to fix their breakfast in the morning. From Angela's point of view, nothing in her life had actually changed.

For Michael, it was a different matter. Neil had assured her that he was old enough to take their divorce in stride, but he had been wrong. Right after their father-and-son talk yesterday afternoon, Michael had gone up to his room and closed his door. He'd stayed there for the rest of the day, and when Neil had knocked to tell him that Taylor had baked his favorite meatloaf for supper, Michael had said to just go away and leave him alone.

Michael's reaction was another reason that Taylor hadn't been able to sleep last night. She had to talk to him and explain that his life really wouldn't be all that different. He'd still see her at the bakery, and he could come over to her house any time he wanted. Most important of all, she had to convince him that she wasn't deserting him, that she loved him just as much as ever.

Taylor poured glasses of juice and set them on the table. She knew Michael was awake. She'd heard him moving around in his room when she'd passed his door. He'd gone without dinner rather than face them, and he must be hungry by now. She'd take him a meatloaf sandwich—an unusual breakfast, but one that he would enjoy. She'd say all the things she'd wanted to say yesterday, and perhaps they'd both feel better.

When the sandwich was ready, Taylor carried it up the

stairs and tapped lightly on Michael's door. "Michael? I really need to talk to you. Is it all right if I come in?"

There a long silence and then the door clicked open. Michael stood there just looking at her, the pain clear in his eyes. He didn't say anything and Taylor didn't either. She just gathered him into her arms and hugged him tightly.

"I know how upset you are, Michael." Taylor stroked his hair "I'm upset, too."

Michael pulled back to stare at her. "Why are *you* upset? We're not leaving you. You're leaving us."

"I know. But I don't want to leave you. You must know that. It's just . . . well . . . maybe it's a good thing that your father and I are putting some distance between us. It's very difficult to live with him when I love him so much."

Michael looked hopelessly confused. "You still love Dad? Honest?"

"Yes, I do." There was no reason to lie to Michael. "I don't want to move out, Michael. I want to stay here with you."

"Dad's an idiot!" Michael stared down at the sandwich in her hand. "Is that sandwich for me?"

Taylor handed him the plate. "I thought you might be hungry."

"I'm starving, but I decided to protest by going on a hunger strike. It worked for Gandhi."

"I see." Taylor bit back a grin. "Eat, Michael. Starving yourself isn't going to make your father love me."

Michael motioned her in, closing the door behind her. He patted the edge of the bed, waited until Taylor had seated herself next to him, and then practically inhaled the sandwich. "I guess that Gandhi act was a dumb idea. So you don't want to divorce Dad?"

"No. I'd like to stay married to him for the rest of my life."

"I just don't get it." Michael wiped his face with a napkin and shook his head. "I was almost positive that Dad loved you."

"So was I, but your dad doesn't want another wife. Melissa hurt him very much."

"I know, but that's in the past, and Dad's always telling me that when life gives you hard knocks, you're supposed to get right back up and shake it off. It's too bad he's not following his own advice. He's being a hippopotamus."

Taylor smiled. "Is that another one of Angela's words?"

"Yeah. She can't say 'hypocrite.' Dad loves you. I know he does. And he's throwing away the best thing that ever happened to us. I just don't get it."

"All we can do is accept it, Michael. Maybe he'll realize that he's made a mistake and ask me to move back in again."

"I wouldn't count on it." Michael gave an exasperated sigh. "He's too stubborn for that. But there's got to be something we can do."

"What? I've tried everything I could think of and nothing's worked."

"Don't give up, Taylor." Michael reached out to squeeze her hand. "Maybe I can think of something."

Taylor smiled and hugged him hard. "I love you, Michael. You know that, don't you?"

"Yeah." Michael shrugged it off, but he looked pleased. "Go on, Taylor. You'd better get breakfast for Angela. I heard her get up a little while ago."

"Don't you want breakfast?"

"I'll grab something later. Will you do me a favor and keep Angela out of the way? I need to have a talk with Dad."

"Where's Michael?" Taylor turned to Neil with an armload of dresses in her arms. "I thought he was going to help."

"He caught me this morning and asked me if he could go to the movies with Robby. It looked like he wanted to cry, and I knew he didn't want to act like a baby in front of you, so I told him he could. He's having dinner over at Suzanne's, too."

Taylor gave a relieved sigh. "You did the right thing, Neil. This move is really hard on him."

"I know. I was wrong about him, Taylor. I thought he'd take it in stride, but he didn't. He was home the day Melissa moved out, and I should have realized that this was bringing back bad memories for him. Sometimes I forget that he's only a kid."

"I don't think either one of the kids should have to watch me move out. That's why I took Angela over to Becky's house to play."

"That was smart. Once we get everything moved, we'll pick her up and go out for a pizza. She'll feel a lot better when she sees that nothing's really changed."

Taylor didn't say anything, but she bit her lip hard. Neil was dead wrong. Everything had changed, and none of it was for the better.

The move was accomplished quickly, even without Michael's help. Taylor had very few possessions, and it was really just a matter of moving her clothing and personal items back to Grandma Mac's house. When they were through, they picked up Angela and took her out for pizza. Then Taylor went home, after promising to come back in time to tuck Angela into bed for the night.

She was sitting in her den, staring at the television and feeling as if her world had come to an end, when there was a knock on the back door. It was Angela, and she was carrying her pink backpack.

"Can I sleep over here with you, Mommy?" Angela was lisping slightly, and she looked very small and frightened.

"Ollie came, too. He didn't want to stay home with Daddy either. It's no fun all by ourselves."

Taylor opened the door wider and helped Angela in. "Of course you can. I told you that you could come over here any time you wanted. Come on, Ollie. I'll put some food in your bowl."

"He loves you, Mommy." Angela giggled as Ollie stood on his hind legs and licked Taylor's face. "He can sleep here with me, can't he?"

"Of course he can." Taylor filled Ollie's bowls with food and water.

"You should have a special door for Ollie." Angela followed Taylor into the den. "Then he can come over to see you any time he wants to, like me."

Taylor got one of Grandma Mac's quilts for Angela. "That's a very good idea. I'll call Ted tomorrow and have him put in a doggy door. Sit right here by me and let's wrap up in this quilt. When we get warm, I'll make us some popcorn and cocoa."

"I brought us a movie." Angela pointed to her backpack. "It's in there."

"Good. Does your daddy know that you're over here with me?"

"I told him, but I don't think he was listening. He was watching war on the History Channel, and he didn't even say anything when I switched it to cartoons. He had a funny look on his face, like he was thinking about something he didn't like very much."

"Then I'd better call him and tell him you're here." Taylor reached for the phone. "We don't want him to worry."

Angela snuggled a little closer. "Okay. This is nice, Mommy. Your TV's not as big as Daddy's, but I like it."

Taylor punched out Neil's number. It rang several times before he answered. When he did, he sounded groggy, as if he'd been sleeping.

"Neil?" Taylor felt shaky just hearing his voice and knowing that he was only a few feet away. She could picture him on the leather couch, his feet propped up on the coffee table. The image was so real, she had to swallow past the lump in her throat. "I thought you should know that I have two members of your family over here."

"Great! I was wondering where they were." Neil sounded very relieved.

"They want to spend the night, if that's all right with you."

"Sure, if you don't mind. Did Michael bring his books with him?"

"Michael?" Taylor began to frown. "Michael's not here. It's Angela and Ollie."

"I wonder where he is. He said Suzanne would have him home by seven and it's already eight. Maybe I should call and go pick him up. She might be having car trouble."

"That's a good idea." Taylor began to relax slightly. Neil was sounding like his old self. "Call me back and let me know, okay?"

They were just settling down to watch the movie when the phone rang again. Taylor reached out to answer it. "Hello?"

"Taylor, we've got a problem."

Neil sounded worried and Taylor began to frown. "What is it?"

"Suzanne says she hasn't seen Michael all day. And Robby didn't go to the movies with him. They just got home from her parents. They were there all afternoon."

"Did Michael go to the movies alone?"

"No. I checked with Al Cooper, and he said Michael wasn't there."

"Is it possible that Al just didn't see him?" Taylor experienced a sinking feeling in the pit of her stomach. It was after eight and the matinee was over at four.

"Al said he looked for Michael. He wanted to give him

a note for you about increasing his cookie order. He said he asked around, but nobody knew where Michael was."

Taylor didn't like it. Michael had been very responsible lately, and it wasn't like him to say he was going somewhere and fail to show up. She supposed she should let Neil handle it. She was about to become his ex-wife and Michael's welfare was now his full responsibility. But those legal technicalities didn't matter. She was worried about Michael, and if he was in trouble, she'd move heaven and earth to help him. "Angela and I will be right over. We can call Michael's friends. One of them must have seen Michael today."

"What's the matter, Mommy?" Angela looked up from her spot on the couch.

"It's Michael. He's not home yet and your dad is worried about him. I said we'd go over and help him make some phone calls."

Angela got up. "I can watch the movie at Daddy's house. Is Ollie coming, too?"

"Yes." Taylor noticed that Angela didn't look worried, and that was strange. "Do you know where your brother is, Angela?"

Angela shook her head. "I asked, but he wouldn't tell me. He said I was too little to go with him. I told him not to take all the peanut butter, so he left me some on a paper plate."

"The peanut butter?"

"Yes. He took the apple jelly, but I said he could have that. There's another jar in the cupboard."

Taylor helped Angela into her jacket and called for Ollie to follow them. "Did Michael make a sandwich to take along with him?"

"No. I told him he should, because the jelly was getting his backpack all sticky, but he said he'd do it later."

Taylor was thoughtful as she followed Angela and Ollie through the gap in the hedge. Michael had taken food with him. It was beginning to sound as if he'd run away from home. But where would he go? The thought of Michael all alone in the darkness was frightening. If he had run away, Taylor hoped he'd gone to a friend's house. But Michael's best friend was Robby, and he wasn't with him.

"Taylor." Neil opened the door before they'd even had the chance to knock. "I'm really glad you're here."

Neil's face was drawn and he looked every bit as nervous as she felt. "Any new developments?"

"No. I called Jim Burkholtz, but Michael's not there. And Gary says he hasn't seen him."

Taylor turned to Angela. "Go put on your movie, honey. I'll bring in a snack for you."

Neil watched as Taylor grabbed a big bag of potato chips and a soft drink. "I thought you told me not to give her junk food right before bedtime."

"I did, but this is an exception. It'll keep her happy and out of the way. I don't want her to see how worried we are."

"Good thinking. What do you want me to do?"

"You start calling Michael's friends and I'll get Angela settled in the den. Then I'll come back and check the pantry to see what Michael took with him."

"He took food?"

"Angela told me he packed a jar of peanut butter and some jelly. I need to see what else is missing."

"Do you think he ran away?"

"It's possible. He was really upset when I talked to him this morning. I just hope he's spending the night with one of his friends."

Neil looked hopeful for a moment, but then he shook his head. "Why would he take food if he was going to a friend's house?"

"I don't know."

"That just doesn't make sense. And wouldn't you think his friend's parents would call me?"

"Not necessarily. Michael may have convinced them that he had your permission to sleep over. Go ahead, Neil. Call his friends and see what you can find out."

TWENTY-NINE

"Thanks, Shirley." Neil hung up the phone with a sigh. He'd called everyone in Michael's class, but no one had seen him. He glanced over at Taylor, who was sitting at the kitchen table with a list in her hand. "What's missing?"

"A loaf of bread, a jar of peanut butter, apple jelly, five cans of tuna, a small jar of mayo, two boxes of cereal, and six packs of microwave popcorn."

"He's run away." Neil began to frown. "And it's pretty clear he took enough food to last him for awhile. I've got to find him before he freezes to death out there!"

"Calm down, Neil. I'm on the edge of panic myself, but that won't do Michael any good. I'm sure he's found some kind of shelter. We just have to figure out where to look."

"Just how the hell do we do that?" Neil knew he was snapping at Taylor and he felt very ashamed of himself. "I'm sorry, Taylor. I'm just so worried about him."

"I know. So am I. What was Michael wearing when he left here?"

Neil forced himself to concentrate. He was losing control, and that wouldn't help to find Michael. "Uh . . . he was wearing his parka. I'm almost sure of that. And jeans. And I think he had on his boots. I didn't really notice."

"We know he took his backpack. Angela told me that. It's large enough to hold all his food and some extra clothing."

"I can't just sit here. I'm going out to look around."
Neil felt the panic rising again. "Should I call a baby-sitter
for Angela? I'd like you to come with me, but somebody's
got to stay here by the phone."

Taylor got up and came over to hug him. Just holding
her in his arms made everything better, and Neil wished
she could stay there forever. Damn Ted Swanson's hide
for taking away the only woman he'd ever really loved!

"You have to think rationally, Neil." Taylor's voice was
soft in his ear. "Driving around town without knowing
where you're headed won't help Michael at all."

"I know. It's just crazy, that's all. Michael's been really
mad at me a couple of times, but he's never even threatened to run away."

"We'll find him." Taylor gave him a kiss on the cheek.
When she stepped away, Neil felt as if he'd just lost a part
of his own body. She was his anchor, his rock, his founda-
tion, and he didn't blame Michael for bailing out. He'd
like to run away, too, away from the pain of losing Taylor,
but he had to stay and put on a good face for his friends
and not let anyone know that his heart was breaking.

"We should check his closet." Taylor brought him back
to the present with her calm, controlled voice. "I'll be able
to tell which clothing he took, and that may give us a clue
to where he's gone."

Taylor had said *us*, not *you*, but they weren't a couple
any longer. Michael was his problem and he had no right
to involve Taylor. But just looking at her anxious face, he
could tell that she was every bit as worried as he was.

Taylor felt relief wash over her like a healing balm as
she went through the clothes in Michael's closet. She'd
already discovered that Michael had taken his toothbrush,
his toothpaste, and the sleeping bag and pillow that had
been rolled up on his closet shelf. His textbooks were

gone, along with several sets of school clothing, and he'd taken his freshly laundered apron and the cap he wore when he worked at the bakery.

"It's okay, Neil." Taylor turned around and hugged him. "Michael is just fine."

"How do you know that?"

Taylor noticed that Neil didn't pull away. He just hugged her as if he never wanted to let her go, and it felt wonderful. Taylor wanted to stay in his arms for the rest of her life.

"Michael took his school clothes and the apron he wears at the bakery." Taylor nestled her cheek against Neil's chest. "I should have realized where he was going when I noticed that the microwave popcorn was gone."

"You know where he is?"

"I think so. I gave him a key to the bakery so he could go in to turn on the ovens while I took Angela to pre-school. He's got to be there."

"I'll drive down there and get him."

"Not quite yet." Taylor leaned back so that she could see Neil's face. "He'll just do it again, if we don't get this whole thing straightened out. And we might not be so lucky the next time."

"You're right. We've got to find out exactly why he ran away."

Taylor thought she knew precisely what Michael was trying to do, but telling Neil wouldn't do any good. All she could do was guide him and hope that he discovered the truth for himself.

"Let's go down and talk to Angela. I'm sure Michael said something to her before he left."

"How do you know that?"

Taylor pulled back, but she kept her arm around his waist. "She just wasn't upset enough when we discovered that Michael was missing. I don't think she knows where he is. I asked her and she wouldn't lie to me. But she may know more about why he ran away."

They walked down the stairs together, Neil's arm around her shoulders and her arm around his waist. It was a narrow staircase, but Neil didn't seem to want to let her go. That made Taylor hopeful. Perhaps he was beginning to realize what she meant to the kids and to him.

"We need to talk to you, Pumpkin." Neil kept his arm around her as they walked into the den. "We think we know where Michael is, but we need to know why he left."

Angela looked very serious. "I don't know exactly why, Daddy, but Michael was really sad. He said he had to do something to keep you and Mommy together."

Neil winced. "Do you know where he went?"

"No. He wouldn't tell me. He said I might say something before it was time."

Taylor nodded. Michael really shouldn't have worried them this way, but his scheme appeared to be working, because Neil was holding her close. "Before it was time for what, Angel Fuzz?"

"I don't know. But I'm pretty sure Michael went shopping."

"Shopping?" Taylor was surprised. That certainly didn't fit in with her theory! "What gave you that idea?"

"He told me not to worry, that he'd be okay. And then he said that he had to give Daddy an alarm clock."

Taylor turned to stare at Neil in confusion. "An alarm clock? What does that mean?"

"I don't know, unless . . ." Neil stopped in midsentence and began to grin. "Try to remember, Pumpkin. Did Michael say that he had to give me a wake-up call?"

"That's right, Daddy. That's exactly what Michael said. And then he told me that he had to go away until you woke up."

"Did he say anything else?" Neil's voice was shaking

slightly, and Taylor suspected that he was trying not to laugh.

"Yes, but I can't tell you. You don't like me to say things that are aren't nice."

"Let's make an exception this time." Neil reached out to ruffle her hair. "You can tell me."

Angela sighed. "Okay, Daddy. But you won't like it. Michael said that you were brain dead."

"Why did he say that?" Taylor bit back a smile. She was sure she knew exactly what Angela would say.

"Michael said that Daddy would have to be brain dead not to see that you loved him. You do, don't you, Mommy?"

Taylor knew she had to answer honestly. "Yes, I do."

"And Daddy loves you, too. Michael told me that he did. He said that Daddy was a hippopotamus because he didn't get right up and dust himself off after he got hurt the first time."

"I see." Taylor risked a sideways glance at Neil. He looked embarrassed, but the corners of his lips were twitching.

"What do you think I should do about that?" Neil bent over to kiss the top of Angela's head.

"You and Mommy should kiss and make up. And then you should go get Michael so we can have popcorn. These potato chips have green things on them."

"They're chives."

Neil and Taylor spoke in unison, and Taylor began to laugh. Then she looked up to find Neil staring at her with a question in his eyes.

"Do you really love me, Taylor?" Neil reached out to touch her face.

Taylor drew a deep breath and let it out in a sigh. "Yes, I love you. I loved you when I married you and I love you even more now."

"What about Ted?"

"Ted Swanson?" Taylor stared at him in shock. "What does Ted have to do with it?"

"Didn't Ted propose to you at our victory party?"

"To me?" Taylor's eyes widened. "Of course not! Ted proposed to *Suzanne.*"

Neil stared at her for a moment and then he gathered her into his arms. "Then I'll propose to you. Will you marry me, Taylor?"

"I will." Taylor stood on her tiptoes so that she could place a light kiss on his lips. "But we're already married, Neil."

"Great. Then we won't have to go through any of the formalities. But I'm warning you, Taylor: I'm talking about a real marriage this time."

Taylor put her arms around his neck and pulled him down to kiss him deeply. And then she gave him a radiant smile. "Later, Neil, but not too much later. We've wasted too much time already."

EPILOGUE

June of the following year

"It's beautiful out here, Taylor." Suzanne shifted her position in one of the patio chairs that Taylor and Neil had arranged around the glass-topped table. Taylor could tell that she was uncomfortable, but soon she'd be back to her old self. Suzanne was approaching the ninth month of her pregnancy, and it wouldn't be long now.

"Try your pillow, honey." Ted handed his wife a small pillow and helped her tuck it into position behind her back. "Do you think I should build us a screened porch? You could sit out there with the baby and not have to worry about mosquitoes."

Suzanne smiled. "That would be nice, but only if you hire the same fabulous contractor Neil and Taylor used. I understand he's very good at his work, and his wife thinks he's extremely sexy."

Taylor laughed. Ted looked a little embarrassed, but he was grinning good-naturedly.

Neil came out with the pitcher of lemonade and refilled their glasses. Then he turned to Taylor with a rather sheepish smile. "I just went up to check on the baby. She's sleeping."

"We know." Taylor gestured toward the baby monitor that was sitting in the middle of the table. "You don't have to check on her every five minutes, Neil. We'll hear her if she wakes up."

They were silent for a moment, enjoying the warm summer night and the chirping of the crickets in the grass. Then Ollie raised his head and gave a soft woof. A moment later, they all heard the sound of a car turning down their block and pulling up in the driveway next door.

"Motherhood calls." Suzanne exchanged a smile with Taylor. "It's been great, but we've got to go. My parents are back with Robby."

After they'd said good night to Ted and Suzanne, Taylor cleared away the glasses and carried them into the kitchen. Neil wiped down the table, flicked off the twinkle lights that ran in a long strip around the ceiling of the porch, and whistled softly for Ollie to come in for the night. When he rejoined Taylor, she was just stacking the dishes in the dishwasher. He walked over to put his arms around her waist. "I really like having them right next door."

"So do I." Taylor turned to hug him back. "I'm glad I decided to sell Grandma Mac's house to them. It looked so lonely sitting over there all by itself, and their apartment would have been much too small with the new baby on the way."

Neil nuzzled the side of her neck. "Let's go to bed."

"Good idea." Taylor shivered slightly. They'd been married—truly married—for more than a year, but every time Neil touched her, she still felt like an eager bride.

Arms around each other, they went up the stairs. First they peeked in at Michael. He was sprawled out on his bed, sleeping peacefully, and Neil tiptoed over to turn off his reading light. Then they went on to Angela's room. They found her curled up in a ball, cuddling the life-sized baby doll that Taylor had given her several months before her new baby sister had been born.

"It's a good thing that doll's not a real baby." Taylor

spoke softly so that she wouldn't wake Angela. "She's practically smothering it."

"I don't think you have to worry about that with Belinda. Angela's really careful with her."

"I know. She's a perfect big sister." Taylor tucked in Angela's quilt and they went on to the nursery. Three-month-old Belinda was sleeping like an angel, and they stood there watching her for a moment in the soft, rosy glow from the carousel lamp that Taylor had chosen for a nightlight.

"She's perfect," Neil whispered, "just like her mother. Do you think we should try for another?"

"Not quite yet," Taylor whispered back, "but you know what they say: Practice makes perfect."

Neil chuckled softly and moved her toward the door. "And you think we need more practice?"

"Hours and hours, maybe even months and years." Taylor turned and raised her lips to his for a kiss that promised love forever.

GRANDMA MAC'S COWBOY COOKIES

(Everybody's favorite cookie! This is a double batch. It makes a lot, but you'll need a lot.)

2 cups melted butter (4 sticks)
2 cups brown sugar
2 cups white sugar
4 beaten eggs
1 teaspoon baking powder
1 teaspoon baking soda
1 teaspoon salt
2 teaspoons vanilla
4 cups flour
2 twelve-oz. pks. chocolate chips (4 cups)
3 cups rolled oats

Preheat oven to 350 degrees. Melt butter in large microwave-safe bowl or on the stove. Add sugars and let cool a bit. Add eggs and stir. Add baking powder, baking soda, salt, and vanilla. Stir some more. Add flour and stir. Then add chips and oats and mix everything really well. (The dough will be quite stiff. Don't worry. It's supposed to be that way.)

Use a teaspoon and drop by rounded spoonful onto a greased cookie sheet, 12 to a sheet. (Each spoonful should be about the size of a walnut with its shell on.)

Bake at 350 degrees for 12 to 15 minutes. Cool on cookie sheet for 2 minutes. Then remove to rack. (The rack is very important—it makes them crispy on the outside and moist on the inside.)

(These freeze well if you roll them in foil and put them in a freezer bag, but they probably won't last that long.)

ABOUT THE AUTHOR

Gina Jackson lives with her family in Granada Hills, California. *Cookies and Kisses* is her second contemporary romance for Bouquet. Gina also writes Regency romances under the pseudonym Kathryn Kirkwood and her latest, *A Valentine for Vanessa,* is now on sale. She loves hearing from readers and you may write to her c/o Zebra Books. Please include a self-addressed, stamped envelope if you want a response. You may also contact Gina by E-mail at yrwriter@aol.com.

In addition, Gina has her own Web site at:

http://www.Lilacs.homepage.com